Books by Bella Settarra

The Cowboys of Cavern County

Carla's Cowboys
Maggie's Man
Two for Trinity

Two for Trinity

ISBN # 978-1-78686-194-8

©Copyright Bella Settarra 2017

Cover Art by Posh Gosh ©Copyright 2017

Interior text design by Claire Siemaszkiewicz

Totally Bound Publishing

Published in 2017 by Totally Bound Publishing, Think Tank, Ruston Way, Lincoln, LN6 7FL, United Kingdom.

The Cowboys of Cavern County

TWO FOR TRINITY

BELLA SETTARRA

Dedication

This book is dedicated to all my readers who have told me how much they love a ménage story. I hope you enjoy it! ;)

Chapter One

"Hey-oll—you didn't tell us she was *that* cute!" Jarrod whistled as the petite, pink-haired girl climbed down from the train.

"Behave," Frank murmured under his breath as they walked toward her. "Remember what I told you."

Cordell rolled his eyes at his buddy, shaking his head in disbelief, but said nothing. *Trust Jarrod...* He gazed over at the girl and had to admit she was beautiful.

"Trinity, my, how you've grown." Sylvia was the first to approach the elfin girl, and the hug she gave her niece looked like it might snap her right in two.

"Aunt Sylvia, it's so nice to see you again." Trinity smiled, although her eyes maintained a melancholy expression. "And Uncle Frank, how good of you to fetch me. I was expecting to call a cab. How's your arm?" She frowned as she studied his left arm, encased in a sling across his chest.

Frank stood forward and gave her a hug, too. "It's fine, sugar. Don't you worry about that. I just fell a little awkwardly, the doctor said. Dang horse got spooked by a mouse or something and reared up suddenly. I didn't realize what was happening until I hit the ground." He chuckled. "Still, like I always say, where there's no sense, there's no feeling." He tipped his head as he let her go. "This here's Jarrod and Cordell." He gestured toward the two guys who stepped forward to join them.

Cordell watched Jarrod smile broadly at the pretty waif and cringed inside, unsure of how she would react to them. To his surprise, she held out her hand.

"Pleased to meet you. I'm Trinity Ellis," she said.

Jarrod seemed a little bemused as he shook her hand, though he was still smiling. "Jarrod Parker. Good to meet you, darlin'."

Cordell noticed her blush slightly before she turned to him, holding that hand out again.

"Hi Trinity, I'm Cordell Bray." He took her tiny hand in his, surprised that such a little woman had such a firm shake. She wore bright pink nail varnish that matched her hair, and her palm was warm and soft against his skin. He couldn't resist prolonging their shake a little as he continued, "Welcome to Cavern County."

She gave him a shy smile before withdrawing it. "Thank you."

"We came to carry your bags—and to do the driving, of course," Jarrod told her, glancing around.

"Oh, that's very kind. But I've only got this." She had a yellow, oversized handbag she was clinging to for dear life. "Everything else is gone." Tears filled her big, green eyes as she said it, and Cordell's heart went out to her.

"Well, let's get you home and settled in," Sylvia offered quickly, throwing an arm around Trinity and leading her toward the car. "I'll bet you haven't eaten in a while, have you?"

Cordell hung back a little as Frank followed the women.

"Looks like she hasn't eaten in a month of Sundays," Jarrod whispered, getting closer to his friend.

"Shh." Cordell rolled his eyes again. Jarrod was a lovely guy, but tact had never been his strong point.

"I'm only saying," Jarrod said, holding his hands up in surrender. "She seems like she'll get blown away if the wind springs up."

"Cut it out," Cordell murmured. "You know dang well she's been through hell and back. The last thing she needs is your smart-ass comments. And don't think I didn't notice you giving her the eye, either. She's off limits, remember?"

"She's still beautiful. You can't deny that," Jarrod muttered with his sing-song tone. "I saw the way you gawked at her, bro. You can't tell me you don't fancy her."

"That's not the point. Just cut it out, will you?" Cordell was muttering through clenched teeth as they neared the car.

Jarrod grinned.

Cordell sighed.

"Stop worrying," Jarrod whispered into his ear before disappearing around the other side of the car.

Cordell couldn't help smiling as he climbed into the driver's seat. Nothing fazed Jarrod. That was one of the many things he liked about his best friend.

"I've got the guest room all ready for you," Sylvia was telling Trinity as they drove toward Pelican's Heath.

"That's very nice of you," Trinity replied, in a small voice. She was sitting in between her uncle and aunt, who seemed to dwarf her, although they weren't exactly large people.

Cordell watched her through his rear-view mirror. She looked bewildered and he realized she must still be in shock after what had happened. "Do you like to ride, Trinity?" he asked, trying to keep the conversation light.

"Yes, I used to," she told the back of his head. "I haven't ridden for quite a while, though. Think I might be a bit rusty by now." Her voice sounded a little more cheerful, and he noticed in the rear-view mirror how she flushed slightly.

"Well, you'll get plenty of opportunity in Pelican's Heath," Jarrod offered. "Although I'd advise you to stay on the horse. Your uncle's method of riding isn't quite what we'd recommend."

They all laughed, and even Trinity sniggered, Cordell noticed. *Good.*

"I'll have you know that wasn't my fault, young man," Frank admonished, playfully.

Jarrod turned to face him. "What? Surely, you're not blaming that poor horse, Frank?"

Cordell glanced over to see the fake expression of shock on Jarrod's face as his buddy put his hands on his cheeks.

Trinity giggled. It was quiet, but it was definitely a giggle.

"That's not what I said and you know it," Frank protested with a tut. He was clearly well-used to Jarrod's teasing.

"Sounded that way to me. What do you think, Trinity?" Jarrod goaded.

"I'm not getting involved," she told him. "I wasn't there, remember?"

"None of us were," Cordell offered, still watching her in the mirror. "In fact, we've got our suspicions that there wasn't even a horse involved at all. Seems to us your Uncle Frank might have had a little too much of his elderflower wine and simply fell over his own feet or something."

Jarrod hooted with laughter, and Cordell was pleased to see Trinity snigger, too. Her face seemed a little more relaxed now, and she was even more beautiful.

"That's a load of baloney and you know it," Frank protested, shaking his head. He was in his seventies, very well-dressed and had an authoritative air about him. Luckily, he also had a keen sense of humor.

"Oh, Frank, you know the guys are only kidding," Sylvia soothed him with a smile. She turned to Trinity. "They do this all the time, hon. You'll soon get used to it."

Trinity smiled, and Cordell noticed her glance up at him in the mirror then blush as she quickly turned away, obviously seeing that he was watching her. He grinned. She was a hard one to figure out. Her bright pink hair and nails gave the impression of a girl who oozed confidence, although she seemed anything but right now. He hoped that spending some time in Cavern County would help her recover from her ordeal and get back to her normal self — whatever that might be.

"Here we are," Frank announced as they pulled up on the drive outside his large house. "Let's get you inside, young lady. You must be worn out."

"No, I'm fine, honestly, Uncle Frank. I slept on the train," Trinity said.

Jarrod was already waiting to help Sylvia and Trinity out of the car so Cordell slowly made his way toward the house where Frank was unlocking the front door.

"I don't like it," the older man whispered. "I know she's just lost her home, but I reckon there's more to it than that. She used to be so bubbly and lively. Hell, it was hard to get a word in edgeways last time she was here. I'm gonna get to the bottom of all this if it kills me." His face tightened as he spoke.

Cordell frowned, but, noticing the women catching up to them, said nothing.

"I'll put the coffee on," Frank offered as they all piled into the hallway. It was a beautiful home, with high ceilings and large rooms.

"Let me show you your room," Sylvia told Trinity with a smile. She led her up the stairs while the guys went through to the kitchen.

"Where have you been hiding her?" Jarrod asked, hoisting himself up to sit on the counter. His long legs dangled and he rolled up the sleeves of his white cotton shirt to reveal his ripped arms.

"I told you. She lives in Nebraska," Frank told him gruffly. "She used to come out here for holidays and stuff when she was growing up, but since she's started working, we've hardly seen her."

"She's sure grown into a gorgeous woman," Jarrod remarked.

Cordell was expecting Frank to berate Jarrod, but instead, the old man frowned thoughtfully. "She has." He nodded.

"But she's got a boyfriend, right? I noticed she's wearing a ring with a heart on it."

Cordell stared pointedly at Jarrod, recalling how Frank had filled them in on the situation earlier. "Here, let me help." He took out the coffee cups and pointed to a high stool where Frank obediently plunked himself down with a sigh.

"That ring was her momma's. It's probably the only thing she's got left of her now." He pursed his lips. "She did have a boyfriend, though. I presume they're still together."

"Then where the hell is he?" Jarrod fumed. "He should be with her right now, not leaving her to deal with all this by herself. What sort of a man is he?"

Frank shook his head. "I never met him."

"Maybe that's part of the problem," Cordell offered. "If it was a bad split, it could have left her in a state, without her home going up in flames on top of it all. I think we need to tread carefully for a while, at least until we know the situation." He gave Jarrod one of his *I hope you're listening to this* stares before resuming preparation of the drinks.

He could feel Jarrod staring at the back of his head and knew his buddy had gotten his message loud and clear, although Cordell realized Jarrod wouldn't like it. Despite being one of the biggest flirts in Cavern County, Jarrod had a heart of gold. Cordell could see he liked Trinity—who wouldn't?—but he would need to tread carefully to avoid upsetting her. Jarrod's stunning appearance never failed to turn women weak at the knees, but in Trinity's case, that was the last thing she needed. The poor girl looked weak enough already.

He'd noted that Jarrod listened intently when Frank had told them last night that he would need a helping hand today, and he guessed the old man wasn't just referring to physical help. The poor guy had turned pale when he had explained to them that his niece had recently lost her home when a gas pipe exploded right outside her apartment building. Sylvia's sister—Trinity's mom—had passed away a few years ago, and the girl's dad hadn't been on the scene for a long while before that. Frank and Sylvia were worried sick about their niece and had insisted that she come to stay with them for a while. They were determined to care for her whether she wanted them to or not. She was quite independent, apparently, so had been a little reluctant to take them up on their offer.

It was hard to imagine Trinity as being a self-reliant chatterbox. Her face was pale and tired and her tiny frame made her seem fragile and weak. She was wearing jeans and a white T-shirt with Converse sneakers, and if it weren't for her bright pink hair, she would simply blend into any crowd. Her penchant for vivid pink made him think there was much more to Trinity Ellis than her manner suggested...

While the coffee pot gurgled away, Cordell turned around to face Frank, who looked lost in his thoughts as he sat at the counter staring into space. "How long will she be staying here?" he asked.

Frank quickly started in surprise, as though dragging himself from his muse. "As long as we can get her to," he murmured, half to himself, Cordell surmised.

"You said she worked from home. Has she got anything to go back to Nebraska for?" Jarrod frowned.

"I don't know. I suppose it hinges on this guy of hers," Frank replied. "If it's serious, she might want to get back to him as soon as she can." He pursed his lips thoughtfully. "It depends how she feels."

Cordell felt a jolt in his stomach at the thought of her boyfriend abandoning her at a time like this. "Can't be much of a man if he doesn't stick around when she needs him," he muttered.

"Ain't that the truth?" Jarrod chimed in with a sneer.

"Now, come on, guys. We don't know the whole story. Let's not jump to conclusions, shall we? There could be a perfectly good explanation as to why he's not here." Frank put a hand up to pacify them as he stood.

"I can't think of anything that would be counted as a good reason for not being with a girl when she needs him," Jarrod protested. "Any guy worth his salt would rush to be with her at a time like this. That girl needs comforting, looking after. Whoever this guy is, I could punch his dang lights out for not being there for her. He doesn't deserve a girl like Trinity. I don't care what his excuse is, it's not good enough. What sort of guy leaves a girl right after her home gets burned down?"

A sudden noise from the doorway made them all turn

around.

"A dead one," Trinity replied.

Chapter Two

Trinity trembled as the heavy atmosphere threatened to suffocate her. Everyone was staring at her and she could feel their shame and horror. She was tempted to run out of the house and free those tears that were burning the back of her eyes, to sob her heart out at the whole unfairness of it all, but she wouldn't. She was stronger than that. She had to be. Besides, Aunt Sylvia was right behind her.

"Is that coffee ready yet?" she asked, forcing her legs to move as she made her way toward the counter. Aunt Sylvia rested a hand on her back and she knew the old lady was probably desperate to hold her, which was the last thing she needed right now.

Cordell was gaping at her, his handsome face tense and uncomfortable. The thick mustache that cradled his top lip twitched as he quickly closed his mouth and obviously struggled to find the right words to say. "Yeah, sure." He turned his attention to the pot and began pouring out the coffee. "I'm real sorry about—"

"It's fine," she told him, putting a hand up to stop him apologizing. She could just about cope with his awkwardness, but she knew she was screwed if he was about to be nice to her. "Are there any cookies in that jar?" She nodded to the container on the counter and Cordell quickly grabbed it and passed it to her.

"Trinity, sugar, we didn't know. I mean, you said your apartment had been hit in that explosion, but not that—"

Uncle Frank sounded devastated and she couldn't help feeling sorry for him.

"It really is all right," she told him as nonchalantly as she could manage, pulling out a chocolate-chip cookie. "He was in the apartment when it went up in flames." The lump that had formed in her throat threatened to choke her, and she knew the cookie was a bad idea. She wasn't going to cry in front of everyone, though. *No way.* She sniffed, climbing onto the stool next to her uncle. Her legs dangled, not quite reaching the bottom rung, let alone the floor.

"Why didn't you say?" Aunt Sylvia threw her arms around Trinity's shoulders, smothering her in the scent of lavender. She knew her aunt meant well, but her kindness melted the heart she was trying so vehemently to keep hardened — for the time being, anyhow.

"It's okay," she said, clearing her throat as she tried to gently push her aunt's arms off her. "Honestly, I'm fine. You really don't have to worry."

She was ashamed, noticing the hurt expression in her aunt's eyes, and she quickly looked away. Unfortunately, her gaze automatically fell on the handsome guy who was handing out the coffees and she noticed he was watching her with a slight frown. She really didn't need Cordell's disapproval on top of everything else.

"Any cookies left in that jar?" Jarrod was sitting at the end of the counter and bent across to reach the container that was right in front of Trinity.

Grateful for the distraction, she quickly put her hand out to pass it to him, just as his long fingers covered hers. He leaned over and she was suddenly surrounded by his fresh cologne and the warmth of his body as it homed in on hers. Closing her eyes to savor the moment, she was surprised at how peaceful she suddenly felt, amid all the tension and awkwardness of the situation. She took a deep breath, as though breathing the guy into her, letting his calmness wash over her tightly-coiled soul.

A low chuckle made her quickly open her eyes and she stared right into his. Jarrod was dark-haired and had a thin layer of scruff around his face, which gave him a slightly laid-back appearance. Tiny creases at the sides of his deep-brown eyes indicated his jovial nature and his wide smile relaxed her. She flushed and her stomach suddenly burned with need.

She went to pull her hand from under his but his palm held her firm. Although she quite enjoyed the feeling of his fingers wrapped over hers, she was a little surprised at his reluctance to free her. She glanced up at him and caught him give her a quick wink before finally releasing her. She shook her head with embarrassment. He was certainly a charmer. She had to admit he was gorgeous, but she wasn't looking for another guy and, besides, he was gay, wasn't he? He and Cordell seemed so close, and they lived together. *That has to be the reason, right?*

"So, what are your plans for tomorrow?" Cordell asked, making her jump around as she suddenly remembered they weren't the only ones in the room.

"Um…" Trinity was tongue-tied, probably for the first time in her life.

"I thought we might go over to Almondine, do a little shopping," Aunt Sylvia replied before taking a sip of her coffee. Her aunt had remarked on how few clothes she had left, and Trinity knew she was worried about her. She was sitting opposite Uncle Frank at the counter, and Cordell slid into the seat next to her, making him directly opposite Trinity.

"Anything else you'd like to do, sugar?" Uncle Frank asked, turning to her.

Trinity shrugged. "It's been a while since I was here, Uncle Frank. I wouldn't mind doing a little exploring, if that's okay? See how much it's changed in the past couple of years."

"Quite a bit, I should think," Aunt Sylvia told her with a smile.

"Oh, Pelican's Heath hasn't changed that much," Uncle Frank said, pursing his lips, thoughtfully. "Maybe one or two more shops, but that's about it."

"We've even got our own beauty salon," Aunt Sylvia

announced proudly.

Trinity perked up at the thought. "Have you?"

Jarrod chuckled. "Now don't get too excited," he told her. "What your aunt means is that we've got a hairdresser who also paints nails."

"What more do you need?" Trinity replied with a weak smile. She became hotter as she gazed at the handsome cowboy and inwardly admonished herself.

Feeling a little more relaxed now, she bit into her cookie. It was yummy. Aunt Sylvia had been right about her not eating for a while. She hadn't had much appetite for weeks, since before that awful incident, in fact. It was surprising how ravenous she suddenly was now. It must have been because of the country air.

"I'll get some dinner on soon." Aunt Sylvia had either read her mind or noticed how she'd devoured that cookie. Either way, she was grateful.

"There's a group playing in town on Saturday," Cordell remarked. "Do you like country music, Trinity?"

She glanced over at him, a little surprised. "Yeah," she replied cautiously.

"Hey, great idea. We can take you. It's only at the bar down the road, but it's a first for Pelican's Heath. We never get stuff like that going on, so it's kind of a big deal." Jarrod became quite excited as he spoke. "What do you reckon, Trinity? Fancy a night out?"

"We quite understand if it's too soon," Cordell interjected quickly, as he and Uncle Frank exchanged a quick look.

Trinity sighed. Although the thought of a night of drinking and dancing to a live band would usually get her all revved up, now really wasn't the time.

"Can I think about it?" she asked.

"Of course, darlin'." Jarrod nodded.

"Sure thing. Well, we'd best get going, anyhow." Cordell stood, staring pointedly at his friend.

"Yep. We'll let you folks get some supper," Jarrod agreed as he got up to go. "It was lovely meeting you, Trinity. Hope to see you tomorrow, maybe?" He peered questioningly as he came over and held out his hand.

She took a deep breath, enjoying his scent as he neared her. "Probably." She nodded as they shook, then reached out for Cordell's hand. Cordell was definitely a hard worker, judging by the roughness of his palm. His cologne was spicier than Jarrod's, too, she noticed.

"I'll see you out, guys." Uncle Frank got up.

Aunt Sylvia was studying her carefully as they were left alone in the kitchen. "Are you all right, honey? They didn't upset you, did they?"

Trinity frowned. "No, of course not. But I hope they didn't think I was rude not to accept their invitation."

Aunt Sylvia chuckled. "I'm sure they didn't, hon. They're a couple of lovely guys. They don't mean any harm, but, I'm afraid they're not the most tactful people." Aunt Sylvia was renowned for seeing the best in folk.

"So, how do you know them?" Trinity got up and cleared the dishes into the washer while Aunt Sylvia started preparing supper.

"They work over at the Fielding Ranch," her aunt replied, slamming the oven door. "Ben reckons they're a real boon. Jarrod trains the horses. He's excellent at it, by all accounts. Ben and Aiden reckon they're lucky to have him. Cordell took over as foreman when Jeremy left to be with his girlfriend up north. Been there about a year or so now."

Trinity rolled her lips thoughtfully. "So, what are they doing here?"

Aunt Sylvia glanced over in surprise. "They're friends of ours. They help out with odd jobs around the place."

Trinity studied the large kitchen. She'd always loved this house. Uncle Frank and Aunt Sylvia were quite wealthy, having held good jobs until they'd both retired.

The house was set away from the main road, up a long drive, and had ample grounds all around it. She recalled how Aunt Sylvia loved gardening and would spend hours tending the flowers while she'd played on the swing Uncle

Frank had fashioned from some rope on a low-hanging branch. He had often promised to buy her a new swing and maybe a climbing frame to play on whenever she visited, but Trinity had insisted that she preferred to climb the trees and play on her 'special' swing. She'd also been unable to bear the thought of cluttering up Aunt Sylvia's immaculate garden with big lumps of ugly metal.

"Do you need some help there?" she asked when she'd finished wiping over the counter and straightening the stools.

"No, I'm fine, honey. It's all ready to cook now. Why don't you go put your feet up? You must be tired."

"No. I thought I'd take a stroll around the garden, if you don't need me for a while."

"Of course. Do you want me to join you? I can go get my other shoes on and —"

"No, you get some rest, Aunt Sylvia. I only mean to take a meander."

Aunt Sylvia smiled and Trinity headed out the back door.

She could hear muttering coming from the front of the house and realized that her uncle was still chatting with the two cowboys.

As she wandered down the garden, she marveled at how impeccably it had all been kept. Aunt Sylvia clearly hadn't lost her touch. The well-manicured lawn and precisely-trimmed hedges took her back to the days when she and her mom had stayed here. Long, sunny days that her mom and Auntie Sylvia would spend lazing on the sun-beds while she would run around with her imaginary friends and make secret dens in the bushes. She toyed with a little gold heart-shaped ring that she always wore.

To her shame, she realized she hadn't been back here since a short while after her mom had died. Aunt Sylvia and Uncle Frank had been contacted by the hospital at the same time she had been called to say that her mom had been taken in. She still blamed herself for having been away at university instead of staying at home to care for her mom.

But Mom hadn't seemed ill at all. She had been in remission and everyone had expected her to be fine. They'd had no reason to suspect that the breast cancer would suddenly return and attack her body so violently. By the time the doctors had realized what it was, it had already spread too far. Mom had died in her arms with Aunt Sylvia and Uncle Frank sitting at the bedside.

She would always be grateful for the way Aunt Sylvia and Uncle Frank had taken over the handling of Mom's affairs. As soon as she had been diagnosed with cancer for the first time, Mom had written her will and had put money aside for her funeral, just in case. They'd even laughed about it when she recovered, making light of the fact that it would all 'come in handy one day.' That day had come much sooner than anyone could have imagined, and Trinity had been grateful that Mom had put everything in place.

After the funeral, Aunt Sylvia had insisted on bringing Trinity back here while she straightened out her thoughts. She had already been attending university in Nebraska and was lucky to be far enough ahead in her studies that taking a short time off to come to terms with her bereavement hadn't affected her grades. Mom had been so proud of her getting into college that it was only fitting for her to go back and finish her exams. The day she'd graduated, Uncle Frank and Aunt Sylvia had been there to support her, assuring her that her mom had been watching, too.

As she ran her hand over the scented lilacs that blossomed on the old tree, she recalled how much her mom had loved it here. She was ashamed that she hadn't come back to visit more often in the couple of years after her mom had passed on. Her aunt and uncle weren't getting any younger, and they might need some help around the place—help that family should provide, and that meant *her*. It rankled her that they were relying on their neighbors to lend a hand while she was miles away in Nebraska.

Two gorgeous faces flashed in front of her eyes and she cursed herself for being so affected by them. There had been moments earlier when she had actually felt something toward those guys. *Attraction? Affection?* Whatever it was, it had to go. Kevin had only been buried a couple of weeks ago, and she sure wasn't after any kind of a relationship now — if ever.

Chapter Three

Aunt Sylvia had already organized a cab to take Trinity and her into Almondine the next morning.

"Your aunt's been looking forward to spending some girly time with you," Uncle Frank announced as Trinity took her chair at the breakfast table. "I don't know what it is about you girls and shopping." He teased with a smile. "Did you sleep all right, sugar?"

"Yes, thanks, Uncle Frank." Trinity smiled at them. "I can't get over how quiet it is out here. I could get used to this." She had been surprised how well she had slept. It had been the first time in the eight weeks since the incident that she hadn't spent the night tossing and turning. The little room she had stayed in at the Fuchsia Falls Hotel, back in Nebraska, had been constantly stuffy and the bed was the most uncomfortable contraption on God's earth.

Uncle Frank smiled. "Good. You stay as long as you like."

"I do have to get back to Nebraska sometime," Trinity told him, munching on a croissant. "Hmm, these are lovely."

"I thought you worked freelance?" Aunt Sylvia frowned. "Surely, you could work from anywhere? I mean, I don't know much about these things, but don't you do it all on computers these days? Surely, you could set up anywhere?"

"I think your aunt has got plans to kidnap you and keep you here forever," Uncle Frank told Trinity with a conspiratorial grin. "She kinda likes having another woman about the place."

"It makes a change from all the guys we get hanging out here," Aunt Sylvia protested, playfully. "I think a little female company will do me the world of good." She winked at Trinity, who grinned.

"You don't normally complain about all the male attention," Uncle Frank teased. "You're practically a momma to most of those young men."

Trinity frowned. "Like who?"

"Well, Aiden and Ben Fielding, for a start." Frank turned to Trinity. "You might remember them. They own the ranch right across the way there."

"Vaguely. They had a sister, too, if I recall correctly. Josie, wasn't it?" Trinity was pleased at how easily she was able to recall how it was when she had last been here. It felt so homey.

"Yeah, I keep asking Josie to get on over here with little Curtis, but she's so busy I hardly get to see either of them." Aunt Sylvia pouted.

"Curtis?" Trinity frowned, racking her memory.

Aunt Sylvia smiled. "Josie had a little boy. He's getting on to eighteen months now. He's gorgeous. And Aiden's married now, too. His wife Maggie is wonderful. You'll love her."

Frank nodded. "And, of course, Cordell and Jarrod, who you met last night. They may as well move in here altogether, the amount of time they spend here." He feigned grumpiness, but Aunt Sylvia was laughing.

"I wouldn't mind in the slightest," she told him. "They are welcome anytime. I've told them that. They're worth their weight in gold."

Trinity looked up in surprise.

"Well, I have to admit I don't know where we'd be without them," Frank conceded, "especially when that dang pipe burst last winter. They turned up and got on with the job without any fuss, despite working full-time at the ranch at the same time. Worked around the clock they did, making sure we had some kind of heating and somewhere dry to sleep."

"Only because you refused to move out for a while," Aunt Sylvia reminded him.

"I didn't want to just go off and leave them to sort out our mess," Uncle Frank replied.

"They wouldn't have minded," she said.

"Well, we had a lot of fun, didn't we? Despite all the hours those boys worked, they were so cheerful, always cracking jokes and stuff. It was a riot with them around." He chuckled, clearly remembering the incident.

Aunt Sylvia laughed. "They had us in stitches, Trinity," she told her, shaking her head. "It was a fun time."

Trinity said nothing but continued to eat her breakfast while her aunt and uncle reminisced about all the hilarity that had clearly ensued while the guys had been helping get their house fixed up after the pipe had flooded the ground floor.

"So, you know them quite well then?" she asked after a while. She didn't know why, but the thought of her aunt and uncle getting on so well with the young men irked her somewhat. *I should have been here to help.*

"Oh, yeah, they're almost like family. Aren't they, Frank?" Aunt Sylvia smiled.

That wasn't what Trinity wanted to hear.

"You could say that," Uncle Frank replied, patting his wife's hand.

Trinity suddenly lost her appetite and stood. "I'll go get my purse," she told her aunt. "How long before the cab gets here?"

Aunt Sylvia glanced up at the clock, startled. "It's due any minute," she said, quickly standing.

"I'll do the dishes. You go powder that pretty little nose of yours," Frank told her, as Sylvia started stacking the plates.

"If you're sure?"

"I insist. Now go on. You don't want to keep the cab waiting."

Trinity smiled at the affectionate exchange between them. They were obviously still very much in love and she wished she could be in a relationship like that one day. It wouldn't be any time soon, though, she mused as she went upstairs.

At one time, she had hoped that she and Kev would have some kind of future, but that boat had sailed even before the dang gas pipe had blown up and claimed his life.

* * * *

Almondine sure was a busy town and much larger than Trinity had remembered. Aunt Sylvia seemed to enjoy showing her around the shops and she'd insisted on treating her to some new clothes, although Trinity was determined that her aunt wasn't to pay for everything.

"I'll repay you as soon as the insurance coughs up," Trinity told her aunt for the umpteenth time as the old lady added another couple of tops to the pile of jeans they'd already selected.

"We'll see," her aunt replied with a shake of her head.

Trinity knew Aunt Sylvia didn't want reimbursing for all the things she had bought her today, but she planned to repay the money, anyway. She had always paid her own way and wasn't comfortable taking anything from the elderly couple. She had no choice right now, though. Until the insurance paid out on the contents of her apartment, she was relying on her savings to get her through. Most of that was money left to her when her mom had passed away, which, until now, had been termed her 'emergency fund'. Although she felt quite justified that this situation was certainly an emergency, it was worrying to see how quickly her inheritance was dwindling.

"Your Uncle Frank said he'd meet us at the diner in Pelican's Heath later," Aunt Sylvia announced when they left the boutique and went back out onto the crowded street. "But we can grab a coffee and a bite to eat for now, if you'd like?"

Trinity smiled. She guessed this was her aunt's subtle way of telling her she was getting tired and was about ready for a break. Aunt Sylvia was much grayer than the last time she'd seen her and Uncle Frank's hair had mostly turned white.

"Is there anything *you* need?" she asked the older lady, as they headed toward a small cafe. "We've got all this stuff for me but you've hardly got a thing."

Aunt Sylvia laughed. "I've got all I need, honey," she told her, putting an arm around her.

Trinity smiled, knowing that she wasn't referring to clothing or the type of 'essentials' they had been buying all morning. Aunt Sylvia sure seemed content with her life, and Trinity was happy for her. She hadn't kept in touch with her relatives half as much as she should have, and it had somehow slipped her mind what a loving couple they were.

The sun had gone AWOL and it was another cool day in Cavern County, so they were grateful for the warmth of a small café tucked away down a side street. Trinity guessed that not too many people were aware of the little building, as it was easy to find an empty table, which had surprised her, given how busy Almondine was.

"Do you come in here often?" she asked, as they sipped their coffee.

Aunt Sylvia smiled. "I don't get over this way much," she told her. "It's not so much fun on your own." Trinity recognized a pang inside her, realizing how lonely her aunt must be. She evidently didn't get much female company, and she clearly missed it. Trinity thought how much she would love to live out here and meet up for regular chats with her aunt. Her relatives were right about not getting any younger and she was all the family they had left now.

"We seem to have bought you nothing but jeans and tops," Aunt Sylvia commented with a frown. "What about some nice clothes for going out or something?"

Trinity declined politely with a smile. "I don't need anything else," she replied. "I don't need to dress up for work as I do it all from home, and I can't see me going out gallivanting anywhere for quite a while."

Her aunt pursed her lips thoughtfully. "Must have been a

dreadful business losing your boyfriend like that," she said, softly.

Trinity sighed. "It was awful, to be honest, Aunt Sylvia," she admitted. "Kevin and I had planned to go out that night, but we'd had a fight—another one." She grimaced, recalling how things had gone.

"So, you weren't getting on too well?" Her aunt frowned sympathetically.

"No. It was my fault. I accused him of some awful things. I was surprised he stayed with me as long as he did, to be honest."

Aunt Sylvia took a sip of her coffee but didn't say anything.

It was warm and quiet in the café with a radio playing some gentle country music somewhere in the background. Trinity relaxed into the easy atmosphere as her mind drifted back to the way things had been in Nebraska.

"We'd been together about six months or so when I first began to notice things," she explained, "things that hadn't seemed to matter before. Kev was a sales rep for a pharmaceutical company so he didn't stay with me all the time. He had to travel so much with his job that he often booked into hotels and stuff on weekends. It hadn't bothered me at first, but I began to realize just how many times he had to stay away. When he was with me, he was usually working on his computer.

"He didn't leave much stuff at my place because he was always living out of a suitcase. I expected to get all his laundry to do every week, but he said that most of the time he'd had it done at the hotels he stayed at."

"He must have been making a good wage, then," Aunt Sylvia commented.

"That was exactly it," Trinity said, shaking her head. "When we first got together, he seemed to have plenty to keep him going and to take me out occasionally. We went to some real nice places, too. I don't know if he was just trying to impress me or something. Anyway, it wasn't long before he started saying he had to tighten his belt a little, as his money wasn't as good as it used to be. I thought it strange because he was working even more by then."

Aunt Sylvia frowned. "Did you ask him about it?"

She nodded with a grimace. "Plenty of times. He told me I was nagging. I only wanted to understand, you know? See if we could find a solution to the problem. It seemed that the harder he worked, the less money he made. I wasn't worried about the cash, as I was making quite a good wage and I knew we could always fall back on Mom's money if things got too tight." She flinched, noticing the unhappy expression on her aunt's face.

"That's not exactly an ideal solution, honey," the older lady interjected.

Trinity sighed. "I know. I just wanted to work things out so we could spend more time together," she told her.

"And did you?"

"No. We just only ended up arguing more and he spent even longer away working. I thought he was actually trying to avoid me sometimes."

"Didn't you talk about it properly?" Aunt Sylvia's concern was etched across her face.

Trinity chewed her lip. "He seemed to think I was accusing him of something — which I wasn't — not at the time, anyhow," she explained. "He asked if I thought he was seeing someone else, spending all his money on another woman or something. I told him it hadn't occurred to me, but then it got me wondering if maybe he was."

Aunt Sylvia frowned. "You honestly thought he might have been cheating on you?"

Trinity huffed. "I don't know. At first, I told him he was being paranoid for even considering that I'd think like that. It honestly hadn't crossed my mind. But the more time he stayed away, the more suspicious I got. Then a flowery handkerchief fell out of his jeans pocket when I was tidying his clothes." She cringed, glancing warily at her aunt.

"Did you ask him about it?"

She nodded. "It was that day — the day it happened," she

explained. "He went mad at me for touching his clothes. He said I was snooping, but I wasn't. I asked him where the handkerchief had come from and he said he'd picked it up off the floor in the hotel foyer. He's assumed some old lady had dropped it and he was going to hand it into the concierge but he'd gotten distracted by a business call and had forgotten all about it."

"And you didn't believe him?"

Trinity felt a lump well in her throat as she recalled the massive falling-out that had ensued that evening.

"It smelled of expensive perfume, not the kind of thing you'd expect an old woman to wear." She noticed a pang of guilt as she stared at her aunt. "Not that I think—"

"It's fine. I understand." Aunt Sylvia put up a hand to reassure her she hadn't taken offense.

"He got real mad at me. Told me he knew I didn't trust him."

"And did you?"

"I don't know," she admitted quietly. "I wanted to. But the more I thought about it, the more things didn't add up. He was always tired when we were together. He didn't want to take me out anymore. I never knew which hotels he was staying in as he said he often changed his mind about where to stay at the last minute, so it was best to contact him on his cell if it was important. And that was it. In the early days, he used to love hearing from me, even if he was in a meeting. Then it became a case of only being able to call if it was real important. If not, he'd call me at some point when he was free. His voicemail was on or his cell was off altogether most times I rang."

"Did he offer any kind of explanation?" Aunt Sylvia frowned.

Trinity shook her head again. "Not exactly. He claimed that he was busy. Anyhow, we were in the middle of this huge fight when his cell rang. He'd left it on the coffee table and I got to it before he did. It was someone called Poppy. I asked him who it was but he whipped the dang thing out of my hand and quickly switched it off. That was it. He accused me of all sorts of things then, claiming I snooped through his stuff, checked his cell and asked questions all the time. He said he seemed like he was under a microscope every time he came home. I told him he shouldn't be so dang secretive. Then he came right out and asked me if I thought he was having an affair. I didn't know what to say. I told him it sure looked that way, given how riled up he was about the whole thing."

Hot tears began to roll down her cheeks and Trinity wiped them away angrily. "We were supposed to be going out for a drink that night with some friends, but he didn't want to come after that. He was still yelling at me when the cab arrived. I was so mad that I told him I'd rather go on my own, anyway, so I did." She sniffed hard. "It wasn't long after that we heard this huge explosion while we were all drinking a few blocks away. I just knew something bad had happened to Kev. I could feel it."

Aunt Sylvia placed a cool hand on her arm. "It wasn't your fault, honey," she assured her.

"But he should have come with me," Trinity insisted. "If we hadn't had that dang argument, we would both have been out of there when it happened."

"You can't blame yourself for that," Aunt Sylvia told her. "He was a grown man and made his own decision not to go with you. That's not on you."

"But if we hadn't had that squabble—"

Aunt Sylvia came to sit next to her and took her in her arms. Trinity sobbed into the comfort of the soft lady, letting all the guilt and hurt flow from her tense body. She didn't know how long she cried for but was relieved to have finally told someone. It was the first time she had spoken about the whole affair—and she hoped it would be the last.

Chapter Four

"Thought I might hit the diner over at Almondine for some lunch if you're up for it?" Jarrod appeared around the side of the stables early that afternoon with a massive grin on his face. The bright sun made his hair shine, and his perfect teeth gleamed through his tanned face.

Cordell hung up the saddle he'd removed from one of the horses and turned to gawk incredulously at his buddy. "You wanna stop work and go all that way just to eat?" he clarified with a knowing nod.

Jarrod grinned. "Or the café. It's a nice day. Thought it might make a change. I don't have too much on for the next hour or two and I know you've got enough hands here to cover you. What do you say?"

"I say you're not fooling anyone," Cordell muttered, patting the horse and walking out the side door. "You're hoping to see Trinity Ellis down there and you dang well know it."

Jarrod chuckled. "Me? How could you think such a thing?" He gave his friend a gasp of feigned shock and burst out laughing again. "Okay, maybe there's a *slight* chance Sylvia could decide to drop into her favorite coffee shop with her beautiful niece. Who knows?"

Cordell rolled his eyes. He called over one of the hands.

"Sam, can you give Caspar a good brushing? And check he's got plenty of water in there. He's had a good run and it's hot up on the mountain." He indicated to the foothills where he had recently exercised the horse. Sam nodded happily and set to work.

"Come on then, Captain Obvious. Let's go see who's

about, shall we?" He led the way toward one of the pick-ups and they both jumped in.

"You haven't forgotten that this girl's off limits, have you?" Cordell checked as he drove down the track.

"No, I haven't," Jarrod replied firmly. "But that doesn't mean we have to ignore her altogether."

Cordell sighed. "She's been through so much. It wasn't too long ago that she lost her mom. Now, to lose her boyfriend, as well as her home... I can't imagine how she must feel."

"*I've* got an idea how she feels," Jarrod replied quietly.

Cordell hit the steering wheel, angry at himself. "Man, I'm so sorry. I didn't think —"

"Hey, it's fine," Jarrod assured him, putting a hand up to reassure his friend. "All I'm saying is I know what it's like to lose someone. Everyone tiptoes around you, afraid to say the wrong thing. Trouble is, they end up not saying anything. They avoid you. Then you feel like it's all your fault for making them feel uncomfortable. You can't win."

"I'm sorry," Cordell repeated, shaking his head slowly. "I didn't think."

"Good. That's the whole point. I don't *want* you to have to stop and think every time you open your mouth. Christ, if you spent all your time wondering if what you wanted to say was likely to offend me, you'd never get the words out. Mom and Dad died. It's shit. I hate it, but it happened. I have to face it and get on with my life. I can't keep looking forward if everyone around me is looking backward, now can I?" Jarrod smiled.

"You're something else, you know that?" Cordell couldn't help admiring him.

Jarrod had been so cut up when his parents died in a car crash, at one time it seemed as though he'd never smile again. He knew Jarrod blamed himself for not being there. Somehow, he'd made it his fault for not going around to see them enough. Guilt had weighed so heavily on his friend's shoulders that Jarrod had appeared as though he'd disappear through a hole in the ground.

"That's why we're such good friends," Jarrod replied with a cheeky wink.

Cordell chuckled. It was so good to see Jarrod back to his old, cocky self again. They'd been friends since they'd first started high school and had been caught cutting class together. They'd bonded over a mutual dislike for their math teacher and been best buddies ever since. Jarrod had always had a laid-back attitude, and it had been awful to see him so down, but he'd certainly improved once they'd moved to Cavern County. There were no memories here, no sympathetic locals telling Jarrod how sorry they were. Nothing to remind him of what happened. It had been a year now since they'd moved out here and they both agreed it was the best thing they'd ever done.

"You really like her, don't you?" Cordell asked as he pulled up outside the diner.

"And you're telling me you don't?" Jarrod looked incredulous, clearly because of the conversation they'd had the previous night after leaving her. Jarrod had always wanted a ménage with a girl, but Cordell had been a little hesitant about the idea. They felt more like brothers than best friends. But having met Trinity and knowing the effect she had on both of them, Cordell had had to admit to a slight change of heart.

"If and when the time's right."

"I hear ya." Jarrod laughed as they left the truck and headed inside.

They managed to find a table near the window.

"No sign of her," Cordell murmured, surreptitiously peering around. "Though I can't see a thing through that line." He nodded to where the cashier was making her way through a crowd of people waiting to pay. "And I sure didn't notice them in the diner as we came past, either."

"Probably still shopping," Jarrod said with a grin. "You know how women are once they get started."

"Don't let them hear you saying that." Cordell chuckled.

"Let who hear you saying what?" Rhona, the waitress,

was suddenly standing by their table with a notepad in her hand and big grin on her face.

"Oh, nothing," Cordell replied. "I'll take a quarter-pounder with fries please, darlin', and a root beer."

"I'll have the same." Jarrod smiled.

"Coming right up," she promised.

Cordell leaned forward once they were alone again. "Frank's very worried about that niece of his," he murmured. "Said she's nothing like her usual self."

"What does he expect?" Jarrod frowned. "She's just lost everything and everyone she had, by the looks of things. She's hardly gonna be all smiles and rainbows, now is she?"

"Keep your damn voice down," Cordell hissed, noticing a few people glancing over. "It's not like that."

Jarrod huffed. "Well, what is it like, then?"

"He said she's—" His gaze wandered over to the counter as he spoke. "She's here," he said quickly.

"Well, what in hell is that supposed to mean— Oh." Jarrod had clearly followed his gaze.

Cordell had noticed the two ladies sipping coffee at a small table on the other side of the café. Now that the crowd had cleared, it was plain to see them.

"I'll go call them over," Jarrod offered, standing up.

"No." Cordell stopped him.

Jarrod frowned. "Is something wrong, bro?"

"I'm not sure." Cordell licked his bottom lip thoughtfully, as Jarrod sat back down.

"I don't think Trinity will want to see us right now," he confided, leaning into his partner.

Trinity was shaking and wiping her face with her handkerchief.

"She's upset," Jarrod surmised after watching the women for a few minutes.

Rhona brought their meals over and they delved into them, though their cheerful moods of earlier had dissipated.

"Sure seems like they did some shopping," Jarrod remarked.

Cordell had also noticed the bags that surrounded their little table. "If all she owned was in that bag last night, I'd say she needed to."

"It's hard to imagine losing all your stuff like that," Jarrod said. "I mean, all your personal things—photographs, mementos from your childhood..."

"Keepsakes from her parents, too, I'd imagine," Cordell added, thoughtfully.

"What about her work stuff? Didn't Frank say she worked from home?"

Cordell hadn't thought of that. "She's some kind of artist or illustrator or something. Fuck, she must have had all sorts of irreplaceable stuff."

"Most of it would have been done digitally, I'd have thought," Jarrod commented, finishing the last of his fries. "I hope she had it all backed up somewhere safe."

Cordell nodded. He couldn't finish his burger. His stomach was churning too much. Trinity looked real cute with her Barbie-pink hair and bright canary-yellow bag. Her image was sure at odds with her melancholy demeanor, and he knew she was usually much livelier than she appeared. Frank had told him that she was a real live wire, the life and soul of the party. That had been before all this had occurred. It didn't seem fair that such a disaster had happened to this lovely girl. He hoped those shopping bags of hers contained some bright, cheery colors and the sort of outfits she would normally wear. The plain T-shirt and jeans she had on were definitely not her normal attire, he guessed.

"You okay, bro?" Jarrod frowned at the half-eaten burger.

"Yeah, just not as hungry as I thought I was."

"You sure it's not got something to do with a certain pink-haired girl sitting over there?"

Cordell sighed. "Maybe. Anyhow, I don't know about you, but I've got a shed-load of work to get through this afternoon, so I guess it's time to get moving."

"Okay, I've got this." Jarrod whipped the tab from the

table and made his way over to the counter to pay.

Cordell walked up behind him and was surprised to hear his name being called.

"Cordell, over here." Sylvia was waving to him from her table.

Cordell had been avoiding looking that way, but now he turned to face the women. "Sylvia, Trinity, hey there." He smiled, walking slowly toward them. "How was the shopping trip?" He eyed their bags.

"It was fun, wasn't it?" Sylvia replied, nodding at Trinity. "I think we wore ourselves out, though."

"Are you all right to get home? We've got the truck, but—"

"Oh, no, it's fine, thank you. I thought I'd show Trinity around Almondine for a while then we'll get a cab back to Pelican's Heath where Frank'll meet us. He's just gone to visit Matt Shearer up at their ranch. There's no rush."

"Well, if you're sure?"

"Yes, of course, dear. Thank you, though."

He noticed that Trinity was nodding, too, but she didn't speak. She was beautiful, despite her face being red and her eyes puffy. He had to fight his natural instinct to throw an arm around her.

"Frank's meeting us in Pelican's Heath," Sylvia went on. "We wanted to know if you boys might be free to stop by later. It's not urgent if you're busy, of course."

"No, not at all," Cordell assured her.

"Thank you. He's boxed up some old books he wants to store for a while. He's making some room in the study for Trinity, so he needs them out of the way. They're way too heavy for us to lift, though."

Cordell raised his eyebrows. "We'd be happy to."

"Sounds like I'm being volunteered for something over here," Jarrod piped up from behind him.

"Hi, Jarrod. I was just asking if you guys wouldn't mind moving some old books later. Frank's having a bit of a tidy up." Sylvia smiled.

"Seriously?" Jarrod gawked in surprise. "Is he feeling all

right?"

Sylvia tutted playfully. "He's fine. He only wanted to clear the spare desk so Trinity could do some work there."

Jarrod smiled at Trinity. "Work, eh? Does that mean you're planning to stick around for a while, darlin'?"

Trinity's voice was a little croaky. "I haven't decided what to do yet," she replied slowly, clearly trying not to catch his eye.

"She wants to keep her hand in. Can't have her getting bored while she's with us, now, can we?" Sylvia interjected.

"And there was me getting my hopes up," Jarrod replied, putting his hand to his chest, jokingly.

"We'll be there after supper, ma'am," Cordell said quickly, noticing the strained expression on Trinity's face. "Come on, buddy."

He led his friend outside and over to the pick-up.

"What in hell was that about?" Jarrod asked, obviously annoyed at being urged away.

"You saw her. That poor girl was obviously upset," Cordell replied as they climbed inside.

"Not by us. I was actually trying to cheer her up a little," Jarrod protested.

"I know exactly what you were trying to do," Cordell told him, shaking his head incredulously. "You seem to forget how well I know you."

* * * *

Trinity felt a little better that evening as she helped Aunt Sylvia clear away the supper dishes. Having had a good cry and telling someone about what had happened with Kev seemed to have done her the world of good, although she hadn't thought that at the time. She'd been embarrassed to see Cordell and Jarrod in the coffee shop afterward and was glad they hadn't asked how she was. She knew they'd have been able to tell she'd been crying and was grateful that they'd taken it in their stride. They seemed like a kind couple of men — not to mention handsome.

She noticed a tiny flutter in her stomach, knowing she would see them again tonight, and she was pleased that she'd washed her face and put on a little makeup. She couldn't help thinking how lovely they were and she relished spending more time with them.

"Why don't we go sit out on the terrace for a while?" Aunt Sylvia suggested when they had finished clearing up. "We could have some of that elderflower wine, Frank, if you like?"

"Great idea."

The sun was beginning to set and a soft haze came over the garden. Wrought-iron chairs surrounded a large matching table and they sat down to enjoy the tranquility of the late-summer's evening.

"I remember last time I was here," Trinity remarked. "It was just as beautiful then. I often imagine sitting here watching the roses and those lilacs." She smiled.

"Your mom loved the lilacs," Aunt Sylvia said, nodding over to the large tree. "We all used to sit under that shade on a big blanket when you were small, making daisy chains."

"I remember." Trinity smiled, longing for those carefree days again. "You've kept the garden lovely, Aunt Sylvia. It's exactly how I recall it when I think of this place."

"She's very particular about her garden," Uncle Frank shared as the sound of a pick-up hummed around the front of the house. "And that'll be your gardeners now, I expect." He chuckled. Without getting up, he raised his voice. "We're around the back, fellas."

Trinity frowned. "You mean you don't still do all the gardening yourself, Aunt Sylvia?" She had always imagined her aunt puttering around the garden with a basket on one arm and a pair of clippers in her hand.

"I wish I could, dear," the old lady told her with a slight grimace.

"Could what?" Jarrod's voice rang out as both guys sauntered around the corner of the house. He easily turned one of the heavy chairs backward and sat astride it, opposite Trinity.

"Hey, boys." Aunt Sylvia poured out more wine for them all with a smile. "We were just discussing the garden."

Jarrod rolled his shoulder, rubbing it hard. "Yeah, it sure takes some work, but it's worth it, ain't it?" He grinned.

"Jarrod had a little accident last time he was trimming that lilac," Cordell explained, taking the chair next to Trinity.

"You were supposed to be holding that dang ladder." Jarrod pouted childishly.

"I was until my cell went off. It was urgent, so I had to answer it," Cordell protested, looking a little sheepish. "I thought you were well-balanced up there."

"There I was, trimming that branch," Jarrod went on, pointing, "when I reached up to nip off some dead flowers and pow, I went hurtling to the ground. Next thing I know my shoulder's dang near broke and I'm off to the hospital." His incredulous expression might have made Trinity giggle had she not been so annoyed that they had been working on her mom's favorite tree.

"I thought *you* normally tended to that tree, Aunt Sylvia," she said in a small voice. She fiddled with the small heart-shaped ring she always wore.

Her aunt sighed. "I did until it became too much for me, honey," she explained. "That tree's a darn sight bigger than it used to be. I can't go climbing up and down ladders to keep it neat nowadays. Good thing I've got these boys to come and help out."

"The lawn's not too bad, though," Uncle Frank added, smiling at Trinity. "When I haven't got this dang thing in a sling, I can usually keep up with it quite well." Trinity knew he was trying to make her feel a little better about it all.

"Only 'cause he's got one of them state-of-the-art ride-on mowers," Jarrod piped up. "We only do the edging for him." He chuckled, clearly oblivious to how unhappy Trinity was with the situation.

She took a sip of her wine. She had been so used to seeing her aunt and uncle tending the garden themselves that it hadn't occurred to her they could no longer cope with it. She knew she should be grateful that these men were so willing and able to come by and help out, but it still rankled. Her earlier amorous thoughts of them dwindled with her annoyance.

What with the flood, all this gardening and now driving them around while Frank's arm was out of action, she couldn't help wondering what else the two were up to with her relatives.

Chapter Five

"I don't think she likes us," Cordell moaned as he stood in the large kitchen of their newly-built house. He was pouring out some strong coffee to counteract the effects of Frank Crowthorne's homemade elderflower wine.

"Now, come on, bro. What have I told you before about thinking?" Jarrod came up behind him, his hair still wet from his shower. He reached around and took a mug from the counter. "Did we run out of milk again?"

"I thought it would be more effective black," Cordell explained as they sat around the oak table.

"You could be right there," Jarrod conceded, taking a sip of his drink.

"About the coffee or the girl?" Cordell clarified with a grimace.

Jarrod frowned. "The coffee. I reckon you're paranoid about Trinity."

"Aw, come on, man. She wasn't happy to see us at the diner, though I get that she might have been a little embarrassed that she'd been crying. We know how women are. But tonight she looked like she could've killed us when she found out we'd been helping with Sylvia's garden. And when we were in the study, she seemed mortified that I knew all about Frank's first-edition law books. I didn't realize it was a secret." He shrugged miserably.

"She doesn't know about Frank's heart attack. Maybe there's other stuff she's not aware of." Jarrod frowned. "He said it had been too soon after losing her mom, so they kept it quiet. If they also haven't told her how bad Sylvia's arthritis is these days, she might be wondering why we've been keeping up the garden for her."

"Maybe you're right," Cordell conceded, licking his bottom lip as he often did when he was thinking.

"There's no 'maybe' about it." Jarrod feigned indignation. "Of course, I'm right. If you ask me, there's too many secrets in that family. It can only lead to heartache and misunderstandings. Hell, you know that."

Cordell nodded. He had to agree. Cordell hardly spoke to his family since a misunderstanding over his dad's funeral had ripped his kin apart. Although he made a point of keeping in touch with his mother, his brothers and his sister hadn't spoken to him in nearly two years. His aunt and cousins only contacted him at Christmas. "Do you think Trinity's keeping secrets?"

Jarrod pursed his lips. "I dunno. She hasn't said anything about what happened in front of us, but that doesn't mean she hasn't spoken to Frank and Sylvia about it."

Cordell nodded. "I wonder if that's what she'd been upset about in the diner. I mean, you could see she'd been crying, so there's a good chance she'd confided in Sylvia about it all."

"I sure hope so," Jarrod replied. "If you ask me, that girl's like a coiled spring, keeping a load of stuff bottled up inside her. She needs to let it all out before she explodes, you know?"

Cordell nodded. He knew, all right.

* * * *

It had been a little over a week since the guys had been over to the Crowthorne's place. It was the first time since they'd met the elderly couple that they hadn't popped around to check on them, although they had rung a few times to ensure everyone was all right. They had been disappointed, though not surprised, when Frank had told them that Trinity was too busy with work to go to the bar with them to see the band.

"We can't avoid her forever, bro," Jarrod commented as they ate their lunch together in the shade of the stables.

"I know. It just feels a little awkward. That's all." Cordell sighed.

"Is that why you told Aiden you were too busy to go over there with him this afternoon?" Jarrod asked, before taking a bite from his sandwich.

Cordell grimaced. "He told you, huh?"

"He was afraid we'd had some kind of argument with Frank or something," Jarrod told him with a frown.

"As if."

"I know. But you can't blame him for thinking it," Jarrod went on. "After all, we're usually over there almost every day doing something or other to help out."

"Yeah, well, maybe they've got Trinity to do that for them, now," Cordell remarked, gritting his teeth.

Jarrod faced his best friend head-on. "What the hell are you talking about? You know she wouldn't be able to do half the stuff we do for them. Not only is she a girl, but she's tiny." He stared at Cordell incredulously.

"Don't you let anyone hear you talking about a lady like that," Cordell admonished. "Haven't you ever heard of women's lib?"

"They can burn their bras all they like. It still ain't gonna put muscles on their arms—or anywhere else for that matter." Jarrod was adamant.

Cordell shook his head. "I got the impression she thinks we've been intruding on her family," he said. "You can't blame her for that."

"Watch me," Jarrod replied.

"Oh no, I can see where this is going," Cordell put a hand up to try to stop his friend from continuing, but it was a waste of time.

"Good. You and your mom were right to do what you did, bro. You know dang well you were. It was the rest of your family who were intruding, if anything. They hadn't been to visit your dad in years. They had no right to come in at the end and start making demands."

Cordell felt a pang in his chest. How many times had they had this conversation? "I get that, but he was their dad, too."

"Yep. And, as such, they should have done what you and your mom did, and that was to stick to what he wanted. It was written in his dang will, for Christ's sake. What kind of family contests that sort of thing in someone's will?" Jarrod was clearly becoming annoyed about it, as he always did whenever the subject raised its ugly head.

"Daddy had always said he only wanted a simple cremation," Cordell said with a sigh of resignation. "Momma and I thought we were obeying his wishes."

"I know, bro, and I agree with you. I just can't see why the rest of your family couldn't do the same. How the hell anyone could accuse you both of holding on to his money was pure trash. It didn't even make any difference to their share, anyhow, being as he'd already put a set lump sum aside for each of you. It was downright disrespectful, if you ask me — to you, your mom *and* your dad."

The whole business with his daddy's funeral haunted him to this day. It had been almost two years and it still hadn't been resolved. How could it? Daddy was gone. Nothing would bring him back.

Had the rest of the family been around more often, they would have known that the old man had always insisted on a simple, no-frills funeral. Once he was gone he was gone, in his mind. No amount of partying or fancy headstones was going to change that, and he had always had a fear of being buried alive, so there was no way he wanted to be shoved into a wooden box under the ground. He had made up his mind how he wanted to go. He had discussed it with his wife and youngest son, as the rest of the family had all moved away as soon as they were old enough, and he'd had it written into his will to avoid any confusion.

When the rest of the family had been told he had passed on and was going to be cremated, they had been wild with indignation. His eldest brother had accused him and his mother of organizing a 'pauper's funeral', which Cordell took as a personal insult. Daddy had had plenty of money to have had any kind of send-off he'd liked, and Cordell's brother Jacob had been determined that he would have liked a much more elaborate affair. Unfortunately, Jacob had always been quite influential as the eldest boy in the family and the others fell in line with his way of thinking. Martin agreed that Dad warranted a more salubrious affair, and Nancy-Ruth, the youngest sibling, went along with her older brothers. Even when they had been shown the will, they wouldn't budge on their points of view.

Cordell had supported his mother—and his father's wishes, of course—which made the rest of the family angry as hell. Jacob had somehow thought that if he had agreed with the rest of his siblings then they would have had a much better chance of contesting the arrangements. They went ahead with the legal proceedings, anyhow, dragging out an already-traumatic situation for their mom, then blamed Cordell when they failed to get the decision overturned.

The funeral had been much harder than it had needed to be, with Cordell and his mother being snubbed by the rest of the family and Jacob and Martin inviting a load of local dignitaries to share in their grief, despite their dad's specific wish that his funeral was for the family only.

The whole debacle had left a nasty taste in Cordell's mouth, and there was no way he was about to allow a rift to develop within the Crowthornes' on his account. Much as it pained him, he would rather never see any of them again than be accused of tearing another family apart.

Chapter Six

Trinity leaned back in Uncle Frank's swivel chair and sighed. She had been sketching some ideas for a book she was working on and was itching to see how they would appear as graphic images.

"They're real good, honey," Aunt Sylvia remarked, reaching over her to put a cup of coffee on the desk.

Trinity winced. She knew her aunt meant well, but it wouldn't take much to ruin the whole week's work with a simple spill of her drink. She had tried to take regular breaks so that she could join her aunt for a coffee out in the kitchen — away from her precious drawings — but she'd become so engrossed in her work that the old lady had kindly decided to bring the drink to her.

"Thank you." Trinity quickly picked up the cup and cradled it safely in her hands.

Uncle Frank peered up from his desk where he had been busy with the household accounts. "Have you finished?" he asked, glancing over at her work.

"For now." Trinity nodded with a smile. It was good of her uncle to allow her space in his office and to let her use the chair. He sat on a high-backed kitchen one, saying that he was only 'messing about with his correspondence' and 'not doing anything important, unlike her'. Luckily it had been his left arm that had been injured, leaving his right free to write with, although he had huffed quite a few times as it was obviously taking much longer than he had hoped.

"Sounds like your delivery's here," Aunt Sylvia announced excitedly as the sound of a diesel engine chugged up the drive.

Trinity took her drink with her and carefully left it on the kitchen counter while she followed her aunt and uncle down the hall and out the front door. Her new laptop had finally shown up and she couldn't wait to get started with the graphics program she had bought with it.

"I'll still be able to keep to my deadline," she told them as she quickly connected everything. Relief spread over her. Her uncle resumed his work over at his own desk, while Aunt Sylvia hovered, watching Trinity with interest.

When the explosion had destroyed her apartment, she had lost all her equipment, and she was still waiting to hear whether or not the little fireproof safe had saved her most precious works and the many memory sticks and disks she had stored everything on. As the building had been so badly hit, it was still deemed unsafe for her to return to the rubble to check. In the meantime, she had to console herself that the most recent of her projects had been saved on the memory stick she had thrown into her bag, not having had time to lock it away as she had been so busy fighting with Kevin.

"Damn," she cursed a while later, as she watched the little icon whirring away in front of her before suddenly stopping. "I can't get the graphics program to load."

"There's a computer shop in Almondine. We can go in tomorrow to ask for advice, if you like?" Aunt Sylvia offered, glancing up at the clock. It was almost five and the shops would be shut by the time they got into town.

"I think I might have to," Trinity replied with a despondent sigh. "I can't see what's wrong with it. It keeps trying to load then aborting. It doesn't make any sense." She frowned. She had been so excited when the machine had finally arrived, and now it seemed as though it had all been for nothing.

"Well, I'm about finished for today. I think I'll go outside and enjoy the rest of the sunshine while I can," Uncle Frank announced, getting up from his desk.

Trinity grimaced, wondering if he was actually leaving

because he could see how frustrated she was becoming.

Aunt Sylvia followed her husband out the door, while Trinity continued to stare at the screen. It seemed to have connected to the Internet all right, so she decided to google the problem. It was worth a try.

The open box appeared in front of her, cursor waiting, inviting her to investigate the whole world. She drummed her fingers on the desk, thoughtfully. It felt odd to be using the laptop here in her uncle's study instead of on her tiny dining table where she used to work back in Nebraska. She wondered when she would go back.

As her mind drifted, a thought suddenly struck her. She hadn't seen the obituary for Kevin in the local paper before she'd left, and she had heard that the funeral had taken place without her. That didn't mean that the details were dead and buried with her boyfriend, though. If she was ever going to get any sort of closure on his death, she would need to see some kind of notification in writing that it had actually happened. It still felt surreal.

She tapped at the keys and brought the details up on the screen in front of her. Notification of the funeral had been published, but not in the local paper. They had been entered in one of the large nationals, with a note asking for only family to attend.

Trinity seethed. It was obvious why it hadn't been placed in the local paper, as one would have expected. Kevin's family didn't want his friends there. Hot, angry tears began to blur her vision as she read the notice. 'Beloved son of Oliver and Patricia Pulver' it read, 'brother to Bernice and Timothy'. She blinked hard to read the following line. 'Fiancé to Poppy Witherington'.

"*What?*" she yelled at the screen in disbelief. Her stomach churned with bile and she began to shake. She read the line over and over, somehow not believing her own eyes. It didn't make sense — or did it?

* * * *

"Are you about finished here, bro?" Jarrod jerked around as Cordell poked his head into the stable where he was settling one of the thoroughbreds.

"Just about," Jarrod replied, with a grin. "Why? You got plans for tonight?"

"Maybe. I fancied going for a drink later." Cordell stood back to allow Jarrod to open the stable door.

"Ooh, sounds like a plan." Jarrod chuckled as he joined him outside. He turned to fasten the door as Cordell's cell rang.

"It's Sylvia."

Jarrod frowned.

Cordell's tanned face dropped as he took the call. "We're on our way, ma'am. Call the paramedics."

Jarrod pulled the keys to his truck out of his pocket and started running toward it, closely followed by his friend. They were already seated and he was gunning the engine before Cordell spoke.

"It's Frank. Seems Trinity found out some bad news and the old boy took some kind of a turn. Sylvia's calling nine-one-one."

"Shoot! Like that family needs anything more to worry about." Bile rose in Jarrod's stomach as they tore down the road.

Cordell was staring out of the windshield, curling his bottom lip thoughtfully. "Sylvia's really worried, especially after last time."

Jarrod leaned over and gently slapped him on the shoulder. His own mind was in turmoil but he could see Cordell was worrying enough for both of them, so there was no point in voicing his concerns. "Paramedics got here quick." His pick-up screeched to a halt next to the ambulance.

The front door was open so they went right in.

"Thank goodness you're here." Sylvia rushed toward them as they reached the study. "The paramedics are with him now."

Cordell put an arm around the old lady and led her toward

the kitchen. Trinity was already pouring out coffees.

"What happened?" Jarrod took one of the cups and handed it to Sylvia.

She sat at the table while Cordell soothed her, still holding her. Her face was white. She was trembling. "We rushed into the study to see what the problem was and he just stopped short. Said it was his arm."

"His left arm?" Cordell clarified.

Sylvia stared up at him and nodded.

"Shoot! You think it's his heart again?" Jarrod asked, as he and Trinity joined them at the table with their drinks.

"His heart?" Trinity's speech was curt as she frowned at him.

"Yeah. Once you've had one heart attack, it's quite—"

"Let's see what the paramedics have to say," Cordell interrupted.

Jarrod's heart hammered as he remembered too late that Trinity hadn't been told of her uncle's health issues. *Damn!*

Trinity turned pale and her jaw clenched.

"He was a little short of breath, but we *had* rushed to see what the problem was," Sylvia told them, her face riddled with worry-lines. "I should have realized…" She shook her head helplessly.

"I shouldn't have shouted out like that. I worried everyone," Trinity mumbled.

"I'm sorry. I didn't think." Jarrod sighed, peering at Trinity's beautiful but anxious face. "Maybe I'll go see if there's any news." He stood up, eager to get out of there.

"No, I think *I* should," Trinity replied pointedly as she rose to her feet.

Jarrod turned to her, surprised.

"It might be best if Jarrod went, dear," Sylvia suggested. "He knows all the details."

He watched Trinity's face tense right up and knew she was angry at not having been told about her uncle. He grimaced. It had been Frank's and Sylvia's decision not to tell her, and he had to respect that, even though he didn't entirely agree with it.

Slowly Trinity sat back down, and Jarrod nodded at Sylvia before heading for the study.

Frank was sitting on the floor, breathing heavily through an oxygen mask.

"We were just going to come and fetch someone," a ginger-haired medic told him with a grin. "There's nothing to worry about. He's fine."

Jarrod heaved a sigh of relief. "Was it his heart again?"

The guy looked at Jarrod. "Nope. His heart's fine. We've given him a thorough check and he's absolutely okay."

Jarrod frowned. Frank did look a lot better than he had expected, and he was sure a good color—better than his wife right now, in fact.

"Sylvia said he was breathless and his arm hurt."

The other paramedic, who was putting away their equipment, turned to him with a smile. "He'd been sitting in the garden and suddenly got up and rushed into the study. He was afraid something bad had happened and he panicked a bit. That's the only reason he's on the oxygen, to calm him down a little. His arm hurt because he'd been trying to use it." He pointed an accusatory finger at Frank, who appeared a little bashful. "It's in that sling for a reason."

Jarrod glanced up at the desk and saw a pile of books that he knew hadn't been there last time he and Cordell had been over. Papers were placed in order, too, so he guessed the old man had been going through the household accounts or something. He felt himself slowly relax. "Is he up to visitors?"

"Yeah, may as well spread the good news." The ginger-haired guy nodded.

"I think we can dispense with this now," the other medic said, carefully removing the oxygen mask from Frank's slightly flushed face.

"He's fine. Come on through." Jarrod leaned on the door jamb of the kitchen and smiled at the hopeful faces that stared up at him.

Aunt Sylvia burst into tears as Cordell helped her up, and Trinity held back a little as Jarrod followed them down the hall.

"You don't have to worry," Jarrod told her. "He truly is all right."

Trinity swung around to face him, glaring angrily. "Yeah, well, you should know, right? You seem to know everything about *my* family!" She spat the words at him, and Jarrod stared at her for a moment.

Luckily, Cordell had already taken Sylvia into the study and Jarrod could hear her talking to her husband. He would have hated it if the old lady had witnessed this outburst. Blood boiled within him and he grabbed Trinity's arm as she went to flounce past him.

"And just why is that a problem?" he murmured, surprised at the fire in her eyes. "You had your own shit to deal with, so they didn't tell you. Cordell and I happened to be here when Frank was taken bad again about a year ago now, so we took care of him and your aunt. We've been keeping an eye on them ever since."

"Yeah, I'll bet you have." She bit the words out.

Jarrod had been about to release her, but her reaction made him hold her a little tighter. Her bright pink nails clawed at his face, and he pulled back in time to avoid being scratched. "You really are a feral cat, aren't you?" He bent forward and murmured the words as soon as he was satisfied that her hands were far enough away from him. As he did so, he breathed in her heady perfume.

"You sure you wanna find out?" She sneered.

Jarrod was surprised at how much he was enjoying being so close to her, and the way her bright green eyes glinted and flashed with anger was most attractive. He hadn't seen so much life in her before, and it was a refreshing change. He and Cordell had spoken about their suspicions that she wasn't as shy and retiring as she appeared. Her bright hair and nails had suggested that much.

"Maybe." He kept his voice seductively low as he breathed

the word into her ear and noticed her whole body suddenly stop fighting him as she stilled momentarily.

She softened in his touch, and for a second, her face seemed to glow as she stared up at him, her eyes shining.

"Come and see. He's absolutely — " Cordell stopped in his tracks as he emerged from the study.

Jarrod knew his buddy was afraid he was interrupting something — which he was. "What do you think? Do you want to go see how your uncle's doing or would you rather stand there berating me for caring about him?" He half-hoped she would give a self-deprecating smile, realizing that he was only goading her, but she didn't.

Trinity's face tensed right up again and she narrowed her eyes at him angrily. "*I* care about *my* uncle." She bit the words at him and he shook his head at her reaction.

Jarrod freed her arms and she stalked off toward the study.

"Everything all right?" Cordell frowned, walking up to him as soon as she had disappeared. "I've obviously missed something here."

Jarrod grinned at his partner. "Everything's fine, bro," he assured him.

Cordell eyed him a little suspiciously. "I didn't exactly get that impression from Trinity."

Jarrod chuckled, shaking his head. "That girl has got a few issues to work through, I'd say," he told him.

"Anything we can help with?"

"Possibly." Jarrod thought for a moment. "Although we've got our work cut out for us convincing *her* of that."

Chapter Seven

Trinity was more relieved once the paramedics had gone and Uncle Frank was sitting in the living room with the guys while she and Aunt Sylvia prepared supper.

"It was real good of those boys to come straight over like that," her aunt said, as she closed the oven door. "I don't know what I'd do without them."

Trinity's stomach lurched. When she had shrieked about the news of Kevin's fiancée, she'd had no idea that her aunt and uncle might think she had been hurt. They'd rushed to her, despite their age. She'd felt so guilty when she'd seen Uncle Frank fighting for his breath and clutching his arm.

"It was my fault," she mumbled, wiping her hands on her apron. "I shouldn't have made a fuss."

"Don't be so silly," her aunt admonished. "You weren't to know your uncle would take on like that."

Trinity's blood boiled. "No, I didn't," she told her aunt. "But only because I didn't know he'd had a heart attack before."

She was surprised to see her aunt's expression as she turned to face her. Instead of looking apologetic and hurt, Aunt Sylvia appeared annoyed — angry almost.

"Your uncle had a heart attack a couple of years ago," the older lady told her firmly. "It wasn't long after your mom had passed on and you'd just gone back to university. He was at the bank when it happened and they called me to say he was being rushed to the hospital. He was wired up to all sorts of machines when I got there. They said he was lucky to be alive after that. He's a strong man."

"I know," Trinity told her, feeling wretched.

"Anyhow, he was taken bad again about a year ago. I was terrified I was gonna lose him. The boys were here when it happened. In fact, they saved his life. We were all out in the garden. I was weeding around the lilac tree and your uncle was nipping the deadheads off the last of the summer flowers in that bed over there by the wall." She nodded toward the window. "The boys had kindly come around to tidy the hedges for us, as that old hedge trimmer's far too heavy for your Uncle Frank now."

Trinity swallowed hard.

"He reached down to top a flower and suddenly he gave out a loud groan. As he collapsed, he was heading straight for the edge of that wall. Jarrod leaped over and caught him before he hit it. That boy held on to him, easing him gently down to the ground while Cordell called an ambulance."

"I didn't know," Trinity whispered, sickness roiling in her stomach.

Aunt Sylvia looked down at her hands. "It was his heart again. I stayed at the hospital with him. There was nothing you could have done if we'd dragged you all the way up here, so I decided it was best not to worry you." She shrugged. "He made a full recovery."

"I wish I'd known, Aunt Sylvia," Trinity told her softly as guilty tears flooded her cheeks.

Her aunt peered over at her. "Why? So you could have worried about us? We didn't want that. It wouldn't have done any of us any good."

"But still..."

"He's been fine ever since. Well, he fell off that horse, but he didn't break anything. And today it wasn't even his heart anyhow. See? Nothing to worry about."

Trinity was about to argue when a voice at the door stopped her in her tracks.

"Sorry to interrupt, but Frank's asking for a drink. Shall I get him some milk?" Jarrod appeared at the door, one hand on the frame of the jamb above his head. He was utterly gorgeous.

Trinity gasped at the sight.

"Of course, dear." Sylvia smiled. "Here you go." She passed him a glass from the cupboard in front of her.

Jarrod smiled.

Trinity watched him go to the large refrigerator and grab the carton. She couldn't help feeling that he looked as casual as though he did that all the time. Maybe he did. He sure seemed at home here.

"I'll put it back." She swooped behind him and took the carton from his hand once he'd poured the drink. Her intention had been to show him that he was, in fact, a guest in that house and not part of the family. She was hoping he'd get the message loud and clear and back off from her aunt and uncle. He'd be seriously irked by it, too. Good.

"Thanks, darlin'," he told her with a smile then winked. His spicy cologne surrounded her and she knew her plan had failed drastically. "I'll just get this back to him. Says he's parched. Must have been the oxygen." He smiled again and sauntered back through the door, leaving Trinity holding the carton as she gaped after him.

"Handsome guy, isn't he?" Aunt Sylvia murmured in her ear.

Trinity went hot. She busied herself in the kitchen until the meal was ready, then helped her aunt serve it. They all sat around the oak dining table and tucked in eagerly.

"You sure are a couple of good cooks," Cordell said.

Trinity glanced up from her plate, surprised that he was looking right at her. He was sitting opposite her, next to Aunt Sylvia, while her uncle was at the head of the table. Jarrod had slipped into the seat next to hers, and she couldn't escape his sultry scent or the warmth of his body as he sat a little closer than he needed to.

"You can say that again," Jarrod echoed, giving her a slight nudge.

Trinity noticed her aunt flush as she peered up at the guys a little coyly.

"It's lovely, darlin'," Frank assured his wife, placing a

hand over hers.

"Well, thank you everyone," her aunt muttered.

It still irked Trinity that the two men seemed to be such a big part of her aunt and uncles' lives, but being so close to Jarrod made it really hard to be angry with him. Cordell was a gorgeous guy, too, and it was good that he'd shown his appreciation for the meal.

"What're we gonna do about this fiancée business, then?" Uncle Frank's question floored her and Trinity dropped her fork as she gaped at him. She had explained about the notification as soon as she'd heard her aunt arrive at the study earlier but had no idea that Frank had heard — or even understood — what the fuss was all about.

"Turns out Trinity's boyfriend Kevin was engaged," Aunt Sylvia explained to the two guys. "That girl got a mention in the obituary."

"Dang!" Jarrod instantly threw his arm around her and Trinity was engulfed in his warmth. His body felt ripped against hers, and his sheer mass offered her protection and security. She closed her eyes, momentarily allowing herself to enjoy his closeness. "I'm so sorry, darlin'. That must have been such a shock for you," he murmured into her ear, and the deepness of it reverberated through his body.

In that instant, Trinity wanted to fling her arms around his neck and sob her heart out into his broad chest. Earlier, she had been too shocked to cry then the fear of Uncle Frank being taken ill had knocked her emotions sideways. But now, hearing the awful fact and having the comfort of such a gorgeous, protective guy made her want to give in to the hurt and sadness that threatened to break her heart in two. But she couldn't. She had to hold her feelings in check. She had to remember that this was one of the guys who was infiltrating her family.

"Trinity, sweetheart, I am so sorry."

She opened her eyes and looked over at Cordell who seemed stunned as he gazed at her across the table.

She quickly sniffed back the tears that were threatening

to flood her cheeks, and she tried to sit up straight. Jarrod wasn't moving his arms from around her shoulder, though, and she wasn't sure whether she was annoyed or relieved. It sure felt good having his body so close.

"I can't imagine how he managed to get away with it," Uncle Frank remarked.

"Trinity wasn't so stupid," Aunt Sylvia announced with a knowing smile. "Were you, honey?"

Suddenly, she was empowered by her aunt's comment and Trinity took a deep breath. Jarrod loosened his grip but still kept one arm firmly around her shoulder. She shook her head. Her immediate embarrassment of having the topic broached in front of the two 'outsiders' was forgotten as she realized that she was in a position to show them she wasn't the helpless victim they might have supposed.

"I wasn't sure, but I suspected something," she told them. "I found a woman's handkerchief in his pocket."

"Are you sure about that, sweetheart?" Cordell frowned with concern.

"I'm certain. It had lace around the edge and flowers on it. Poppies, I think." She noticed a hard lump in her stomach as she realized what she had just said. She stared over at her aunt whose expression must have matched her own. "Poppies." She breathed the word out, shaking her head in disbelief.

"Poppy was the name of the fiancée," Aunt Sylvia explained.

"And the woman who called Kev's cell," Trinity murmured.

"Well, I'm glad you'd sussed it out, darlin'," Jarrod said, squeezing her a little. "Must have been an awful shock, even so."

"It was," she admitted in a whisper.

"Well, there's nothing you can do about it now," Aunt Sylvia told her softly. "You need to put it all behind you and move on with your life."

Trinity tasted bile as she stared at her aunt. She understood exactly what the old lady meant. Kevin had gone and he wasn't coming back. He'd gotten away with it. The sadness she'd suffered from losing him was fast turning to anger. Her guilt about the way they had argued shortly before his death was becoming righteous indignation. The helplessness she had endured over the whole episode morphed into strength. She took a deep breath, sitting up straighter in her chair, despite Jarrod's steady hold.

"I wouldn't be so sure about that, Aunt Sylvia," she replied, jutting out her chin defiantly. "Kevin cheated on me, but he cheated on someone else, too. I wonder how she feels about him now."

Jarrod's body jerked against hers. He clearly hadn't expected that reaction.

"Now, honey, you can't just go find this girl and wreck her life," her aunt admonished. "It may not be her fault any more than it's yours."

"She's right, darlin'," Jarrod told her softly. "Think about what you'd do to her feelings if she suddenly found out now. It might crush her. You won't want to be responsible for that, especially as she thought she was going to marry the guy."

Trinity jerked her head up and stared right into Jarrod's deep, dark eyes. "So, because he'd actually proposed to this woman, I should say nothing?" she snapped. "Because he obviously thought more of her than he did of me, is that it? I'm the one who doesn't matter. It's fine to simply walk all over my feelings because he didn't really love me like he did her, I suppose."

She was surprised that Jarrod suddenly tightened his grip on her as she raised her voice, but it wasn't until she had finished her tirade that she realized why. He was trying to remind her that her aunt and uncle were here and it had only been a few hours ago that it had looked like her news might have given the poor old man a heart attack. *Damn!*

"That's not what I meant," Jarrod told her calmly. "I merely think that maybe you need to think about this a little more. Maybe sleep on it and see how it seems in the morning."

"He's right, you know," Uncle Frank agreed. "This is all too raw right now. You need to think real hard about what you're gonna do about it." His voice was low and he oozed wisdom as he spoke gently to her.

Although she was a little irked that her uncle was agreeing with Jarrod instead of her, she had to admit he was making sense. This other woman, Poppy, might be as much a victim as she was — more, even. What if Kevin had bought a house with her? Got her pregnant? Her feeling of sympathy for his fiancée quickly turned to jealousy at the thought of Kevin having committed to the woman, and her stomach roiled.

She sighed. "You might be right," she told them. "I'll think about it."

"Just don't let it eat you up," Cordell advised her.

Trinity nodded. He truly was a thoughtful guy. She had watched how he had looked after her aunt earlier, holding her while she explained about Uncle Frank and staying with her the whole time. He had guided her and cared for her through the whole incident, then sat with Uncle Frank when Aunt Sylvia had suddenly remembered she had a meal to prepare.

Her aunt had seemed so fragile while Uncle Frank was being seen to, but she'd become much stronger once she knew he was going to be all right. Poor Uncle Frank had said he'd felt like a fraud for not being 'actually ill' but Aunt Sylvia was clearly just pleased that he was okay.

Tonight had been a real eye-opener for Trinity in so many ways. The discovery about Kevin had cut her like a dagger, but the fear of losing Uncle Frank had been an undying ache. She was still aching now. She couldn't bear it if either he or Aunt Sylvia were to go. Not only because they were all she had, but also because they were such loving, caring people. The world would be a worse place without either of them in it.

"Who's for dessert?" Aunt Sylvia was on her feet, smiling broadly as she stacked up all the dirty plates.

Trinity sat back a little to take in the scene. The table was full of people and the kitchen smelled of apple pie. Outside it was already dark, but in here there was warmth and laughter as everyone replied in a delighted chorus. Her aunt and uncle were clearly comfortable and happy with a full house, and the two men seemed quite at home here with them. Although the thought had angered her earlier, she could now see that these two *were* like family to the elderly couple. They appeared as though they belonged here, fitted in. She cursed herself inwardly for feeling so irked by the thought. Now she could see that they honestly cared about her folks the same as she did. The thought comforted her. Maybe she'd gotten it all completely wrong?

* * * *

She was still mulling it over when she got into bed a few hours later. The thought of those guys warmed her as she switched off the lamp and snuggled under her duvet.

Jarrod's flirty nature and blatant good looks made her smile, and her heart beat a little quicker at the thought. Even his dominant demeanor when they had been in the hallway outside the study had excited her, though it had made no sense. Although he'd clearly been angry with her, he had kept his cool and shown her what an idiot she had been, although she never would have admitted it at the time.

She squirmed, suddenly aware of how wet she was becoming with the thought of the handsome cowboy, and she closed her eyes as she imagined his competent hands running all over her skin. His confidence was a real turn-on, and she guessed he wouldn't wait to be asked to remove her clothes and help himself to her body.

Slipping her fingers between the soaking folds of her pussy, she imagined his soft tongue there, lapping at her flesh. She clenched her thighs together as her stomach burned and her breathing became more rapid. Jarrod would tease her mercilessly with that tongue, circling her clit while she begged for relief. As she became hotter, she pushed the cover back then rammed a pillow into her mouth to stop herself from crying out as she swiped the sensitive nub, bringing herself to an almighty climax while a vision of Jarrod's face smiled in her mind's eye.

No sooner had her breathing begun to steady than she imagined Cordell taking her naked frame in his arms. His laid-back nature was calming and reassuring, and she somehow knew he would be more than capable of delighting her body.

Under his ministrations, she would relax and allow herself to wallow in his touch. She spread her arms and legs out like a starfish, stretching deliciously at the thought of Cordell exploring and tasting her with his mouth. His brawn would complement her slender physique beautifully and she would delight in his weight demanding her submission.

The mere thought of him sent a burn through her as she allowed her hand to linger over her pussy, rubbing gently then harder as her heart pounded through her ears. Sliding her heels up the bed, she allowed her knees to fall to either side of her, opening herself up farther to her own ministrations as her hand moved rapidly over her nub.

She only just remembered the pillow in time and she screamed as she lost complete control. Bright lights shone behind her screwed-shut eyes and a pain shot through her temple at the intensity of her orgasm.

Freeing her mouth, she gasped for air, panting hard into the darkness while perspiration trickled down her body. It was an effort to reach over and grab a handful of tissue from the box on the nightstand to wipe down her inner thighs before drifting into a well-earned sleep.

Chapter Eight

"I'm going back to Nebraska," Trinity announced over breakfast.

Despite waking with a huge smile on her face this morning, she was determined to put a little distance between herself and the temptation that was the gorgeous cowboys. Besides, she didn't think she could face them after the thoughts she'd had about them. Part of her was afraid they would read her mind and realize how she thought of them, while the other part was disappointed that they must be gay and the whole situation was worse than hopeless anyhow. Not that she would be able to choose her favorite, even if they were heterosexual and available.

Uncle Frank frowned. "Have you properly thought this through, darlin'?"

She glanced at her aunt and uncle's worried faces and forced a smile. "It's okay," she assured them. "I'm not going to cause trouble. It's Kevin's internment tomorrow, so I'm only going to attend and see how it all goes."

"You're going to the *internment*?" Aunt Sylvia was clearly horrified. "But surely that's for family only? You can't just show up!"

Trinity shook her head. "Oh, no, I'm not going to show my face," she told them. "I'll hang around and see who's who — get the gist of what's going on."

"What's going on is that poor family's laying the boy to rest," Uncle Frank told her firmly but kindly. "No matter how you feel about him now, you have to allow them to do that without any incident."

Trinity stared at him. "Uncle Frank, I'm not going to make

a scene. I won't even talk to anyone. I only want to see for myself. Besides," she said, chewing her cheek thoughtfully, "I wasn't at the funeral. I want to see where he's laid to rest."

"I can understand that, honey," Aunt Sylvia said, placing a hand over hers. "But do you really want to go when the family's all there? Can't you simply find out where the gravestone is and go a little later? There's no hurry, is there?"

Trinity sighed. She had felt so much better this morning when she'd finally made the decision to travel there today. Tomorrow she would merely go along to the crematorium and see for herself who showed up and maybe overhear a conversation or two. She was desperate to see the woman Kevin had chosen over her. She wasn't intending to ruin the poor woman's life. She just wanted to know.

"I want to do it now," she told her aunt in a small, determined voice.

Uncle Frank sighed. "Where will you stay when you get there?"

Relief swept through her. If he was thinking this far, he had already conceded that she was going. "I'll find a motel or something," she told him with a shrug. "I might also get to go back and see what's happening about my apartment. I need to see if they found the safe."

"It's a long way," Aunt Sylvia reminded her.

"That's why I thought I'd go today. According to the information on the Internet, the internment is happening in the morning, so I'll take the train then find somewhere to stay when I arrive. Once I've been there tomorrow, I can see about the apartment. My insurance is holding back with the payment until they know what happened to that safe. I've got a lawyer handling it for me there, but I haven't heard from him in days. I'll be able to sort it out easier face to face, I'm sure. I'll be back here in a couple of days — if that's okay with you, of course?" It suddenly occurred to her that she was being very presumptuous, thinking that she could casually move in here, go back to Nebraska whenever she decided to then come stay with her relatives again afterward.

"Of course. We want you to stay here," Aunt Sylvia told her incredulously. "It's your home."

Trinity had a warm feeling on hearing those words and got up and gave her aunt a big hug.

"Well, thank you, honey." Aunt Sylvia laughed in surprise.

"Thank *you*," Trinity replied.

"You'll need to book your accommodation before you leave," Uncle Frank told her, getting up from the table. "I'll arrange your transportation."

"I can easily check the train times while I'm online," she assured him.

"I said *I'll* do it." Uncle Frank's firmness was a surprise, and she smiled. It was good to know he was looking out for her. She had become so used to doing everything for herself that it was lovely to have someone to help.

"Thank you," she told him, giving him a big hug, too.

Uncle Frank chuckled and went off toward his study.

After helping Aunt Sylvia with the dishes, Trinity went through to the study herself and fired up her laptop.

"You just let me know what time you need to leave, darlin'," Frank told her, peering up from the morning paper which he had spread over his desk.

"Okay." She smiled.

There was a small hotel near to the crematorium, so she booked herself in for a couple of nights. She wasn't sure how long she would need to stay, but it was a start.

"I'll need to leave right after lunch," she said, having checked up the distance she would be traveling.

"That's fine," Uncle Frank assured her with a nod.

"I'd best go pack then."

She went up to her room and studied her clothes. She had nothing formal, only jeans. All her tops were in muted tones, mainly black, navy and burgundy. She sighed. Her closet in Nebraska had been full of vibrant colors and vivid patterns. Even her jeans had big, bright patches or embroidery on them.

She glanced at her face in the mirror. Her hair, which had been stark, in-your-face cerise pink only a few weeks ago, was now dull and lifeless. Where she used to spike it up at the top with funky gel, she had now left it to lie in boring layers against her head. She hardly bothered with her makeup these days, and when she did, it was natural shades instead of the thick, black eyeliner and bright pink lipstick she used to wear.

The girl who stared back at her in the mirror sure wasn't the same girl who had left her apartment for the last time. It was a shame. She recalled how having her hair done and putting on her makeup always used to cheer her up, even when her life was shit. Now it seemed every day was shit and there was no reason to cheer up. She'd lost her guy, her home and, if that safe wasn't found intact, her livelihood. And that was all on top of losing her momma.

It didn't take long to bundle a few clothes into her large yellow bag, and she spent the rest of the morning helping Aunt Sylvia weed the front garden. She noticed how her aunt's hands no longer straightened properly, and the old lady winced a time or two as she worked. That arthritis sure was playing up.

They ate lunch on the cast-iron dining suite on the back terrace. It was a warm day and the sun glinted off their cutlery as they devoured a large ham salad.

"You got that cell all charged, darlin'?" Uncle Frank asked as the sound of a car could be heard around the front of the house.

"Yes, it's right here." She held it up to show him.

"Good, now you give us a call as soon as you get there, ya hear? And on the way, too, if you like. We simply need to know you're safe."

"I will, Uncle Frank. Don't worry. I'll probably fall asleep on the train, though," she warned him with a giggle.

She was giving them a big hug when she heard footsteps coming around the side of the house. At first, she ignored them, assuming the cab driver had come to see if she had any cases to carry.

"I'll let you know what's happening," she assured them.

"Or we will," a familiar voice added.

Trinity darted around and stared right into the bright-blue twinkling eyes of Cordell Bray. Jarrod was right behind him, looking equally as gorgeous. Her heart pounded painfully with a mixture of excitement and embarrassment—not to mention shock. For a split second, she thought their arrival right at the point when she was expecting a cab was purely coincidental, but the knowing expressions on their faces soon put paid to that idea.

"Good. You do that, boys," Uncle Frank told them with a nod.

"But I thought…" Trinity frowned.

"You didn't honestly think I'd let you go all the way to Nebraska on your own, did you? All fired up and baying for blood? I might be old but I'm not stupid, sugar." Her uncle winked at her with a grin. "These boys'll take care of you. Make sure you don't go doing anything stupid."

Trinity stared at him. She had assumed they were merely going to take her to the station. Clearly not. "I don't need a chaperone," she told him. "And I'm quite capable of traveling on my own, Uncle."

"I'm sure you are, honey. Your Uncle Frank simply wants to make sure you're all right. That's all," Aunt Sylvia soothed her. "Now, you take good care of her, boys. We want her back in one piece as soon as she's done whatever it is she has to do."

"Yes, ma'am." Cordell smiled at the old lady and went to pick up Trinity's bag.

She snatched it before he could take it. "I'll see you soon," she assured the elderly couple and gave them a hard stare before she left. She could hear them chuckling as she led them around the side of the house and was surprised to see a highly-polished SUV waiting for her on the drive.

Her mood shifted slightly. She had imagined a journey in the pickup she had seen them driving, not a comfy, top-of-the-range utility vehicle. Not that she should be anywhere near them anyhow after the unholy thoughts she'd been having. *This is all wrong.*

"Is this yours?" she asked Jarrod, trying not to look him in the eye as he opened the passenger door for her. She was fighting a losing battle trying to keep her mind from straying.

"Yup." He grinned, "Do you want to ride shotgun?"

"I thought you drove a truck," she said to Jarrod, as Cordell climbed in behind her.

"Only for work," he replied with a smile.

She watched, bemused, as Jarrod took the driver's seat and the car hummed back down the drive. Both were certainly dressed neatly today in crisply-pressed shirts and shiny boots. As usual, they wore jeans that hugged every desirable inch of their taut butts.

"You got a plan for when you get there?" Cordell asked as they drove out of Cavern County.

"I'm staying at a small hotel tonight, then I'm going to the crematorium tomorrow. How about you guys?" She had turned around to face him, and almost regretted it when she saw the same handsome expression that had haunted her dreams the previous night.

"The same," he replied with a grin.

She frowned. "Wait—you're not actually planning on going *with* me, are you?"

"Yup. We promised your kin, remember?" Jarrod piped up with a chuckle.

"Yeah, but, I didn't think you'd really wanna…"

"Someone has to keep an eye on you," Cordell told her with a cheeky smile.

"Where exactly are you planning to stay?"

"Where are *you* staying, sweetheart?" Cordell asked, taking his cell from his pocket.

Her heart pounded as she suddenly imagined sleeping in the same building as them. She wasn't so sure that was such a good idea but reminded herself for the umpteenth time that they were probably a couple. "The Winchester Hotel," she relented. "It's near the crematorium."

Cordell grinned as he tapped the keys of his phone.

"Have you thought what you'll say to this woman if you actually see her?" Jarrod asked.

"I think I'll just see how it goes," she replied. "I'm not planning on making a scene, if that's what's bothering you."

There had been a time yesterday evening when she'd thought she would love to face up to the woman, saying exactly what she thought of her conducting an affair behind her back, but it seemed pointless now — not to mention possibly unfair. It was, of course, possible that Trinity had been the 'other woman' in the whole relationship. The thought saddened her, but not as much as it had. Having such vivid dreams about these men had certainly put things into perspective, despite the impossibility of anything coming of it.

Jarrod narrowed his eyes and she guessed he was remembering how she had acted in the hallway of her uncle's house last night. She had shown him that she wasn't the kind of shrinking violet who would take kindly to being walked all over. She had an opinion and wasn't scared to voice it.

"I've got us booked in," Cordell announced. "I booked three nights, in case we need it. We can always change the reservation if necessary."

Trinity turned to see him smiling at her. He sure was a looker, with his dazzling smile shining through his tan. He wore his usual laid-back expression, his eyes twinkling and his fair mustache neatly trimmed around his lip. She rolled her eyes but didn't say anything.

Cordell chuckled, slipping his cell back into his pocket.

"Must have been hard to find out he'd been unfaithful to you," Jarrod went on. "Did you have any idea besides that handkerchief?"

She sighed, sitting back around in her seat again. These guys did seem easy to talk to, and despite her earlier suspicions about their motives, they honestly gave the impression that they cared about her and her family.

She told them all about how she and Kevin hadn't been getting on too well for a while, and how guilty she was about it now that he had died. The fight they'd had the night of the explosion weighed heavily on her mind and hot tears threatened the back of her eyes as she related the conversation to them. With hindsight, she could see that he was goading her to accuse him of being the cheat that he was to make her feel bad about even considering it. The guy who'd died that night wasn't the guy she had thought she'd been living with. That hurt like the devil.

The whole journey was spent in conversation. The men were good listeners and they let her cry when she needed to and made her giggle when it was appropriate. She couldn't fail to feel closer to them by the time they arrived back in her home town.

"That's where I used to get my hair done," she told them, pointing out a beauty parlor in one of the main streets. She experienced a twinge of guilt. It had become part of her regular routine to go there and get her hair and nails done every few weeks, and she loved having a massage or waxing done when her money came in. They probably wouldn't recognize her in there now. She really had let herself go.

"Wow! Won't ya look at that." Cordell pointed to a large boutique that stood on the corner. Some strikingly outlandish clothes hung in the window, brightly patterned and every hue imaginable. Some were even luminous.

"I love that shop," Trinity told them. "I used to get loads of stuff from there. You should have seen my closet when I lived here."

Jarrod placed a hand over hers and guessed he'd noticed how her voice had faltered a little as she'd thought about what had happened. She had never thought she was very materialistic, but it was surprising to recall some of the things that she missed.

She'd been away for a few weeks now, and already felt like a stranger in her own town. Although the place still seemed familiar to her, she didn't feel like the same person who had left. She certainly didn't look like the kooky, vibrant trend-setter she used to be.

"This is it," Jarrod announced a few minutes later when they pulled up in the parking lot of a small hotel.

Trinity had passed this place many times but had never had cause to venture inside. She was surprised at how salubrious it was. Highly-polished wooden furniture adorned the foyer and reception area, with plush, well-stuffed sofas lining one wall.

"I'll take you to your rooms," the receptionist offered when they had registered. "You're actually right next to each other on the third floor."

Trinity noticed the guys grin at each other and wondered if Cordell had planned it this way. She quickly admonished herself for being so suspicious as she recalled that he had made an online booking and therefore wouldn't have had the chance to choose their room. Besides, he couldn't know which room she had been allocated. She sighed, wishing she could stop feeling so skeptical about them.

"There's a restaurant downstairs. Shall we eat there?" Jarrod asked as they walked down the corridor.

"That would be good," Trinity replied with a yawn. "Though I'm not all that hungry."

"We'll knock on your door when we're ready to go," Jarrod told her with a smile. "Just give us ten minutes to freshen up."

Trinity was relieved to be shown to her room first and she immediately closed the door and flung herself onto the massive bed. The room smelled of flowers and polish, and it had a classy feel to it. She hadn't realized quite how tired she was, although it was past seven o'clock. She must have fallen asleep as she was woken by the sound of knocking on the door. *Damn!*

"You all right in there, sweetheart?" It was Cordell.

She quickly jumped off the bed and swung open the door. "I'm sorry. I won't be a minute," she promised.

Cordell grinned, stepping into the room. "That's all right. We can wait."

She huffed as the two hunks sauntered in, peering around as they did so.

Trinity grabbed her bag, which was still on the bed, and pulled out her toiletries. She rushed into the bathroom, wishing they had decided to wait outside. She quickly washed herself and pulled on a clean, navy T-shirt. She brushed her teeth and dragged a comb through her hair that had become matted at the back. *Great!* The sound of laughter came from the two men who were waiting patiently for her, and she sighed. Although a little embarrassed at being caught out, she was quite comfortable having them around now that she had convinced herself that they couldn't possibly know about the ungodly thoughts she'd had about them. The idea of making this journey on her own and sitting at a table for one tonight certainly hadn't appealed. She smiled at the pale face in the mirror. Uncle Frank was sure looking out for her. She finished then went with them downstairs.

The meal was delicious and Trinity was proud to be dining with the gorgeous pair. She took the opportunity to find out a little about them, when she realized she had done most of the talking on their journey here.

"We moved to South Dakota from Georgia about a year ago," Cordell told her when she asked about their past. "It was shortly after Jarrod lost his parents and we both needed a change of scenery. We'd been close for years, so we knew each other's folks well. It was just right to get out of there together."

She flushed and a thud hit her stomach. "I'm so sorry for your loss," she told Jarrod.

He smiled. "Cordell had lost his dad, too, so we both know how it is to lose somebody," he told her.

Somehow that only served to make her feel worse. She had spent so much time feeling sorry for herself. It hadn't occurred to her that the people around her were suffering, too — first Uncle Frank with his heart, Aunt Sylvia's arthritis and now this.

How selfish can I be?

Chapter Nine

Trinity had a restless night and woke up feeling cranky and tired. As she had tried to sleep, she had imagined the scene at the crematorium. Kev's fiancée was bound to be beautiful and classy—everything she wasn't. How would she react to seeing Trinity? Would she suspect anything? Her stomach had roiled with anxiety. Then she'd heard the guys in the room next door, laughing. She was surprised at how turned on she had become and had tried her best to ignore the feelings they re-ignited inside her. The walls of this hotel must have been wafer-thin, as she practically heard every word. They were so close. They had to be gay, for heaven's sake. As she went down for breakfast she realized she'd lost count of how many times she'd reminded herself of that fact in the past twenty-four hours.

"Morning, sweetheart." Cordell joined her at the counter in the dining room where she was pouring herself a glass of fresh orange juice. "How're you feeling today?"

"I'm okay, thanks," she told him, forcing herself to smile. He was as handsome as ever.

"Hey, gorgeous!"

She spun around and was relieved that Jarrod was speaking to her and not Cordell. She was sure they had to be a couple. They were so close and seemed to do everything together—although she hadn't seen any physical evidence that they were lovers. Oddly enough, that thought gave her hope.

"Morning, Jarrod."

Trinity cradled her cold drink in her hands, trying to quell the heat that rose in her at the sight of the two hunks. She quickly made her way back to the table where the waitress was waiting to take their order.

They joined her a few moments later, laughing easily as they sat down.

Trinity watched as the waitress blushed slightly when Jarrod flirted with her before leaving them to serve another table. She noticed that the couple placing their order was wearing black suits.

"I wonder if any of Kev's family's staying here," she whispered, leaning forward, since they had sat opposite her.

Jarrod followed her gaze and nodded. "Sure looks that way."

A few more guests arrived, all dressed in dark colors and Trinity tried to decipher who they were. She recognized Kev's parents, although they had only met once. His mother was the center of attention, of course, and everyone sought her out before turning to the food.

There were several young girls, any of which might have been Poppy Witherington. Trinity watched them all with interest.

"You're staring, sweetheart," Cordell murmured after a while.

Trinity glanced at him. He had obviously been watching her, though she had hardly taken part in any of their conversation. She blushed.

"What are you two going to do today?" she asked.

"Well now, that all depends on you," Jarrod replied, quietly. "Do you still want to go to the crem? I mean, you've seen everyone already. What good would it do?"

Trinity felt a little irked, though, she knew it made sense. "I need to go," she told them. "I have to check it out for myself."

"All right. Then Cordell's going with you." Jarrod clearly had this all planned.

"Why?" Trinity frowned as she studied the fair hunk.

Cordell smiled. "Even if you don't get too close to the

party, it might seem a little conspicuous for a girl on her own to be hanging around somewhere like that," he whispered softly. "At least if we act like a couple, it might seem a little more…casual."

"Casual?" Trinity giggled, noticing them all in their jeans while everyone around them wore smart suits and dresses.

Cordell grinned, his eyes flashing with mirth. "You know what I mean. We could merely be a couple who happened to be passing. Or two people who happen to be walking by while they're all gathered around talking. No one notices a couple, do they?"

Trinity nodded. "Okay." She turned to Jarrod with a frown. "So, what're you going to do? Won't you be left out?"

The dark-haired guy shrugged with a grin. "I'll casually mingle, find out what I can. Don't you worry about me."

"They're making a move," Cordell muttered.

Trinity tried not to stare at everyone as they slowly made their way toward the door. Her heart thumped against her ribs. None of the family looked their way and she guessed they had more important things on their minds. Her thoughts drifted to Kevin and she felt bad that all these people were mourning his passing. She was sad, too, of course, but it was mixed with a lot of anger and confusion in her mind.

* * * *

A short while later, Trinity and Cordell walked casually up the path of the Garden of Rest where the family had gathered at the side of one of the plots. They surreptitiously glanced at the graves at either side of the track, which meandered through well-manicured lawns and flowerbeds.

Cordell was clearly holding back a little, but Trinity wanted to get close enough to hear what was being said.

"Don't go upsetting yourself now," he murmured kindly. "We can wait here if you like, simply get a lay of the land."

"Please, I desperately need to know what they're saying," she whispered past the massive lump in her throat.

Cordell obliged and strengthened his grip on her hand. He couldn't have known quite how much his comfort meant to her right then.

A pretty girl in her twenties was reading a poem as a man whom Trinity recognized as Kevin's dad stood next to her holding a wooden box.

"That's got to be her," Trinity whispered.

Cordell immediately let go of her hand and put his arm firmly around her shoulder. Trinity breathed him in. He wore a fresher scent than his buddy, and Trinity couldn't decide which she preferred. Cordell's body was a little broader than Jarrod's, too, and she felt safe and protected in his embrace. His body was taut against hers and his muscles rippled through his cotton shirt, which was partially unbuttoned. She let him pull her a little closer to him as she stared at the woman who now had tears streaming down her face.

They watched as the box was placed inside the vault and Trinity's stomach roiled with nausea. She grabbed Cordell around the waist at the same time that he turned, wrapping his toned body around her. She was vaguely aware of him leading her away from the congregation and they took a path that led in a different direction.

In the peacefulness of the late morning, they stood, shaded by a massive oak tree while Trinity cried into his chest. There was something very relaxed and serene about Cordell that enabled her to simply let go and pour out all her sorrow in a never-ending stream of tears and sobs. It wasn't all for Kevin, though. Her mind had drifted to the last funeral she'd attended, that of her mother. Aunt Sylvia had been right about her not having grieved properly for her momma. She'd been too busy convincing everyone that she was fine and eagerly went back to college to bury her head – and her heart – in her studies. She stroked the tiny gold heart on the ring her momma had left.

In Cordell's safe arms, she was able to let all the sadness of both bereavements flood right through her. He held her patiently, stroking her hair, her cheek, her fingers, as her heart melted into his warmth. She had thought that she was all cried out after the other day with her aunt, but it seemed not.

"I'm sorry," she whispered when she finally caught her breath.

"It's all right, sweetheart. You've nothing to be sorry for," he assured her gently, caressing her cheek with his finger.

She peered up into his kind face and sniffed. "I'll bet I look a mess," she muttered.

"Not to me, you don't." The sincerity in his eyes drew her even closer to him, and she blinked hard as she gazed into his handsome face.

The sound of muffled voices surprised her and she glanced over to where the paths forked. She recognized some of the party as they slowly made their way toward the parking lot.

"What time is it? Should we be going?" she asked with a sniff. She suddenly felt a little panicked and her mind raced with the idea of them all taking off somewhere she didn't know and her losing her chance to find out any more about Poppy and her relationship with Kevin.

Cordell shook his head slowly. "No, take as long as you need," he told her gently. "There's no hurry. Jarrod's on it, don't forget."

She *had* forgotten. Her mind had been so lost in her own misery that she hadn't given him a second thought.

Cordell stroked her cheek again and she stared into his pale blue eyes. Her stomach burned as she gazed into his beautiful face and she was drawn to him like a moth to a dancing flame. Her emotions were running high right now, but they weren't the emotions she had expected to feel. Guilt washed over her for missing her mom while she was supposed to be here for Kevin. She *was* sad at losing Kevin, but even sadder that he wasn't the person she had thought he was. He seemed like a stranger, almost, now that she knew he had been cheating on her. He seemed to have this whole other life that she wasn't a part of.

Her anger had dissipated for a while and she now was numb—numb and confused. She wanted answers, some way of piecing everything together. How long had he been with Poppy? When had they got engaged? Did she have any idea that Kev had been living with her, Trinity, when he was supposed to be her fiancé and therefore dedicated to her?

She could still hear people mumbling as they strolled away from the vault, and she was sorry that they all had such a warped impression of the man they had just laid to rest. She didn't bear them any malice. She pitied them.

Her mind returned to the Adonis in front of her and she sighed. Cordell would never be untrue. She knew that. She had seen how he and Jarrod were with each other and knew they were extremely close. No one should ever come between them. Every fiber in her body was crying out for him. Why was this fire inside her raging in desperation for his touch? *And why are his soft lips rubbing up against mine?*

Trinity closed her eyes as she felt his kiss right down to her core. His fresh scent surrounded her and he held her like he would never let go, while his kiss seduced her into his warmth. She suddenly wanted to spend forever here in his embrace, in his affection. The outside world disappeared and all that mattered was the feeling that engulfed her right in that minute. A feeling of being wanted, needed, loved.

Loved? She opened her eyes and pulled herself from his arms. "I have to go."

She ran down the path and almost bumped into an elderly couple who were slowly walking toward the parking lot. Her brain was too befuddled to worry that they were probably part of Kevin's family or that anyone would think it strange that a young girl with pink hair was running through the grounds of the crematorium. All she could concentrate on was getting out of there and away from Cordell Bray.

When she arrived at the hotel, she was surprised to hear voices and horrified to note that they were coming from the bar where she had planned to drown her sorrows in a neat gin. Instead, she ran up the stairs and let herself into her room, slamming the door behind her and sliding down it in a torrent of tears.

She couldn't believe that she had just kissed Cordell. *How could I?* She had seen how close he and Jarrod were. No one on this earth had the right to come between those two, and yet, there she was, kissing him.

Things had only been made worse by the fact that it had been in the Garden of Rest where the family had recently placed Kevin's ashes. Even though she didn't have the same feelings for her boyfriend as she'd had before, it still felt wrong.

And where was Jarrod? Off somewhere helping *her*. He had trusted her and Cordell to act as a couple so as not to attract any attention to her being on her own or raise suspicion as to her motives. And this was how she had repaid him!

She got up and went to the bathroom to swamp her face in copious handfuls of cold water. She berated herself for crying. *She* was not the injured party here!

Her mind raced as she considered her options. She could simply rush off and get the next train back to Cavern County, but what good would that do? The guys lived there and would be returning home soon themselves, so it certainly wasn't a way of avoiding them. Her aunt and uncle loved those two and as soon as word got out that she had tried to split them up, no one would want her around, anyhow.

She still had an appointment booked with her lawyer tomorrow and it made sense to stick to it, if she was ever going to have a chance of seeing her work again. Jarrod would be off finding out the intel on Poppy what's-her-face and she couldn't see Cordell showing up here anytime soon, knowing he would have to either act as though nothing had happened or 'fess up to his lover. Either way, he wouldn't be in a hurry.

Her eyes had puffed up and reddened and her face was flushed as she stared at her reflection. *How in hell have I let it come to this?* She sighed at the state she was in and reached for her cosmetics bag. She'd hardly put on any makeup this morning so there hadn't been much for her tears to wash away.

She did her best to conceal the redness of her skin and smeared on some eyeliner before adding a few coats of waterproof mascara. Although her bright pink lipstick still lay in the bottom of her cosmetics purse, she automatically grabbed the more neutral one she had favored of late.

Taking a deep breath, she jutted out her chin. No way was she going to stay cooped up in her room for the rest of her stay. She was going to have a stiff drink downstairs and make a plan of action. After she grabbed her purse, she headed for the stairs.

It was still noisy when she reached the foyer and she rolled her eyes as she made for the bar. She was shocked when she got there to see so many people dressed in black. *Damn!* She hadn't considered that being the nearest hotel to the crematorium, it had been the obvious place for a family gathering following the internment. Well, she was here now and was darn well going to have that drink.

"A double gin and tonic, please."

The bartender smiled at her and reached for the bottle.

"I hope that's your first," a familiar voice chided her as Jarrod leaned on the bar next to her.

"It might be. But it sure as hell won't be my last," she told him dryly, taking her drink from the bartender.

He appeared a little taken aback. "Are you okay?"

"Just dandy," she assured him with a nod. The knot in her stomach twisted a little more at the sight of the handsome guy and she straightened her back a little and took a big drink as she wrestled with the guilt that threatened to engulf her.

He frowned, then leaned into her a little closer. She was immediately swathed in his lush, spicy aftershave and she breathed in the scent with relish.

"The girl with the flower in her hair's the fiancée," he muttered conspiratorially as he gestured to a group of women who had gathered at a small table nearby.

Trinity cursed herself for enjoying his proximity so much and quickly turned her attention to where he had indicated. A pretty girl with a nose piercing and long, mousey-brown hair seemed to be holding court with her three friends. Sure enough, she had been the one reading the poem earlier. Trinity smirked. "No shit, Sherlock. It's a poppy."

Jarrod rolled his eyes. "The blonde girl next to her is her kid sister, Avril. She's a piece of work, but I think she might be useful in getting the lowdown on the situation—if you still want me to, that is?" He seemed a little concerned.

Trinity narrowed her eyes, swallowing the last of her drink. She noticed Jarrod eying the almost-full bottle of tonic water on the counter in front of her and knew he was wondering exactly how much she'd drunk. *Not nearly enough!*

"Yeah, I wanna know everything," she told him firmly.

He appeared a little surprised, but nodded. "You're looking great, by the way," he whispered into her ear.

"Thanks." She didn't even try to lower her voice. He certainly was smooth. She knew she looked like shit.

"I can tell you that they *were* engaged but hadn't picked the day, yet," he murmured.

She felt his hot breath on her ear and inwardly admonished herself for enjoying the sensation. She spun around on her stool to face the four girls who were huddled together over the small table near the bar.

"What I want to know," she murmured slowly, "is how long he was with her."

"Are you sure that's a good idea, darlin'?" Jarrod frowned.

"Oh, yeah. I think it's a great idea," she told him, nodding slowly. "Was he cheating on me with her—or her with me?"

Chapter Ten

Jarrod watched Trinity order another double gin.

"Hold the tonic," she told the bartender.

As soon as the young guy placed the glass on the counter, Jarrod picked up the bottle of tonic water that still sat in front of her and poured it into her drink, filling the glass to the top.

"Hey, I didn't want that," she told him with a frown.

"And I don't want you getting drunk and ruining this whole operation," Jarrod whispered fiercely.

The stunned expression on her face told him she had understood his message, so he took his beer and left her to it. He knew today must be extremely hard for her, and the sooner they got the information she wanted, the sooner they could all relax. Trouble was, Trinity was already looking a little *too* relaxed.

He frowned as he searched around for Cordell. He was sure he would have accompanied her here, but so far, he was nowhere to be seen. He pulled out his cell and was surprised to see the message button flashing.

Slight problem, bro. Think I've ruined our chances with Trinity. Explain when I see you. Going to look for her now. C.

That explained a lot. He could see there was no point in asking Trinity what had happened — but it sure must have been something bad.

She's in the hotel bar. Drinking! J.

He quickly messaged back.

Whatever had happened between the two of them might well be the reason for her sudden change of mood.

"Hey, there." A short blonde sidled up to him as he stood peering around the bar.

"Hey, yourself. Avril, right?"

She seemed flattered that he knew her name. "How did you know? You a friend of Kev's?"

"How did you guess?" He smiled, aware of the doe-eyes she was giving him. "Can I get you a drink?"

"How about tequila slammers?"

"How about some ID?"

"You wouldn't!" She was clearly horrified. She was also clearly underage. Talk about jailbait!

He winked with a grin. "Coke it is, then."

She huffed but didn't stop him calling over the bartender and ordering her drink.

"Can't I at least get some vodka in there?" She stared into the blackness of her drink as though gazing into the abyss.

"Sure, you can, just as soon as you're old enough." He chuckled, even more amused at the fact that she didn't find it funny.

The bartender sniggered, which seemed to annoy Avril even more.

"You wanna go sit over there?" She pointed to a quiet corner of the room and he followed her lead.

"So, Kev was gonna be your big brother-in-law?" he asked as they sat down.

Avril stared at him disparagingly. "Yeah, right."

"You didn't like him much, I take it?" He was surprised at how blatant she was about her feelings.

"He was never gonna marry Poppy," she told him with a sneer. "She was too starry-eyed to know it, but *I* did. He only asked her to keep her interested — and to keep in Daddy's good graces."

"Is that so?"

She nodded. "He made a pass at me." She was leaning

into him now, muttering conspiratorially.

He raised his eyebrows. "Is that right?"

"Oh, yeah. He kissed me. Said I kissed even better than my sister." She was clearly proud of her assertion.

"That must have been pretty awkward for you." Jarrod frowned. "Did she ever find out?"

"I told her. She didn't believe me. Said I was merely jealous." Avril shrugged.

"Hmm. That must've been hard. Were they together long?" he asked, trying not to sound too interested.

Just then a noise from the bar made them both jerk up.

"Why don't you go and leave me alone?" Trinity was shouting at Cordell, who looked mortified at her outburst.

"Trinity, let me explain —" he was pleading with her, red-faced at all the attention.

Shit!

"I don't need no explanation, big guy," she told him, slurring her words slightly. "I can see right through you. It's just a pity everyone else can't!"

"How much have you drank?" Cordell sounded angry now.

"Mind your own damn business," she slurred slowly.

Cordell sighed, shaking his head.

Jarrod knew his moment with Avril had passed. "I think I need to go rescue someone," he told her, getting up from his seat.

* * * *

Trinity was horrified to see Jarrod stalking toward the bar. She had hoped he'd keep out of it. This was between her and Cordell. It had nothing to do with Jarrod. Well, it had *everything* to do with Jarrod. That was kind of the point. But it would have been better if he hadn't known that, all the same.

"You okay, darlin'?"

She was surprised to see that Jarrod was speaking to her.

She knew they had some sort of strategy in place, but she was sure she was supposed to be *Cordell's* girl, not Jarrod's.

"I only want a quiet drink," she told him. Or, at least, that's what she thought she said. Her brain had gone to mush and she wasn't totally sure what was going on.

"I think you've had enough." Jarrod said, putting an arm around her.

She glanced over at Cordell, who had taken the stool on her other side. Whatever they had hoped to achieve today, their cover was well and truly blown. She couldn't quite fathom what their plan was or why they were there at all, but she knew this was quite wrong. They shouldn't all be together.

"I want another one," she told Jarrod pointedly.

Jarrod smiled. Surrounded by his scent, the warmth of his body and that dang smile of his, she let out a huge, contented sigh. *He sure is a great-looking guy.*

"Why don't you go sleep it off and maybe we can have some more later on?" he suggested calmly.

He was being so nice to her that she truly wanted to go along with his wishes, but she also wanted another drink badly. She wasn't exactly drunk yet, but she was sure on her way to it. Everything was a little hazy in her mind, and she had to concentrate hard to keep her thoughts on track. She bit her lip. She'd hoped to have drunk enough to forget her confusion about her feelings toward these two guys, but unfortunately, that seemed to be the most prominent thought in her brain — except one.

"I really need to pee," she announced as a strangely uncomfortable feeling settled inside her.

"Let me take you to restroom," Jarrod offered, quickly standing up.

"I don't know if I'll make it," she told him sheepishly. This was worse than she'd thought.

"Come on." He hoisted her up into the air and carried her through the bar. Trinity couldn't stop smiling, even when he stood her outside the door. "Can you manage from here?"

The thought of him taking her into the bathroom suddenly seemed hilarious and she burst out laughing.

"Go pee," he instructed her, as a group of girls joined them.

"We'll take care of her," one of them said, giggling.

"Thanks."

Trinity was helped into the cubicle and barely managed to whip her jeans down in time. She was peeing like a racehorse. It seemed like it would never end. As she sat alone in the tiny closet, she closed her eyes. The room seemed to be spinning around and she took deep breaths to try to regain some semblance of normalcy.

"I'm amazed at how well you're coping," she heard one of the girls saying.

"Yeah, well, I don't have much choice," another girl said. "Kevin's gone. No amount of tears will ever bring him back."

Trinity opened her eyes in shock. *That must be Poppy.* The realization seemed to sober her up immediately. It was odd how Kev's fiancée sounded more resigned than upset, she mused, though she knew better than to try to gauge another person's grief.

The fog in her brain had cleared a little now and she recalled what she was here for. This was a golden opportunity to ask Poppy the question. The only trouble was she couldn't stop peeing.

"The poem was lovely," one of the girls said.

"They gave us a list of suitable readings before the funeral," Poppy replied, airily. "Some of them were so morbid, but the woman who was arranging everything picked that one because it wasn't too bad."

Trinity frowned. *They left it to someone else to arrange the funeral? And the grieving fiancée hadn't even chosen her own poem?*

She tried to force the liquid from her body in her hurry to get out there and join in the conversation, but it simply kept draining. *Damn!*

"I noticed Lydia showed her ugly face earlier," someone said. "Fucking cheek!"

"She *was* his ex. She probably thought she had a right to be here," another of the girls said, cagily.

"Yeah, and she should've stayed his ex, too," the first girl replied. "What sort of person dumps a guy then gets back with him once he's with someone else? Talk about a cheap slut!"

"Yeah, well, she didn't get to keep him, did she?" Trinity recognized this as the voice of Poppy.

She gasped. *Kev had cheated on Poppy, too? And she knew about it?* It was a good thing she was sitting already as she honestly felt like she would have fallen down right at that minute.

"Good for you, Pops," one of the girls said as the main door opened. "I'll get another round ordered."

The door slammed shut again and Trinity strained her ears to try to ascertain who, if anyone, was still left in the room.

"Don't cry," one of the girls said, as the sound of sniveling came from the vanity area.

Trinity heaved a sigh of relief. Not only because it seemed that Poppy was still there, but also because her body had finally realized that the world wasn't big enough for another Niagara Falls, and she had eventually stopped peeing.

"I forgot you were in there," the girl who had helped her in said as she emerged from the cubicle.

"Sorry." Trinity flushed and wasn't sure if it was embarrassment or gin that had caused it. She washed her hands, peering warily at Poppy, who was wiping her nose. "Are you okay, sweetie?"

Poppy nodded.

"She's recently lost her fiancé," the other girl told her.

"Oh, I'm so sorry. How long were you engaged?" Trinity held her breath as she waited for the answer.

"Six months," Poppy replied, with a sniff.

The *Hallelujah Chorus* rang through Trinity's head. She had been with Kev for a little over a year, so that meant that she'd had him before Poppy. Somehow, that made her feel better, though, she didn't know why as he had still cheated on her.

"That must have been awful." Trinity tried her best to sound sympathetic, but at the same time couldn't help feeling like a two-faced bitch. Her heart throbbed against her ribs and she warmed as she stared at Poppy.

"It was, especially as we'd been together for nearly a year before he proposed," she went on.

Trinity felt as though she had instantly been turned to stone. Her body became numb as the news sunk in. *He was with her before me.*

"Well. I suppose I'd better paint on a smile and get back out there," Poppy said with a sigh. "People will expect to see me."

Trinity narrowed her eyes as she watched the two girls disappear out the door. She suddenly was perfectly sober as her brain whirled with the realization of what had been going on. Her whole body began to tremble as soon as she was left alone with her thoughts. She leaned against the hand basin, closing her eyes as the quietness of the room started to suffocate her.

"Trinity, are you still in there?"

Jarrod was opening the door, clearly worried that she hadn't materialized yet.

"Yep, I'm here." She almost bumped into him as she came out of the bathroom.

"Are you all right?" He frowned.

"Yeah. I'm fine."

"You don't look it."

"I wasn't the first," she muttered.

"Darlin', I am so sorry."

Suddenly he put his arms around her and she was surrounded by his gorgeous body. Trinity was surprised how natural it was to be held by the handsome hunk, and her mind drifted back to earlier when she had been in Cordell's arms. That had seemed normal, too. What was absolutely remarkable, though, was how spontaneously both men had held her when she'd needed them most. They didn't appear to have any reservations about showing her affection, despite their obvious impermeable bond to each other. These guys truly were something else.

"Let's get out of here," Cordell said softly, coming up behind them.

"Good idea. Come on."

She was still in Jarrod's embrace when Cordell's muscular arm came across her other shoulder as they led her out of the hotel. She still didn't know what to make of that dang kiss, but right now she had other fish to fry.

The cooler air was refreshing as they hit the street and strolled down toward the town.

"There's bound to be somewhere to eat around here," Jarrod remarked, peering around at the shops.

There was a fresh breeze as the evening turned into night, but Trinity couldn't fail to keep warm, encompassed, as she was, in the arms of the two gorgeous hunks. As they strolled down the street, Trinity's mind whirled with hurt and confusion.

"He must have been with her when I thought he was working," she mumbled.

"Surely he must have worked some time? How else did he get paid?" Cordell asked her.

She sniffed. "I don't know. He spent a lot of time on his laptop when he was home. He said it was the only way to catch up with the paperwork as he'd spent so long on the road."

"There's got to be an explanation," Jarrod told her. "I'm sure we'll figure it all out later."

"He seemed to be making less money lately than he had been. He said it was because he couldn't sell as much because of the economy. He must have been spending it all on *her*."

"Now, we don't know that, do we? It's probably best not to speculate." Cordell certainly was the peacemaker.

Trinity sighed. She knew he was right, but it didn't make matters any better. Nothing could do that right now.

Suddenly, she gasped as she glanced up and recognized where they were. They had walked a little further than she had expected and were now right in front of the pile of rubble that used to be her home.

"Ker-ist!" Cordell's whole body tensed next to her and she knew he must have realized what this place was.

"Oh, God, I'm so sorry, darlin'." Jarrod must have caught on, too.

Trinity felt hollow inside as she stared at the mass of bricks and rubble that was interspersed with pieces of rag and personal belongings. Police tape cordoned off the whole area where the apartment block had stood and also encompassed some of the sidewalk and road outside it.

This was the closest she had been able to get to the site since the incident. Death and destruction flooded the whole scene while despair hung in the air like a thick, black cloak.

"Everything's gone," she whispered.

"Come on. Let's go, too." Cordell clearly wasn't taking 'no' for an answer as he ushered them away.

As tears streamed down her face, Trinity followed blindly, glad to be out of there.

"Let's hope they've unearthed that safe of yours," Jarrod said, as they turned a corner.

"Yeah, what time are you seeing that lawyer tomorrow?" Cordell asked.

It was obvious that the men were trying to take her mind off the horror of it all by talking about the practicalities, and she was grateful for it. She sniffed hard.

"Umm, I'm seeing him at ten," she told them, having had to rack her brain for the answer.

"Great. It'll be interesting to hear what he's got to say," Cordell replied.

She couldn't help noticing his subtle way of letting her

know he intended to be in on the meeting—and she knew that meant Jarrod wouldn't be far away, either. Despite her previous misgivings about them, she had to admit that they were both so kind and caring. She didn't know how she would have coped without them. Uncle Frank and Aunt Sylvia were clearly good judges of character—while all this business with Kevin proved that *she* certainly wasn't.

"How about this place?" Jarrod suggested as they stood outside a large restaurant.

"Fine by me. What d'you think, sweetheart?" Cordell turned to Trinity, who gazed up at him, nodding.

"Great. I don't know about you two, but I'm starving," Jarrod announced as he pulled open the heavy door.

Trinity hadn't realized how ravenous she was, too—they had all missed lunch—and they each tucked into a large helping of steak with mushrooms, tomatoes, onions, peas and fries. Mississippi mud pie with lashings of cream followed, and she found herself forcing the last spoonful into her mouth as she sank back in her soft-backed chair.

"Well, that should've soaked up some of that gin," Jarrod told her with a smile.

"Yeah, exactly how much of that stuff did you drink, sweetheart?" Cordell sure sounded shocked.

Trinity shrugged. "I've no idea," she admitted.

"Well, no one can blame you. It's sure been one hell of a day," Jarrod told her, shaking his head.

"In more ways than one," Cordell added, looking a little sheepish.

"Care to tell me what happened?" Jarrod asked

Cordell sighed. "I kissed her," he admitted.

"Well, I can see how that might drive a lady to drink." Jarrod chuckled.

Cordell shook his head. "I'm sorry, sweetheart. I didn't mean to offend you."

At first, Trinity thought he was speaking to Jarrod, but then she noticed that both of them were gazing at her.

"What?" she asked, a little unsure.

Cordell sighed. "I must have misread the signs. I'm sorry if I upset you."

She frowned, shaking her head. She turned from him to Jarrod, expecting some kind of reaction, but there was none.

"I was merely afraid that Jarrod would be upset," she explained in a quiet voice.

"Upset about what? You having a kiss without me?" Jarrod frowned in confusion.

"You're a couple. He kissed me. Doesn't that worry you?" Trinity spoke slowly, well aware that she could be splitting these two up for good. She was shocked that they didn't seem more worried about the fact, though.

"What?" Jarrod gaped at her with an incredulous grin, and Trinity knew then that she had gotten it wrong somehow.

She looked at Cordell who had narrowed his eyes at her. "Did you think we were a couple and I was in some way being unfaithful to Jarrod, sweetheart?" he asked slowly.

Trinity took a deep breath and nodded. "Yeah."

Jarrod hooted with laughter. "Well, I do love this guy, but not in the way you're thinking."

She frowned at them, astonished. *Are they actually telling me what I'd hoped?*

"We're not gay, sweetheart." Cordell said simply.

"What?"

"We're just best friends. That's all. Close friends, but not *that* close, if you know what I mean?" Jarrod explained, his dark eyes twinkling in the candlelight. "And, while we're laying our cards on the table, you may as well know that we're interested in a ménage relationship. Does that make a difference to you?"

Chapter Eleven

Trinity gasped. Why hadn't it occurred to her that this could be the case? She supposed that she'd had so much going on lately that she wasn't thinking straight. Of course, all the signs were there. They had both flirted with her. And although they were clearly very close, there had been no interaction between then that would suggest that they were actually in a relationship. *I'm such a dumbass!*

"We understand if you don't want anything to do with us." Cordell broke the silence that had ensued as her brain whirled with the implications. "I mean, there must have been some sense of security while you thought we were only interested in each other. We can drive you back tomorrow and —"

"No." She blurted the word out, much to the obvious surprise of the two men who stared at her.

"No, it doesn't bother you, or no, you don't want to go home tomorrow?" Jarrod asked slowly.

Her heart thumped loudly as she realized their confusion. "Both."

"Good." Jarrod was still frowning at her.

She flushed. "I mean, I have to go see my lawyer tomorrow," she added hurriedly. "But, of course, if you need to leave, I can easily take the train."

"No," Jarrod assured her quickly, putting his hand up in a pacifying manner. "We've taken a few days off, so we can go back whenever you're ready."

She nodded gratefully.

"So, the non-gay thing," Cordell said quietly after a few moments.

"Yes." She nodded again.

"It bothers you?" Cordell queried.

"No."

"You're okay with it?"

"Yes."

"Sure?"

"More than okay." She blushed. "I-I mean—"

"That's good to know," Jarrod said with a snicker.

"Oh, no, I didn't mean—"

"So, you're *not* okay with it?" Cordell frowned.

"No. Yes. I mean…it's fine." She spoke hurriedly, eager to reassure them.

"You sure?" Cordell seemed as confused as she felt.

Trinity sighed loudly. "Of course it doesn't bother me. Why would it?"

She noticed them exchanging a look, but neither spoke.

"All finished?" The waitress came to clear away their dishes.

Trinity was glad of the distraction and smiled at the girl, nodding.

"Can I get you some coffee?" the waitress offered.

"Not for me, thanks," Trinity replied, holding her hand up. "I don't think even a drink would fit in my stomach right now."

"It sure was a good meal," Jarrod piped up, "but I think we're all stuffed. Just the check, if you wouldn't mind, please, ma'am?" He threw the woman one of his dazzling smiles and Trinity noticed how she blushed. A spike of jealousy rose inside her and she had to turn away in shame.

"I don't know about you guys, but I don't think I can manage to walk home," Cordell announced with a huff. "How about we get a cab back?"

Trinity nodded eagerly. "That would be great. I've been dreading trying to get out of this dang chair, let alone walking all the way out of town."

Cordell grinned.

The check arrived and Jarrod quickly picked it up. "I've

got this," he announced, casually, getting up. "Hmm, think you're right about that cab." His hand went straight to his stomach and he groaned.

A few minutes later, they were all piling into a cab, and before they knew it, they were back at the hotel.

Cordell quickly whipped out his wallet and paid the driver before they made their way inside.

The foyer was quiet, with some piped music playing quietly in the background. The peacefulness of her surroundings was totally at odds with the confusion in her head.

"Are you okay, darlin'?" Jarrod must have noticed how quiet she had been on the way here. She was still trying to get her head around the events and revelations of the day.

"Yeah, just tired, I guess," she told him with a forced smile.

Jarrod's returning smile was much more genuine. "It's been a long one. You should get some rest."

She nodded and followed them upstairs to their rooms, realizing that theirs was probably two doubles, not a queen as she had assumed.

"Sleep well," Cordell told her before putting his arms around and holding her in a warm embrace for a few seconds. She loved the faint scent of his cologne and the feeling of his ripped body next to hers.

"Sweet dreams, darlin'." Jarrod was next to put his arms around her and she gasped. Her hair grazed the scruff on his chin, and his chuckle reverberate through his chest as he kissed the top of her head.

She felt bereft when he pulled back.

"Good night." She hadn't expected her voice to come out as a whisper, but they heard her all right.

Trinity forced her feet to move as the gorgeous men waited by their room, and her fingers trembled as she unlocked her door.

The bed had never seemed so inviting and she quickly got ready and climbed in. She could hear mumbling from next door as she lay thinking. The noise didn't bother her. In fact, she found it quite comforting — almost as comforting as the hugs they had given her. She closed her eyes as the events of the day — and night — whizzed through her mind.

* * * *

Cordell was sleeping soundly when a noise woke him. They were both worn out but the sound of whimpering permeated his brain and a sick feeling tensed his stomach.

"Bud, wake up." He threw one of his pillows over at Jarrod.

As soon as he stirred, Cordell leaned over and switched on the bedside lamp.

"What is it?" Jarrod frowned, quickly sitting up.

"It's Trinity. She's crying."

"Oh, no." Jarrod obviously heard the sound, too.

Minutes later, they were outside Trinity's door, knocking quietly. The noise was louder and more pitiful from here, and Cordell shook his head at the sound.

"Trinity, it's us. Open the door," he murmured into the wood.

He heard a loud sniff. When she opened the door, her room was in darkness, and she looked bewildered but beautiful in the dim lights of the hallway.

"What is it?" She gasped, presumably at the sight of them in only their shorts.

Jarrod scanned the corridor around them and grimaced. "Can we come in?"

She nodded with a sniff, standing back to allow them entrance. Her room smelled of her floral perfume.

Cordell immediately switched on the small lamp while Jarrod closed the door quietly behind them.

"We heard you crying, darlin'. Are you all right?" Jarrod asked softly, turning to her.

Trinity sniffed again, and Cordell immediately offered her a tissue from the box by the bed. She nodded. "I'm okay."

She looked far from okay. Her face was flushed and her eyes were puffy. Tearstains marred her soft cheeks.

"I hope I didn't wake you guys," she said, her eyes big and watery.

"No, darlin'. We were just worried, that's all." Jarrod wrapped his arms around her and Cordell was relieved at how easily she nudged into him and threw her slim arms around his muscular body. It was good to see them together like this. Cordell felt a warmth inside him, hoping that they could somehow persuade her to stay with them.

As soon as Jarrod loosened his grip, Trinity glanced over to Cordell, and he went straight over to them and gave her a hug. Her tiny frame seemed so fragile in his strong arms, and he desperately wanted to protect her and keep her safe.

"You're cold," he told her, gently rubbing her arms. "Come on. Let's get you into bed."

Jarrod was already sitting on the covers, leaning against the headboard, his legs out in front of him. Cordell watched Trinity go straight over and snuggle into his arms.

"I must have been crying in my sleep," she murmured as Cordell joined them, pulling a blanket over Trinity while he and Jarrod remained on the top of the coverlet.

"I woke up in tears and everything came flooding back."

Cordell offered her more tissues as her body racked with sobs.

"I know, darlin'. It's been a horrid day. How about you get some sleep now and put it all behind you?" Jarrod's voice was soothing and Cordell smiled at his kindness. Jarrod was usually joking and messing around, and he could be quite tactless at times, but it seemed that when it truly mattered, he was just as loving and caring as Cordell knew he could be.

Jarrod nodded over Trinity's head to Cordell, who immediately turned out the light. They lay in the quietness of early dawn, holding their girl in their arms. Cordell couldn't help feeling how right this all seemed, and only hoped Trinity felt the same way.

It took a short while for Trinity to stop sobbing, and the cadence of her soft breathing told him she had fallen back to sleep. Jarrod snuggled in a little tighter to her, and Cordell smiled as she idly tickled his right arm before he, too, went to sleep.

Cordell inhaled the sweet scent of the beautiful girl in their arms. She had been through so much, and none of it was her fault. He was so sorry that she had been subjected to so much sadness, and the fact she had been crying in her sleep suggested she was even more affected by it all than she let on.

He stroked her hair and she stirred a little. He knew how Jarrod felt about her, as they had talked about nothing else all night. Cordell must have finally fallen asleep thinking about the gorgeous girl in his arms, as he woke to the sound of birds singing and Trinity giggling. *Perfect.*

"What's so funny?" he asked, peering up at them.

"Jarrod reckons you snore, but I was defending you," she told him, proudly. "I hadn't heard a sound from you all night."

"Yeah, well, you should have been with us earlier," Jarrod told her with a grin.

"I don't believe a word of it," she protested, laughing. "I think you just made that up."

"You'll have to sleep with us again so I can prove it to you," Jarrod told her matter-of-factly.

Cordell winced in amazement at his partner's subtlety. He sure was smooth.

An uncomfortable feeling in his groin made him grab for the blanket and cover himself, and he peered over to see that Jarrod had done the same. He grinned.

"I'll quickly use your bathroom," he said, turning away from them and sauntering over to the other door. He was glad he had slept on the side nearest the en suite. It would have been mighty embarrassing to have to walk past Trinity with his morning wood on display. He sniggered, wondering how Jarrod was going to manage.

A few minutes later, he emerged from the bathroom, feeling much more comfortable and refreshed. Jarrod gawked over at him with an envious expression. Cordell grinned. This was payback time for the snoring comment.

"Well, I guess we'd better be going and let you get ready, sweetheart," he said, smiling at Trinity. "Hope you didn't mind our…er…intrusion last night."

She was sitting up now, and he noticed how hard her nipples were as they jutted through her pale-pink cotton pajamas.

"No, I'm really glad you came in," she told him, crawling out of the bed. "It was very kind of you. Sometimes I shout out in my sleep and I'd have been real embarrassed if I'd done that here. I might have woken up half the hotel."

Cordell couldn't help feeling sorry for her. Even before this business with losing her home and the discoveries about her boyfriend's infidelity, it seemed she had been battling with nightmares.

"I'm sure no one would have minded," he assured her, as she headed straight for his arms.

He held her momentarily, smirking over her shoulder to where Jarrod was seething on the bed. He knew darn well that his partner was going to have to expose himself as soon as he moved.

"We'll be ready in about half an hour, if that suits?" Cordell offered, trying not to smirk at his friend's discomfort.

Trinity nodded. "Yeah, just give me a holler on your way past the door."

Cordell grinned. "Great." He turned to Jarrod who was staring at him. "Come on, bro. Time we were making a move," he told him.

He and Trinity waited by the door while Jarrod chewed his lip. He took the blanket from the bed and wrapped it around his waist. It covered him but still tented out at the front. Then he stood up and strutted proudly toward them, clearly realizing that there was no way of hiding his erection, so he had decided to flaunt it instead.

Cordell watched Trinity stare at Jarrod as he made his way across the room. She seemed totally bemused, as though she didn't know how to react. She couldn't seem to tear her eyes away from his groin at first, then she turned her gaze anywhere but. Cordell grinned as she flitted her eyes all around the room while she spoke.

"Right… Okay, then… Well, thanks for stopping by." She seemed a little reluctant to open the door, so Cordell reached over and took the handle.

He kissed her on the top of her head, stroking her arm. "See you soon, sweetheart."

"Yeah, we won't be long," Jarrod told her, but he didn't get close enough to touch her before almost pushing his buddy out the door.

"Not too long, anyhow," Cordell added, staring pointedly at Jarrod's groin area.

Trinity let out a loud laugh, which she had obviously been holding back. He loved to hear her sounding so happy.

Voices alerted him to the fact that they weren't alone in the corridor, and he looked up to see two girls walking toward them, staring at Jarrod's blanket.

They both burst out laughing, then sneered over at Trinity as she stood in the doorway. Quickly the guys heard her slam the door and they headed for their own room. *Damn.*

"What the hell did you do that for?" Jarrod demanded as soon as they were safely behind closed doors.

"What? We had to get back here and shower," Cordell replied, trying to sound innocent.

"You know full well 'what'. How on earth was I supposed to disguise this thing?" Jarrod pointed at his briefs, having whisked the blanket off.

"You didn't even try, man. I saw you strut your stuff across the room. Poor girl didn't know where to look."

"She soon figured that one out," Jarrod boasted.

"Talk about the elephant in the room." Cordell sneered.

"Yeah, there's no disguising my trunk."

"Oh, is *that* what you were doing with that blanket?

Trying to disguise it? We couldn't tell."

"Yeah, well, in the end, I realized there was no way to hide it so I may as well show it off."

"Yeah, to every passing female as well as the one we were supposed to be impressing." Cordell rolled his eyes.

"You mind if I j go and get rid of it?" Jarrod eyed the bathroom, the twinkle returning to his eyes.

Cordell sighed. "We said we'd only be half an hour."

Jarrod nodded. "Yeah. We don't want to keep the lady waiting" — he chuckled — "although I'm sure she'll understand if we're a little *longer* than we anticipated."

"Always bragging." Cordell grinned as he stood back and Jarrod headed for the bathroom.

Chapter Twelve

Trinity gasped as she slammed the door to her room shut. Those men sure were lovely and it was so kind of them to come and look after her last night. She wondered if they would make a move on her this morning, but it seemed they truly were the gentlemen she had hoped they were—although, on the other hand, she couldn't be sure she would've turned them down if they had. She had to remember, of course, that although they had admitted to being interested in a ménage relationship, they hadn't actually said that they wanted it with *her*. It didn't stop her hoping, though. Even first thing in the morning with their hair disheveled and a few more whiskers than normal, she had to admit they were gorgeous.

She smiled as she remembered the way they had teased each other. It had been so cute. *Poor Jarrod.* He had appeared so uncomfortable when Cordell had said they had to leave while he still had that dang hard-on. To give him his due, though, he had impressed her in the way he'd brazened it out—right up until the minute he passed those two girls in the corridor. She giggled. It was the first time she had seen Jarrod embarrassed.

As she showered, she ran her soapy hands over her body and her mind drifted back to the hunky cowboys. What would it feel like to have one of them nuzzle into her neck? Cordell's mustache would be soft, tickling her as his soft kisses would send shivers up and down her spine. The stubble on Jarrod's face would be a little rougher and would scratch a little as he would nibble and bite at her skin. She felt herself glow at the thought.

They would caress and massage her breasts as she was doing now. Cordell's hands were a little calloused as he was clearly a manual worker, and she'd feel his coarse skin against her soft flesh. The contrast would make her nipples harden, as they were now. Jarrod would caress her gently with his silken fingers, driving her wild.

They would eventually work their hands down her stomach and hips to where her pussy would be waiting eagerly for their attention. She imagined that Cordell's rugged hands would stroke her slowly, while Jarrod's long, velvety fingers would move quicker. Either way, as soon as one of them grazed the tip of her clit, they would make her come with the best orgasm of her life.

She moaned as she flicked her most sensitive spot and had to grab the tiled wall with her other hand to prevent herself from falling over as her legs weakened. Heat ran through her pussy as the evidence of her arousal ran down her leg, mingling in the soap and running with the water that continued to cascade over her. Her eyes were closed as she had imagined the two guys, and she gulped, fighting for her breath as her whole body hummed with electricity.

It took Trinity a while to find the strength to move from the shower cubicle, then she dried herself briskly. As she rubbed her hair, she noticed in the mirror how it spiked up now that it was wet. She liked that style. It was a shame she had stopped using hair gel, as she actually preferred it that way.

She got dressed, contemplating how much she had changed lately. It was hard to remember when she had last given herself an orgasm, having usually waited for Kev to come home—not that they had done much in that department in the past few months. He always seemed to be tired or too busy on his laptop. It was something she had mentioned that night in their argument. He'd told her she was nothing but a nymphomaniac to expect it every time he was there. She had believed him, although all the articles she had read in *Cosmopolitan* suggested otherwise. As she pulled on her navy-blue T-shirt, she recalled the colors she used to wear — any one, as long as it was bright. She'd worn orange or red to perfectly clash with her bright pink hair, or yellow or lime-green merely to cheer herself up. She'd worn colored jeans, too — not just the black or blue ones she had taken to wearing of late. Sneakers weren't usually her style all the time like they were now, either. She'd had several pairs of strappy sandals and Doc Marten boots, as well as high-heeled pumps.

With a sigh, she studied her reflection. Her hair was flat and the color had faded. Her clothes were dull and she was paler than ever.

"I suppose I'm still in mourning," she told herself.

A knock at the door made her jump and her heart beat a little faster, knowing that she was about to see the two gorgeous hunks again.

"Hi, darlin'." Jarrod was leaning against the jamb when she opened the door.

She automatically glanced at his groin and noted that his jeans fit him as snugly as ever. His chuckle told her that he had noticed her checking, and his relaxed expression when she glanced up was a sure indication that he felt a lot more comfortable than earlier.

She flushed and quickly averted her eyes to Cordell. He was looking cool, as usual, smiling contentedly. It wasn't hard to figure out that these guys had had a lot of fun in their respective showers, too.

"What time do we have to leave?" Cordell asked as they walked into the restaurant.

"It'll only take about a quarter of an hour to get to the lawyer's office," Trinity assured him, pouring out three glasses of orange juice. Jarrod had filled a bowl with some fruit and they found an empty table by the window.

"Sure is busy in here today," Cordell remarked, peering around as the waitress took their order.

"Quite a few of the funeral guests were here drinking late last night," she explained with a smile. "They had a few too many so they decided to stay over. None of them were up very early this morning." She rolled her eyes.

Trinity gasped as she saw a familiar girl walking into the room, laughing and joking with a handsome guy. Not only did she have that poppy in her hair again, she also had them plastered all over her cotton dress. They stood out starkly against the white background. Her nails were scarlet, as was her lipstick.

"Trinity?"

She suddenly became aware that Jarrod was speaking to her.

"Sorry, I was…" she murmured.

Jarrod checked behind him to see what she was staring at. "Oh."

"Can I get you a cooked breakfast, ma'am?" the waitress asked.

"Oh-oh, sorry. No, I…er…I'm not that hungry. I'll stick with the fruit, thank you." Trinity nodded to the bowl Jarrod had placed in the middle of the table.

"Thank you." The waitress nodded and left.

"Well, she seems happy." Cordell frowned, following their gaze.

"We shouldn't second-guess another person's grief," Trinity said, as much to herself than to him.

Cordell snorted. "Yeah, right. Or *lack* of it."

Trinity grimaced as she watched Kev's fiancée flirt with the guy she had arrived with, before they took their seats at a large table in the center of the room. More raucous laughter could be heard and Poppy seemed to be soaking up the limelight quite happily.

"Wow, they all seem quite cheerful today, don't you think?" Jarrod remarked.

Trinity glanced around the room at the other diners. "*He* doesn't."

She gestured toward Kev's dad, who was standing behind his wife's chair, glaring disparagingly at the youngsters seated around the center table.

"Perhaps they're not as close as they appeared yesterday," Cordell offered. "Appearances can be deceptive."

"Yes, they certainly can," Trinity replied quietly, thinking how much she'd been deceived by Kevin.

"I'm sorry, sweetheart. I didn't mean…" Cordell reached his hand over the table and grabbed hers, slowly stroking his thumb over her skin.

Trinity gasped, recalling how she'd imagined his touch in the shower earlier, and she began to get hot. "No, it's fine," she assured him, too embarrassed to look him in the eye.

The waitress arrived with the guys' breakfasts and Cordell slowly moved his hand to allow her room to set them on the table.

"Are you sure?" He didn't seem convinced and Trinity felt sorry that he felt so anxious.

"Yes, of course." She peered up, catching his eye as she did so. He seemed a little relieved, and she smiled to reassure him. His gorgeous blue eyes twinkled and those cute little creases appeared in the corners again.

Trinity thought for a second that he could read her mind, and quickly busied herself selecting an apple from the fruit bowl.

It became quite noisy in the small restaurant, with the younger guests on the center table getting rowdier by the minute. As the men ate their meal, Trinity noticed that a couple of the girls sitting with Poppy were pointing toward Jarrod and giggling. She narrowed her eyes, recognizing them as the two who had been in the corridor earlier when the guys had left her room. *Damn.*

"We'd best hit the road," Cordell said, glancing at his watch as he finished eating.

"Okay, I'll go fetch my purse." Trinity was relieved to be out of there and scampered up the stairs to her room. She glanced over at her bed, recalling how she had woken in their arms this morning. It had felt so good.

She heard voices outside her door and guessed they had come to see what was keeping her. Grabbing her purse, she called out to them.

"I'm just coming."

"That's good to know," Jarrod replied with a big grin as soon as she opened the door.

She flushed.

"Let's go," Cordell said, shaking his head with a chuckle. He threw an arm around Trinity and led her back downstairs.

"I hope this lawyer of yours has some good news for us," Jarrod piped up as they climbed into the SUV.

It didn't take long to get into town and they were soon in the offices of Burns, Steadman and Wright.

"Miss Ellis, it's good to see you again." Mr. Montgomery Steadman came out to greet them in the foyer a few minutes later. "Come on through."

She sat in his large, airy office, while the men stood either side of her. Mr. Steadman was probably in his late fifties, with gray hair and a rather large nose. He was quite thin and his brown suit hung capaciously on his puny frame, but he was a darn good lawyer, all the same.

"Pull up those chairs, gentlemen, if you're staying." Mr. Steadman raised his eyebrows questioningly at Trinity.

She flushed as she felt the guys staring at her, too, awaiting her reply.

She nodded. "Yes, they are, sir."

They got a couple of chairs from by the window, and Trinity introduced everyone.

"Well, I've got good news for you." The older man beamed at her. "They managed to retrieve your fireproof box. It's rather battered, I'm afraid, but I've got high hopes for its contents."

Trinity sighed with relief as Mr. Steadman gracefully rose from his chair and went to a wall cupboard. He pulled out the box and set it on his desk. It was cleaner than Trinity had expected, though she imagined it must have taken a lot of water to put the fire out.

"It was a good thing you went for the higher UL rating,"

he went on. "And it took longer than they expected to put the fire out, so we can only hope that your box was among the first of the items to be cooled.

"I got a UL rating of one hundred twenty-five for an hour," she told the guys, as she slowly stood. "It cost a small fortune, but I figured it was worth it. Now, I only hope it was enough." She bit her lip nervously.

"I've still got that copy of your digital hard drive," Mr. Steadman assured her. "I know it's not everything you've got in there, but it's a start." He smiled kindly at her.

"And you've still got your key?" she asked, trembling as she eyed the safe nervously.

"Of course." He took it from his pocket and she was glad that he was so prepared for their meeting. She had left both items in his safekeeping, just in case anything ever happened like this. *Good thing, too.*

He offered her the key and she took it in her shaking hand, hardly daring to use it, but desperate to know if her work and equipment had survived. She was glad to note that the lock still worked, and again thanked her lucky stars that she had paid more for the better quality.

Tentatively, she pulled open the door and felt like she was about to faint with relief as she saw her belongings inside.

"Whoa!" Cordell had obviously noticed her sway slightly as he was on his feet in a flash, wrapping his strong arms around her. "I think you'd better sit down, sweetheart." He carefully helped her back on her chair, where she heaved in great gulps of air.

"Let me take these out," Mr. Steadman offered, reaching into the box. Trinity was only half-listening as he listed everything as he retrieved it. Her copy of the hard drive was in there, along with several memory sticks and the original disks of all the graphics' packages that had been loaded onto her computer. There were also several photographs and some papers that she had kept in there, including her birth certificate and passport.

"I think it's all okay," the old man told them, "although

some of these papers may be a little heat-damaged. You should check them to make sure."

"That's good. Thank you, sir," Jarrod told him.

Mr. Steadman put all her belongings into a large, padded envelope while Trinity continued to take deep breaths. She felt a little embarrassed by her reaction, but also very relieved that they had been there to support her. She could hardly believe how lucky she was to have all her equipment back safely. Years of hard work, important contacts and ideas for future projects were stored in that envelope. Now it seemed she could move on and further her business, after all.

She managed to stand up and thank Mr. Steadman before the men ushered her out of the office.

"Let's go grab us a coffee," Cordell suggested, clutching the envelope to his chest, while his other arm was firmly around Trinity's shoulder.

"Great idea. I'm sure I saw a place just up there." Jarrod pointed up the street.

They were soon sitting around a small table in a quaint café that had the radio playing in the background and checkered curtains at the windows.

"How're you feeling, sweetheart?" Cordell smiled at her.

"I'm fine, thank you. I think it was simply such a relief," she told him, flushing.

"That's good," Jarrod chipped in. "Well, it looks like you're all set to get back to work as soon as you're ready." He tapped the envelope that sat on the table between them.

"Yeah." Trinity frowned as she considered what her next move should be.

"Does that mean we're going home?" Cordell asked softly.

She thought for a moment. "I suppose there's nothing keeping us here," she said.

"Well, we're at your disposal. Whatever you wanna do is fine by us," Cordell replied.

She took another sip of her coffee, gazing up idly as the

door opened. A young couple walked in, kissing as they did so. They strolled, hand in hand, over to a bench-seat by the window where they continued their kiss, which became more heated by the second.

Trinity got hotter as she stared at them.

"Well, that's a revelation." Jarrod spoke slowly, clearly as stunned as she was.

Trinity stared at the bright red poppy in the girl's hair and her stomach roiled. "Guys, we can check out of the hotel later, if that's all right. I've actually got something I want to do first. Can you give me about an hour?"

She quickly stood up and left the café, marching down the street to a familiar building. She heard them behind her, chuckling.

"We'll come back later. Have fun." Jarrod waved to her as she went inside.

"Can you fit me in for my usual, Beverly?" she asked, hopefully.

The owner of the salon stared at her in shock at first, but then she nodded with a massive grin.

"Someone pass me the bubblegum-pink hair dye. The biggest bottle we've got."

Chapter Thirteen

The guys couldn't resist another investigation of the pile of rubble that once had been Trinity's home. There were workmen repairing the sidewalk and part of the road that had been damaged, when they sauntered over.

"Looks like a big job," Jarrod remarked when one of the men took a break.

"Tell me about it," the guy told him with a grimace. "Thirty-one people died that night, and they still don't know exactly what caused the dang pipe to explode."

"They *are* still investigating it though, right?" Cordell checked with a frown.

"Oh, yeah. There'll be millions in compensation to be paid out if it turns out that the gas company's at fault." The guy wiped the back of his hand over his sweaty face. "Well, I guess I'd better get on with it."

"Yep. Take care," Jarrod said as the guy went back to work.

"I hadn't even thought of that," Cordell admitted, pursing his lips.

"Yeah. Who gets it if it comes to that? My money's on whoever had their name on the dang rental agreement." Jarrod grimaced. "I suppose if this Kevin guy held the lease, it'll go to his next of kin."

"Trinity said she was dealing with the insurance company over the contents of that safety box, so maybe she had her name on everything," Cordell mused.

"Let's hope so." Jarrod shook his head. It sure was a complicated mess.

They wandered back toward the salon.

"I wonder how Trinity feels about being in Cavern County after having all this on her doorstep," Cordell remarked, scowling at all the stores and cafés.

It was a lot busier than Pelican's Heath, which had all its retailers in one main street. Here there were businesses and outlets all over the place, and there were several streets leading off each other, like a sort of rabbit-warren with shops.

Jarrod grimaced, considering how long Trinity would want to stay with her family. He dreaded the idea of her coming back and leaving him and Cordell. But would she see it that way? After all, as far as she was concerned, they had nothing between them, and she couldn't stay with her aunt and uncle forever—although he knew the elderly couple would love it if she did.

They strolled on in silence, studying all the modern buildings and wacky stores until they found themselves back at the hair salon.

Jarrod noticed Trinity as soon as Cordell opened the door. Her bright pink hair caught their eyes immediately. Both guys grinned. She was chatting away a mile a minute with the girl behind the reception desk, and she beamed at them. Her hair had been styled slightly shorter and spiked up at the top, making her appear even cuter. It had been dyed a shocking pink, which thoroughly suited her. Jarrod imagined this was how she'd usually worn her hair, and she must have lost interest in it a little lately, as it had been much flatter and paler since he'd known her. He loved this image, though, and it was clear that she was more comfortable like this.

"Wow!" He instinctively put his arms around her. "You look fantastic, darlin'." Her body felt warm and much more relaxed than before in his embrace. He wanted to hold her forever.

"Thank you." Trinity giggled. Jarrod loved that sound.

"What a transformation!" Cordell laughed as he took his turn in giving her a hug. "Sweetheart, you are beautiful!"

Jarrod marveled at how easily she welcomed their arms, and he smiled. He and Cordell had already spoken about their feelings toward the gorgeous girl and they were both smitten. They also knew she might not be around for too long, so they were trying not to get too carried away with their emotions. She sure was a lovely armful, though.

Trinity waved goodbye to her friends at the salon and they went back out onto the street.

"I hope you weren't too bored," she said, linking arms with them both as she steered them toward the corner of the road.

"No, we just had a little nosey around the place," Cordell told her. "There sure is a lot to do and see here."

"Yeah," she said, thoughtfully.

"*You* must be the one getting bored back at Pelican's Heath," Jarrod remarked, watching her expression closely. "There's not half as much there."

"No." She pursed her lips. "There's not as many shops and stuff, but there's plenty of countryside and mountains. Certainly, much more peace and quiet."

"You like the tranquility of it all?" Cordell eyed her curiously.

"Yeah," she said eagerly. "Who wouldn't?"

"Well, a townie like you, I'd have thought..." Cordell replied, again studying her reaction. "We were afraid you might find it too quiet back there."

Trinity giggled. "I haven't *always* lived here," she explained. "I'm a country girl. I came out here when I wanted to go to college." She shrugged. "I suppose I've sort of got used to it all now, but I still love going home."

Jarrod felt his heart sing with the realization that she still regarded the country as home.

"So, you've lived here, what? A few years?" he queried as they continued down the street.

"Yeah," she told them, matter-of-factly. "I left home to go to the university. It was cheaper to rent than to stay at the halls, so I moved into the apartment. I was only going to stay there until I graduated, then I assumed I'd go back home. When Momma passed away, there was nothing to go back there for. The house had been sold and the only family I had were Aunt Sylvia and Uncle Frank, and they were quite well settled without me. It made sense to stay where I was." She shrugged. "I was used to living out here by then, anyhow, so it seemed like the logical step."

Jarrod and Cordell exchanged a relieved expression.

"So, Kevin moved in with you?" Cordell asked, as both guys held their breath for the answer.

She nodded. "Yeah. I met him in a bar when I was out with some friends. We hit it off right away." She grimaced. "I can't believe he was already with Poppy, though. No wonder he didn't bring many belongings over. I mean, he had a few clothes and CDs and stuff, but not half as much as you would think. He told me he sold it all to move in with me so he wouldn't clutter up my place. I stupidly figured he was being thoughtful."

Jarrod squeezed her arm a little tighter, afraid that bringing up the subject might upset her.

She gazed up at him, her big, green eyes bright and shining. "It's okay." She smiled. "Everything's slotting into place now. I can't believe I was so dumb as to not realize it before. He must have been lying to me from day one. I was simply too naive to notice. With hindsight, I can see that all the signs were there. He never loved me." She shrugged.

"He was a damn fool." Cordell's voice was more of a growl, and they both gawked over at him, surprised.

"I've got to agree with you there, bro," Jarrod told him with a grin.

"Um…thanks." Trinity seemed bemused, but smiled. "Is it okay if we go in here?"

They were standing outside the boutique that had caught their eye the other night. Jarrod recalled her saying that she used to shop here all the time. "Of course. Want us to wait out here?"

"No, you can come in if you like."

She glowed with excitement.

They followed her inside. It wasn't too big, but the shop was crammed from floor to ceiling with brightly-colored clothes and shoes. Some shirts with psychedelic patterns adorned mannequins to one side of them, while the shelving opposite stored vivid T-shirts. Piles of jeans with bright patches and embroidery were stacked neatly on the table in the middle of the room, while dresses and tops hung from the ceiling all around the shop.

Trinity went straight to the T-shirts and picked out a bright pink one that matched her hair. Then followed a yellow, an orange and a red. She gazed up at some of the tops hanging on a rail, her eyes shining.

"I like the green one. What do you think, guys?"

Jarrod grinned. He wasn't used to being asked his opinion on womenswear.

"I agree. It brings out the color of your eyes," Cordell replied, thoughtfully.

Jarrod was impressed at his observation and agreed with him. Her eyes were like sparkling emeralds, and the lacy top in pale green and white would certainly enhance them.

"I hadn't thought of that," she said, surprised. "What about those in the corner?"

She was pointing to a rack of handkerchief-hemmed flowing tops with large bell-sleeves in bright orange and blue.

"Yeah, they're great." Jarrod wasn't entirely sure what he was looking at, but if she liked it then it must be good.

Cordell shook his head. "I prefer those." He pointed to a couple of mannequins which sported cotton tops with a sweetheart neckline and pretty cut-out details along the edges of the sleeves and hem.

Trinity gasped when she turned to where he indicated and quickly went over to them. "They're fantastic," she marveled. "I love how the shape follows the contours of the body."

Jarrod grinned, guessing that this feature wouldn't have

gone unnoticed to Cordell, either.

She picked a few bright bandeau-style tops, too, and some thin crop-tops that would show off her flat stomach beautifully, Jarrod noted.

He smiled as she also picked out some bright green jeans and some floral cotton trousers. She even bought a pair of red shorts, which he couldn't wait to see her in.

The shopkeeper recognized her and welcomed her with open arms. "We don't see nearly enough of you," he told her.

She briefly explained what had happened as he rung up the sale.

Jarrod took a meander around the shop while Cordell and Trinity argued about who was going to pay for the goods. He could see how well they got along, and he smiled. Cordell had certainly made some good suggestions about the clothes, which had surprised Jarrod. Cordell was usually so masculine. It was weird to find how much he knew about the subject.

Jarrod approached the counter as the other two left, carrying the bags of clothing.

"Excuse me, sir," he asked the guy who had just served them. "Do you do mail order, by any chance?"

He heard Trinity's breath hitch behind him and smiled.

"As a matter of fact, it's something we're starting to do," the guy replied eagerly. "Let me get you the details."

Jarrod took the leaflet from him with a grin. Instead of handing it directly to Trinity, he stuffed it into his back pocket. She could have it *after* he had copied down the information.

* * * *

Trinity smiled as Jarrod took her bags from her. They were such gentlemen. Cordell had even tried to pay for her shopping, but she had stood firm. Okay, so she was spending the inheritance money that she should have been saving, but in fact, this was one of those occasions emergency funds were for. Besides, as soon as the insurance paid up on the contents of the apartment, she would be able to repay her savings account.

She breathed in the warm air. It was unexpectedly humid today, and with all the traffic, it was quite noisy, too. She noticed that they always stood on either side of her, putting her in the middle so she didn't get jostled around like she normally did. Being so small, she guessed most people didn't acknowledge her — despite the pink hair.

"Wanna get some lunch?" Jarrod suggested.

"That would be great." She hadn't realized how late it was getting and she sure was hungry.

She gave a sigh of contentment as they each threw an arm around her shoulder as they headed for the diner. She hadn't been so relaxed in a long time, despite the horrid circumstances.

"Is there anything else you need to do before we head home?" Cordell asked as they sat at a small table near the window.

Again, she had one hunky guy on each side of her. "No, I'm all done. How about you both?"

Jarrod raised his eyebrows in surprise. "We're only here for you, darlin'. If you wanna stay longer, that's fine by us, and if not, we can take you home this afternoon."

Trinity felt a warmth in her stomach. "It was very good of you both to bring me."

Cordell raised his eyebrows. "We'd do anything for you, darlin'" he told her softly.

She flushed. She saw sincerity in his big blue eyes and she knew he meant every word. Her stomach was burning now, and she could feel herself pant a little as her heart throbbed heavily.

Jarrod put his hand over hers. "What he said," he whispered.

Trinity gazed from one handsome face to the other. "Thank you," she said, her voice much huskier than she'd expected.

She was a little disappointed that the waitress arrived at that moment and Jarrod removed his hand to grab a menu. Her throat had suddenly gone dry and she had to cough several times to clear it before she could order her burger.

"Don't you have to get back to work?" she asked the men once they were alone again. "I'd hate for you to get into trouble for helping me out."

Cordell said, "Aiden Fielding's a real good boss. Besides, we had some time owed us. He was only too happy to let us go for a while. Your Aunt and Uncle are good friends of the Fieldings, so in a way, we were helping them out, anyhow. I'm sure he or Ben would've brought you if it had been a problem."

Trinity gasped. She was real glad it was these guys who'd opted for the job. She wouldn't have been half as relaxed with anyone else.

"I'm not a charity case," she remarked, after thinking it through for a minute. "I was quite happy to take the train. That was my plan in the first place."

Cordell smiled, reaching over to place his hand on hers. It was real warm.

"No one's saying that, sweetheart. We merely wanna help. That's all. It strikes me you've been away from Cavern County too long. You've forgotten what it's like living in a community like ours. Everyone helps everyone else. It's how we roll." He shrugged.

"Yeah, and we were only too happy to help you out. Not only because it gave us a couple of days off work, but we got to hang out with you for a while. What's not to love?" Jarrod piped up with a wink.

Trinity suddenly felt much better. They were right. She recalled how neighborly everyone was back at Pelican's Heath. It was nothing like that here. Living in Nebraska, she had soon learned to fend for herself and rely on no one else. She only wished she'd been a little smarter when it came to picking a boyfriend.

She smiled at them. "I can always count on you to make me feel better about stuff."

"All part of the service, ma'am," Jarrod joked.

Trinity giggled.

As they ate their lunch, she wondered what it would be like between them once they were back into their usual routines.

Gazing out of the window, she noticed Poppy go by with the guy she had been with that morning. They stopped on the corner and had a kiss. Trinity narrowed her eyes. The grieving fiancée had sure gotten over Kevin quickly. It had only been a matter of weeks, and yet here she was in another guy's arms.

Her thoughts turned to the two hunks seated on either side of her. Despite waking up in their arms, her conscience was clear about Kevin—not that she owed him anything, since he had been cheating on her and lying about it. They had also not been getting along too well for the past few months—small wonder—and she had known they would split up before too long. She only wished they had parted ways sooner. Kev would still be here if they had, and she would have been free to find someone else to be with—someone who would make her happy, not that she needed a guy for that. She could manage quite well without a man. Although, she had to admit, things had been much easier over the past few days with these men in her life. She just wondered how long it would last.

Chapter Fourteen

Trinity was a little reluctant to return to Pelican's Heath as it would mean the guys getting back into their routine and she wouldn't see them as much. It had been lovely having their company these past couple of days, and she'd miss them. But she had to admit there was nothing keeping her here any longer, so it was only fair to let them go back to work.

"I expect you'll have loads to do now that you've got all this stuff to load up," Jarrod remarked as he picked up the large envelope with her hard drive and everything else they had retrieved from her safe.

She smiled, wondering if he'd read her mind. "Yeah. It'll give me something to do," she said with a shrug.

"Are you afraid you'll get bored being at Pelican's Heath?"

She was amazed at how concerned Jarrod appeared as he asked her. She shook her head. "No, there's plenty to do there."

"That's good." Jarrod sighed as they left the diner.

Cordell drove them back to the hotel where they went to pack their bags.

"I'll be a few minutes," Trinity told them when they arrived upstairs.

They placed her bags inside the door, and she caught Cordell gazing wistfully at her bed moments before they left.

She delved into one of the bags and pulled out a striking yellow T-shirt to go with her new bright green jeans. With a smile, she quickly changed. She checked herself in the mirror and was happy with what she saw. She looked much more like her old self. There was only one more thing. In the bathroom, she found her makeup bag and pulled out the bright pink lipstick that had lain unused at the bottom for several weeks. It didn't take long to apply some eyeliner, sparkly eye shadow and thick mascara. She giggled at her dramatic reflection. Somehow, she felt whole again. Normal.

She quickly packed all her things and swung open her door just as they were about to knock.

Jarrod gaped at her. Cordell's face split into the most dazzling smile.

"Ready?" she asked.

"For anything, darlin'," Jarrod assured her, still appearing utterly astonished.

"Wow! You are stunning, sweetheart." Cordell nodded.

"Beautiful!" Jarrod agreed.

"Thanks."

"Let's go home," Cordell offered.

They headed downstairs, laughing. Trinity was overjoyed with their reactions. They had never seen her like this and she wasn't quite sure what the cowboys would make of her appearance. They seemed to love it, though, if their whoops and hollers as they went out to the SUV were anything to go by.

"I'm driving," Cordell announced once they'd piled everything into the trunk. "Wanna ride up front?" He flashed that smile at her and she couldn't refuse.

Soon they were on their way, and Trinity was surprised at how relieved she felt as the factories of the town gave way to lush fields and distant mountains.

"You don't look too much like a country girl right now," Jarrod remarked as they admired the landscape.

She turned to face him. He was grinning at her, his face radiant and open.

"Is that a problem, cowboy?" She raised an eyebrow.

Jarrod let out a loud whoop. "No, ma'am. It's not a problem at all. Just an observation."

"Good." She smiled. "'Cause I feel comfortable with the way I look. Besides, I'm still a country girl in here." She pointed to her heart. "Always was, always will be."

"Good for you, sweetheart," Cordell interjected. "I love the way you look. Couldn't quite picture you with pigtails and a cattleman's hat, somehow."

Jarrod laughed. "Or one of them checked dresses," he added.

"Nope. Sorry, guys. That's just not me. I know I might appear a bit out of place in Pelican's Heath, but I guess they'll simply have to get used to it. This is me." She shrugged.

"And we wouldn't have you any other way, darlin'," Jarrod assured her.

She giggled. "Why, thank you." She fluttered her eyelashes flirtatiously.

"Hang on a minute. Does that mean you're planning to stay there?" Cordell asked.

She turned back to face him, a little taken aback by his serious expression. "Certainly, for the time being, as long as Aunt Sylvia and Uncle Frank don't mind. I can work from anywhere, being freelance, so why not? I love Pelican's Heath and I think I'm beginning to make some great friends there. Why would I want to leave?"

Cordell's handsome face relaxed into the most gorgeous smile and his blue eyes twinkled like sapphires. "Sounds good to me, sweetheart."

He leaned over and chanced a quick peck on her cheek, which totally floored her.

"Eyes on the road," Jarrod admonished him, as he bent forward. "I, on the other hand, ain't driving." He reached over and pulled Trinity toward him before planting a luscious, soft kiss right on her lips.

She gasped, speechless as he slowly withdrew with a low chuckle. "I think you've made the right decision, darlin'," he told her in a deep, sultry voice.

"I hope so," she replied in a whisper, gazing from one

gorgeous hunk to the other.

* * * *

Cordell reached over to stroke Trinity's cheek as she slept. It seemed a shame to wake her but he knew she would want to see her aunt and uncle again. They were such a close family.

"Hey, sweetheart, we're home." He kept his voice soft as her beautiful sparkly eyelids fluttered.

As soon as she opened her eyes, she gave him a dazzling smile that warmed him inside. She sure was lovely and had seemed like a different person on the way back here. Trinity had seemed quite tense and suspicious when they had taken her to Nebraska, but now that the whole ordeal was over and she had changed back to her normal look, she seemed far more relaxed and happy.

He knew she still missed Kevin and was devastated at the way he had died, but she seemed to have come to terms with it, somehow. Maybe discovering that he wasn't the guy she'd thought he was had helped. When she had spoken about him this afternoon, her eyes didn't flood with tears like they had before. He was glad. It had broken his heart to see her so distraught.

The passenger door opened and Jarrod stood, grinning. "You had a good sleep, darlin'."

"Sorry. I must have been more tired than I thought." She flushed and Cordell rolled his eyes. Trust Jarrod to make her feel uncomfortable right now.

"It's hardly surprising after last night," Cordell soothed her.

"You're here!" Sylvia's voice rang out into the night as she emerged from the shadows. "We were starting to get worried."

"*She* was," Frank piped up, behind her. "I knew you'd simply be taking it easy, driving carefully with your precious cargo." He smiled lovingly at Trinity who hopped down from her seat and gave the elderly couple a huge hug. She really was affectionate.

Jarrod had already taken her bags from the trunk and they both followed the others inside.

"Sorry we're a bit late," Cordell offered. "We stopped for a meal on the way."

"Yep, my fault," Jarrod admitted a little sheepishly. "I was starving." He placed the bags by the door.

Sylvia frowned. "Does that mean you won't want a slice of my chocolate cake with your cocoa?"

"Oh, no, I can always find room for your chocolate cake, Sylvia. You know that." Jarrod put an arm around her as he assured her.

Sylvia held up the cake, beaming. If it tasted as good as it looked, they were in for a real treat.

Cordell and Jarrod took their seats on the large, squishy sofa facing the fire. Its glow gave a warm, homey feel to the house, and Sylvia's cake and hot cocoa were perfect. Sylvia and Frank took their usual seats in the two winged armchairs that sat nearer the fire, and Trinity smiled as she took her place on the sofa between him and Jarrod.

"You look lovely, hon," Sylvia said, smiling at Trinity. "Right back to your old self. How do you feel?"

Trinity nodded. "More like me," she admitted before taking a bite of her cake.

"I'm glad they managed to find that dang safe box," Frank piped up. "That must have been such a relief for you."

"It was." Trinity sighed. "I've got to load it all onto the laptop to check, but it didn't seem like there was any damage done."

"That's good. We wouldn't want you getting bored out here." Frank smiled.

Trinity giggled. "Why does everyone think I'm going to be bored? There's plenty for me to do, even without work. Honestly, don't worry." She smiled before getting back to eating her cake.

Cordell snickered. She really was a country girl at heart,

although right now she looked anything but. He loved her bright colors and her hair was gorgeous. She appeared much more comfortable in her own skin now, and she glowed with contentment.

She got up to help her aunt collect all the plates after a while, and they disappeared into the kitchen.

Frank leaned forward, his voice low. "We're so grateful to you for all this, you know."

"It's been our pleasure, sir," Cordell assured him.

"It was a great road trip," Jarrod piped up. "Well, apart from the sad bits, of course. That was hard. But we were glad to be there for her. I wouldn't have forgiven myself if she'd had to go through all that on her own."

"It was a darn sight more than a mere road trip," Frank replied, incredulously. "I don't know how you did it, but you took our little waif away with you and brought back our Trinity. We can't thank you enough for that."

The old man reached out his hand and both guys got up to shake it.

"To be fair, I think it was good that she met that Poppy girl," Cordell admitted. "Once she got to the truth of the matter, she was able to start mending."

"Yeah, and seeing how quickly the fiancée had healed sure lit a fire in her," Jarrod added. "She must have thought that if that girl could get over it so easily—and she was supposed to be marrying the cheating dumbass—then what was she still moping around for?" He shook his head. "Who can blame her?"

"Hmm, there's something not right there, if you ask me." Frank frowned, thoughtfully. "I mean, I'm glad Trinity's getting over it—don't get me wrong—but I don't see how the grieving fiancée can be with someone else like that so soon after it all."

Cordell winced. He knew Frank hadn't been happy when Trinity told them what had happened. The old man obviously hadn't voiced his concerns for fear of worrying Trinity, but he was right to be suspicious. Cordell and

Jarrod had already had a similar conversation between themselves.

"We'll keep an eye on the situation. Don't you worry about that," Jarrod assured him. "We'll see if we can't do a little snooping and just make sure it's all kosher. Don't you go fretting. We don't want that heart of yours taking the strain." He seemed quite adamant, and Cordell was impressed. He knew Jarrod thought the world of Frank and Sylvia and would do anything for them. Without any parents of his own, he probably regarded them in that role. And Cordell was only too aware of Jarrod's feelings about Trinity. They were both falling heavily for her.

"Well, we'd best be going. I'm sure Aiden will have a good long to-do list waiting for us in the morning." Cordell grinned.

He heard a gasp behind him and shot around to see that Sylvia and Trinity had returned.

"I'm so sorry. I've put you all behind in your jobs. You'll both have to work twice as hard now to make up for it. I'm really — " Trinity looked ready to cry.

"Now, don't you worry about that, darlin'. We're more than capable of doing whatever the boss has in store for us, believe me. Besides, there's plenty of hands over there to pitch in." Jarrod strode over and put an arm around her. "We were glad to help and we had a real wonderful time with you. Well…it wasn't nice all the time, of course… It was… Well, you know what I mean."

"Yeah, I wasn't complaining or anything." Cordell felt like shit. He hadn't expected them to hear him and certainly wasn't insinuating that the trip had been a hindrance in any way. *Damn.* He rushed to put his arm around her shoulder, too, and kissed the top of her head. Her hair smelled of the salon.

The three of them hugged each other as though it was the most natural thing in the world. Cordell was thrilled at how easily Trinity threw her dainty arms around their huge frames and held them close.

"We'll have to go riding sometime," Jarrod offered on their way out the door, "whenever you're free."

Trinity nodded as they climbed into the SUV.

It was sad driving off without her. Wrong, somehow.

"Do you think she'll take us up on the offer?" Jarrod asked.

"I sure hope so." Cordell tried hard not to sound as doubtful as he was. He wished they'd set up a definite date so they could be sure of seeing her again soon. Now that she had all her work back, he could imagine her getting caught up with that and not having time to see them again.

"She sure is close to Frank and Sylvia," Jarrod commented as they arrived home. "It's good to see."

Cordell frowned. "Oh no, I know where this is going, bro, and you can forget it." He wasn't in the mood for the same old argument tonight, although he had to admit it had crossed his mind lately.

"Come on, man. You've only got one family. Once they're gone, they're gone. There's no chance to make it up then." Jarrod was relentless as they went into the house.

"I know. Bro, I'm tired, now. Can't we go and get some sleep? I really don't wanna go over all this again. Not tonight." Cordell pursed his lips as he waited for Jarrod to relent.

"All right. But we need to talk about it soon, okay?"

"Okay." Cordell knew he needed to address the situation with his family, and he would. Just not right now. Unfortunately, the seed had already been planted in his brain, and even when he was curled up in his warm, oversized bed, he couldn't stop his mind from whirring.

He couldn't change the past, but if the family were going to have any kind of future together, they were going to have to accept the situation and each other. Cordell knew he and his mom had done the right thing. They'd had no choice. Dad had already made the decision for them. There simply had to be a way of getting everyone else to accept that before it was too late. Trinity and Jarrod had each lost both parents, and he wanted to cling onto the only one he had left, his mom. She was a lively woman, always busy, but she was also in her seventies. He desperately needed to make it all right for her before it was too late.

Despite being exhausted, he couldn't sleep. His brain wouldn't shut off, no matter how much he tried to relax. The thought that had struck him the other day at Kevin's vault just wouldn't waiver. His mom might die at any time, with the family standing around her headstone cloaked in guilt instead of love.

Chapter Fifteen

The next couple of weeks passed in a whirl for Trinity. She was so pleased to be able to upload all her files again and access her research and previous projects. She also had copious notes for ideas she had come up with for future projects, as well as contact details for potential, current and previous clients.

Her cell had hardly stopped ringing with queries and offers of commissions, and she was enjoying sinking back into her work.

Aunt Sylvia and Uncle Frank popped their heads into the study from time to time, but mostly she was left alone to get her designs done in peace.

"I'm sorry, Uncle Frank. I feel like I'm keeping you out of your office," she told him one night at supper. "I honestly don't mind some company while I work if you need to use your own desk."

"It's fine. I can see how hard you concentrate. You won't want me huffing and shuffling papers in the background. I'm quite happy to do whatever I need to do out here or on the kitchen table. The house is plenty big enough for us to all have our own space."

Trinity pursed her lips. It was lovely living out here, so peaceful and beautiful. Aunt Sylvia was a great cook, and Uncle Frank was so kind. But she knew she couldn't impose for too long. The last thing she wanted to do was overstay her welcome.

"I might take the day off tomorrow," she announced, thoughtfully.

Aunt Sylvia smiled. "I think you should, hon. You can't

work all the time. Give yourself a break."

Trinity nodded. They were sitting in the conservatory enjoying the sunset. She gazed out at the view of the rolling hills in front of them. The sky was swathed in pink and purple as the sun made its majestic descent.

"I think it would be nice to walk up into the hills, maybe take a picnic. What do you think? Could we all go?" Trinity smiled. It would be nice to spend some quality time with them.

"Don't you think that might be a little too energetic for your Uncle Frank?" Aunt Sylvia asked, frowning. "He has to take it easy now, you know."

"Dang, I hadn't thought of that. I'm sorry, Uncle Frank." Trinity secretly admonished herself. Uncle Frank was so active that it was hard to remember he was supposed to be resting as much as he could. He didn't seem to have any more problems with his heart, and he'd been much happier this past week since the doctor had removed the sling from his arm, but he was still taking pills.

She supposed they could drive up into the hills, but then it would be either her aunt or uncle who would have to drive and that might not be so relaxing for them. Besides, the idea was to get some fresh air, not go for a drive.

"Why don't you go over to the ranch? Jarrod invited you when they brought you home, didn't he? I'm sure the boys'd love it, too." Uncle Frank suggested.

Trinity frowned. The handsome hunks hadn't been far from her thoughts every day, despite her workload, and every night they took over her dreams. Each morning when she awoke, she wished she was back in their arms like she had been the day they left Nebraska. She recalled the feeling of being safe and protected. She had never been as relaxed as she had that morning, and the guys had just oozed affection. She hadn't forgotten the invitation, but she wasn't sure whether Jarrod was merely being polite.

"I'm not sure," she said with a sigh. "They are probably real busy, and I already feel bad for putting them behind schedule by dragging them all the way to Nebraska." Her heart thumped a little heavier at the thought of spending some time with them, though, and she desperately wanted to believe the invitation had been genuine.

Uncle Frank chuckled. "They weren't too busy when I went over there yesterday," he said. "Cordell was chatting on his cell, while Jarrod was drinking coffee in the sunshine, as I recall."

Trinity's heart lightened. She'd almost forgotten Frank saw them most days for one reason or another. She'd been a little disappointed that she hadn't seen them come across to see her aunt and uncle since she'd been back, though, and wondered if she was the reason for their absence. The thought dulled her enthusiasm and she chewed her lip.

"I dunno. They haven't been over or anything. Perhaps they don't like me," she said, thinking aloud.

Uncle Frank guffawed. "I'm sure you've nothing to worry about on that score," he said. "Those boys love you. Even a blind man could see that. Jarrod came over to help mend that bottom fence a couple of days ago. You were all he could talk about. I told him you were working and he said not to disturb you. Same with Cordell, when he rang up the other day to see how we all were. Your Aunt Sylvia was going to take you the phone so you could tell him yourself, but I was afraid you were up to your eyes in that book you were working on. You might not have time for chit chat."

"Oh…no…it's fine," she stammered, horrified that she'd missed them. She certainly didn't want to give the impression she wasn't to be disturbed while she was working, although some of the illustrations for the last book had been quite complicated.

"No worries. He wasn't offended or anything," Aunt Sylvia assured her. "He asked all about you, though. Wanted to check you were all right, and he offered to stop by if there was anything you needed. I told him you were fine, but we'd let him know if there was something. He's a good boy. He likes to take care of us, I think." She smiled.

"Jarrod was exactly the same. Wanted to know what you'd been up to and how you were getting on. He was real pleased you were enjoying your work."

Trinity's excitement that the guys had been asking about her was marred by the knowledge that she had missed the opportunity to speak to them herself. She sorely missed them and would have loved to have had a chat with Cordell or had coffee with Jarrod. *Damn!*

"Why don't we give them a call, see if they're free tomorrow? The weather's forecast to hold out, and it'll be beautiful up in the hills right now. I took a ride up in the foothills with Ben the other day. He wanted my opinion on some weeds. It was nothing poisonous, but it was good of him to check. It's so peaceful up there. You'll love it." Frank was already reaching for his cell as he spoke, and Trinity could see there was no point in objecting. She held her breath while he dialed.

"Hey, Jarrod. Young lady here fancies a ride up into the mountains tomorrow. You got a horse she can borrow?" He grinned as he spoke and his eyes were shining. "Hang on. I'll hand you over."

Trinity took the cell, her hand trembling. "Hey, Jarrod." She held her breath for his answer, hoping to gauge his reaction toward her. She wasn't disappointed.

"Hey, darlin' how are you? We heard you've been buried deep in pictures of some kind. I guess you managed to upload all that stuff onto your computer then." She could hear in his voice that he was smiling. He sounded every bit as relaxed and cheerful as she recalled, and she let out a huge sigh of relief.

"I am so sorry," she told him. "I had no idea you'd been over. I don't mind taking a break every now and then, you know. You should have just hollered."

"Oh, I wouldn't dare disturb you while you're working," he assured her. "It was no great shakes. I was only helping Frank out with a fence. I hear you wanna come riding tomorrow?" He sounded genuinely happy about it and she cursed herself for not mentioning it before.

It had been a couple of weeks now, and she was thoroughly missing them.

"Yeah, if that's okay? I mean, I know you've got to work and all, but—"

"Hey, don't sweat it, darlin'. I can always make time for you. Not sure about Cordell, though. He and Ben are working on something at the minute so he may not be able to join us. You cool with that?"

"Yeah, of course. Are you sure you can spare the time, though?" She couldn't help feeling guilty keeping him from his job.

"Yup. I'll come fetch you if you like? Say about ten? We don't want to be up there at midday. It gets real hot some days. You wouldn't believe summer's supposed to be over. Mind you, it sure is cold at nighttime around here."

Trinity gulped, wondering if he was conscience of the innuendo in that last remark. Knowing Jarrod though, he'd have been well aware of what he'd said. She suddenly felt hot, and fought to keep her mind on track.

"Ten o'clock's fine, as long as you're sure."

He chuckled. "All right. I'll see you then."

"Thanks, Jarrod. And give my love to Cordell, too, okay?" As soon as the words left her mouth she realized what she'd said. *Love?* Where the hell had that come from? It was just a normal thing to say when she was chatting to her family, but with *them*?

She could tell by the brief silence that Jarrod had computed exactly what she'd said.

"Sure thing, darlin'. Same to you."

He hung up and the silence was filled with her heart hammering out what felt like the backing to a Marilyn Manson track.

"Everything all right, hon?" Aunt Sylvia had been clearing away the dishes and she frowned when she returned to the table.

Trinity was still clutching the cell.

"Um…yeah…of course," she murmured, quickly looking up. She handed the cell back to Uncle Frank, who had overheard their conversation. The twinkle in his eyes told her that he'd noticed what she had said, and she wasn't sure whether that sparkle in his eye was acknowledgment or mirth.

Damn, either way.

Chapter Sixteen

Cordell was surprised to see his cell flashing when he climbed out of the shower the next morning.

"Everything all right, bro?" Jarrod poked his head around the bedroom door and must have noticed his frown.

Cordell shrugged. "It's Nancy-Ruth. Said she's got something to tell me and is it okay if she stops by this morning." His stomach churned. The last time he had spoken to his sister, she was planning a trip to visit their momma to apologize for all the shit she and their brothers had put her through.

Jarrod pursed his lips, walking toward him. "Doesn't mean it's something bad," he pointed out. "Maybe she's gonna say she and your momma have made up and everything's okay."

"Hope you're right there, bud." Cordell wasn't so sure. Things had been really bad within their family since they'd lost Dad, it was hard to imagine everyone forgiving and forgetting that easily—not that it *had* been easy. He had spent the last couple of weeks trying to talk to his brothers, to convince them to at least contact their momma, but they obviously weren't interested in anything he had to say. Jacob seemed to think their momma owed *them* all an apology, and Martin simply didn't want to talk to either of them. He licked his bottom lip, wondering what to tell his sister.

"I already told Trinity you had that meeting with Ben this morning." Jarrod handed him a mug of coffee. "Do you think you'll be able to get out of it?"

Cordell shook his head before taking a sip of his drink.

"He's got some big-shot marketing guy coming in at nine-thirty to talk about raising the profile of the ranch. They want to extend the riding school so they're hoping to attract more clients. It's my place to coordinate everything."

"Maybe Nancy-Ruth wouldn't mind dropping by the ranch to catch you when you've finished. She'll understand how important your job is."

"I'll see what she says." Cordell nodded as he hit the 'reply' button on his cell. He switched to speaker-phone so he could get ready while they spoke.

The phone rang several times before his sister answered.

"Hi Nancy-Ruth, I got your message."

"Hi, Cordell. Sorry. I was actually getting on the train. I'm on my way over to Almondine now." She sounded happy enough, although the racket in the background made it a little hard to hear her.

He frowned. "You're already on your way? Is everything all right?" His stomach roiled with concern. She sure wasn't wasting any time.

"Yeah, of course. The train gets in at half past ten. Any chance you could pick me up or should I take a cab?"

Cordell frowned again. "I'll probably still be in a meeting then, sugar—"

"I'll fetch her," Jarrod interrupted.

Cordell spun around to stare at him. "Seriously? What about Trinity?"

Jarrod grinned. "I'm sure she won't mind coming a little later. Maybe we could all go out for an hour or so? Just a gentle trek up toward the mountain. We don't have to go far."

"Sounds great to me." Nancy-Ruth's voice came over the phone. "I haven't ridden in ages."

"It could work," Cordell said with a nod. "I had a few things planned for after the meeting, but I suppose I could get some of the hands to help out. I'd need to get going now to get it organized, though."

"That's settled then. Meet you at ten-thirty, Nancy-Ruth,"

Jarrod shouted.

"Great. Thanks for that." She sounded quite pleased with the idea. "I'll see you both later."

"Bye, Nancy-Ruth," they chorused down the phone.

"I'll call Trinity to let her know I'll be a little late fetching her." Jarrod grinned.

"Think she'll be okay with it?" Cordell pursed his lips.

"Why wouldn't she be? She'll understand."

Cordell hoped his buddy was right. He quickly got ready while Jarrod spoke to Frank. It seemed Trinity was still in the shower, so Frank offered to tell her when she emerged. He noticed the disappointment on Jarrod's face and guessed he had been hoping to speak to her directly. Cordell had to admit he had been looking forward to hearing her voice, too, and couldn't wait to see her later.

"We can grab breakfast on the way," Cordell suggested, eager to get the rosters changed before the hands started work.

Jarrod nodded, handing him his jacket as they passed through the hallway.

"D'you think I'll need it?" Cordell was hoping for a nice day, although it was hard to tell what the weather would be like yet, as it was still dark.

"You never know," Jarrod told him.

* * * *

Trinity was annoyed with herself for missing another call from Jarrod. She would have loved to speak to him again, even if only for a moment. Her stomach fluttered as she remembered his deep voice and how happy he had sounded when they'd spoken the previous night. She grimaced, remembering what she'd told him at the end of the conversation and hoped he hadn't realized what she'd said. Something told her he would have, though.

"He said he had to run an errand," Uncle Frank told her as she sat at the breakfast table. "Needed to go into

Almondine to fetch something, I think. Anyhow, he'll come by afterward. Probably about eleven. He said he's sorry to mess you up."

Trinity's heart sank. They were planning to go for a trek up in the hills, and Jarrod had been concerned about being up there in the midday sun in case it got too hot. If he didn't pick her up until eleven, they wouldn't have much time for their ride.

Having suddenly lost her appetite, she had to force down the slice of toast she had just buttered. Uncle Frank was now telling Aunt Sylvia all about a story he was reading in the newspaper, and Trinity was left to dwell in her own thoughts for a while. She didn't want to show that the call had upset her, so she tried to concentrate on listening to the story instead, though it was virtually impossible. It was something to do with a man who...*how come something had come up so early this morning? Surely he would've known last night if something was happening?*...the house had caught fire...*would they even have been at work by the time Frank took the call?*...the poor dog was barking like mad...*if Jarrod was that busy, then why agree to go riding with her in the first place?*... the dog refused to move...*would it be churlish to ring back and cancel their ride altogether?*...the fire was totally getting out of hand...*she badly wanted to go, though and needed a break for a while*...oh, the dog was guarding its master who had collapsed...*maybe it would be best to merely fall in with Jarrod's plans.*

Trinity spent the morning working on her current project, illustrating a children's book with fairies and woodland scenes. She tried to imagine what the view would be like from up the mountain. There would certainly be plenty of woodland to see from up there.

She pursed her lips, glancing at the clock. It was almost ten already. She googled the number of the local cab-hire firm and stored it into her cell before giving them a call. They could have a car here in ten minutes. Good. That would save Jarrod a journey and enable them to go riding as soon as he was free. She looked forward to having as long as possible out with him. They hadn't exchanged cell numbers yet, so she had to leave a message at the ranch to let Jarrod know he needn't come over.

"I'll see you later, Aunt Sylvia." She waved at the old lady as the cab trundled down the drive and out toward the Fielding Ranch.

The countryside was so beautiful and brought back fond memories of her childhood. Her mother had loved it here. She toyed with her ring, rubbing her finger over the little heart.

It didn't take long to reach the ranch, and she stared at how much it had changed since she'd last seen it. As the cab sped off, she gawked at the additional stables that had been built since she was last here. The horses in them must be thoroughbreds. They were beautiful. As she wandered toward them, she noticed that there were a couple more rows of stables beyond the ones she had seen. Some children were being helped onto some of the smaller palominos by a woman she vaguely recognized.

"Hey there, can I help you?" A young cowboy approached her, smiling.

"Um, I'm trying to find Jarrod Parker," she stammered, feeling herself flush.

"He took a trip into Almondine. Shouldn't be long, though. Would you like a coffee while you're waiting?"

"That would be very nice, thank you." She nodded.

"I'm Ashley, by the way." The guy led her toward a building near to the stables. "This is for the riding school mostly," he explained. "There's often a few parents waiting around for their kids to finish, but not today. They can have coffee while they wait, and there's a viewing gallery up those stairs where you can see for miles." He pointed to a set of stairs to their left then headed straight for the counter.

"This is lovely." The smell of fresh coffee welcomed them, and the comfy sofas and big, soft armchairs made the place quite homey.

Ashley smiled, handing her a cup. He glanced at the large wall clock. "I'm sure Jarrod'll be back soon," he told her.

Trinity was of two minds whether to ask about Cordell, but Jarrod had said he would be held up in an important meeting so there wasn't much point.

"Thank you. That's so nice of you." She smiled, wrapping her hands around the cup.

"Will you be okay on your own for a bit? I have to get back to work. Cordell, my boss, can be a bit of slave-driver, you know?" He winked conspiratorially and she giggled.

"Of course. I don't want to keep you."

"If you go up to the gallery, you can see the whole of this part of the spread, so you'll see Jarrod when he gets here. He normally parks over there." Ashley pointed to a small parking lot not far from the stables.

"Great. Thank you again."

Once he had gone, she studied the large room. The floor was wooden and the furniture was cream, with hand-embroidered cushions scattered around. A large burgundy and cream rug adorned the center. She imagined the parents would love to come here and meet over a coffee while waiting for their children to finish their riding lessons. She wandered upstairs and found the same décor echoed there, although most of hardwoods were covered in a thick brown carpet.

All the walls in the building were made of glass, offering a marvelous view of the ranch and the mountains beyond. It sure was a lovely part of the world.

As she sipped her coffee, she took a seat on one of the large, plush sofas and watched the hands working with the horses. A large training paddock stood to one side and she imagined that would be where Jarrod would spend most of his days. He certainly seemed patient and kind, so would probably be great at his job, she surmised.

A beautiful thoroughbred stallion was being led out of one of the stables and she gasped at the sight. It was dark chestnut with white socks and a white stripe down its nose.

Its majestic poise reflected its pedigree, as it was slowly coaxed out onto the yard. The stable-hand was looking toward the large house, where three men were slowly meandering toward him.

Trinity remembered that house, and she squeezed her fingers together, rubbing the side of her ring as she did so. When she had first visited the ranch, an older couple had lived there—Mr. and Mrs. Fielding. She'd never known their first names, as she'd always referred to them formally, being so young. They had passed away, though—in an accident, she thought—and the next time Trinity and her mother had come to visit, Aiden and Ben had taken over the place. She didn't know their sister very well, although she may well be the lady with the riding school, but Aiden used to take Trinity to see the horses every time she came, and he taught her to ride.

The three guys approached the stallion, one of them clearly presenting the beast to one of the others. They all wore hats and from here it was difficult to see their faces, but she would know the build of the third man anywhere. Cordell. He appeared quite important and nodded to the other two men. One of the men ran his hand down the horse's nose, then they all suddenly burst out laughing. Cordell moved slightly and she could see his face for a brief second as he brushed his hat up from his eyes.

Trinity felt her stomach burn at the sight of him. He certainly was gorgeous. She wanted to go down there now and hug him, but she could see he was busy. Her heart was almost pounding out of her ribs and she couldn't help smiling.

She heard a noise coming from downstairs and turned around as a woman came in, carrying a cup of coffee.

"Sorry. I didn't mean to startle you," the woman said. "I'm just waiting for my granddaughter to finish riding. She's usually through by now, but as it's such a lovely day, they probably let them have a little longer."

Trinity smiled. "That's so nice." She nodded before

focusing back on the men in the yard.

As the woman took a seat by the window, Trinity noticed one of the men shake hands with the other two and he left, walking toward the small parking lot. As the stable-hand led the horse back to its stall, Cordell and the other man waved to their guest as he drove off. The two men exchanged another joke before the man she didn't know returned to the house.

Cordell looked edible, tipping his hat back a little to wipe his brow, his fair hair shining in the sun. Trinity was about to go down and see him when she noticed his line of sight. A large SUV pulled into the yard, and it stopped momentarily to allow a lady to get out.

Trinity recognized the vehicle as Jarrod's and watched as he drove it around to the small parking lot that Ashley had indicated earlier. Her eyes flitted back to Cordell and she was horrified to see him hold his arms out and give the woman a massive hug. Then he held her at arm's length while she told him something which seemed to make him happy and he threw his arms around her once more.

"Well, something's definitely made their day," the woman remarked.

Trinity stared out the window.

Jarrod returned to them and he joined in their hug, as he said something to Cordell. They all laughed and the girl squeezed each of them tightly before linking arms with them. Then they headed toward a small office building.

"Do you know them?" Trinity asked the woman.

"Oh, yeah. That's Cordell Bray in the brown hat. He's the foreman around here. Damn good one, too, I hear. The other guy's the horse trainer, Jarrod Parker. I don't know so much about him, but he seems real nice. The girls seem to like him. I hear he's a bit of a flirt, though I'm not one to gossip."

"Of course not," Trinity mumbled. "Do you know the girl?" She held her breath while the lady answered.

"Nah, she's not from around here," the older woman

assured her. "Whoever she is, she's real pretty, though, eh? You can't argue with that."

Trinity nodded. The girl *was* pretty. She had long, dark curls and seemed to be a little more curvaceous than Trinity. She would have loved to have a figure like that. "The guys obviously know her well."

The woman frowned. "She's probably their girlfriend, I should imagine."

"You think they're in a ménage-à-trois with her?" Trinity felt her anxiety ratchet up another notch, having actually heard her worse fear being voiced.

The woman shrugged. "Probably. This is Cavern County, remember? Lots of people have ménage relationships around here. I'm not one to judge."

Trinity's stomach roiled and she thought she was about to be sick. No wonder Jarrod hadn't had time to fetch her this morning. He had been way too busy with their girlfriend.

Chapter Seventeen

"Great timing." Cordell smiled as he saw his sister climb out of the SUV.

"Hope I'm not interrupting your meeting. Jarrod told me you had some hot-shot marketing guy to impress." Nancy-Ruth looked radiant. She was clearly much more relaxed and happy than the last time they had seen her.

"All done," he assured her. His stomach churned as he wondered what she had come to tell him.

He held his arms out to her and she ran into them, hugging him tightly. She was warm and smelled of fresh flowers. It was so good to have his sister back in his arms again. Finally releasing his grip, he took a step back. He held her hands, peering steadily into her face. She had always been pretty — not strikingly so, like Trinity Ellis, but pretty all the same.

"You'd better get it over with, sis," he told her. "What's happened?"

She laughed. "You men are all the same," she said, shaking her head. "Jarrod quizzed me all the way over here, assuming the worst. It's okay. It's good news. I'm pregnant!"

Cordell felt the weight of the world lift from his shoulders as he whooped and raised her into the air. "That's wonderful," he told her. "I never even considered that."

He wrapped his arms around her, hugging her again. This was exactly what she'd always wanted. Nancy-Ruth used to say she wanted a husband to take care of and a baby to clean up after — or was it the other way around? Anyhow, it was fantastic news.

"What did I miss?" Jarrod had returned from parking the car.

Cordell let go of his sister as she beamed over at Jarrod.

Jarrod said, "Come on. You've got to tell me now. I've waited long enough, don't you think?"

Nancy-Ruth giggled. "I'm going to have a baby."

"Yes!" Jarrod yelled and went straight over and gave her a huge hug. "I'm so happy for you, Nancy-Ruth."

"Hey, should you be standing up? Maybe we should go find somewhere quiet to sit down. And have you eaten lately? We can get some coffee and—" Cordell's mind whirled as he and Jarrod threw an arm each around her shoulders and led her inside.

"Will you stop fussing?" Nancy-Ruth sounded incredulous. "I'm pregnant, not ill. You don't need to mollycoddle me." She pouted thoughtfully for a moment. "Although some coffee and cake would be real nice if you have any."

They all laughed and went through to the staff dining area.

"I'll get this. You go find a seat," Cordell insisted, giving his sister a little squeeze before letting her go.

"Don't argue with him, darlin'," Jarrod warned her with a wink.

Cordell frowned. "Aren't you supposed to be fetching a certain little girl to join us in a trek up the mountain?" he asked.

Jarrod glanced up at the clock. "Shoot. I clean forgot the time. Let me get your sister settled, and I'll head on over there."

"I'm fine. You go fetch her. I can't wait to meet this girl." Nancy-Ruth giggled. "Go."

"You heard the lady." Cordell grinned as his sister shooed Jarrod back out the door.

"Apple cake all right?" he asked, turning back to Nancy-Ruth.

"Perfect." Her eyes lit up, reminding him of how they

always used to when she was excited about something. She sure had a lot to be excited about right now.

"It was real good of Jarrod to come fetch me," she said, when they sat at the little table in the corner.

"I'm just sorry I couldn't come myself," he said.

"Oh, no, I understood you were busy. I could easily have taken a cab if —"

"Not in your condition," Cordell interjected. "In fact, should you be riding this afternoon? We can always do something else if you prefer? Go for a walk or whatever. We've got a picnic all made up."

"I'm sure I can manage a gentle trek up the hills," she told him. "I was practically born in the saddle, anyhow."

"That doesn't mean your baby has to be," Cordell told her with a grimace.

"Cordell. I'm only a few weeks along." She put her hand to her stomach. "You can hardly tell it's there at all yet. Look."

He gazed at her round tummy. Despite what his sister was saying, there was definitely a bump.

She smiled at him. "Wanna touch it?"

Cordell grinned as he reached over and placed his big hand on the tiny lump. "I can't believe there's another life growing inside. Right under my hand. It sure is a miracle." He took his hand away, longing for the day when he would feel his own child moving or kicking or whatever it was little babies got up to in those places. He wondered how Trinity felt about becoming a mother.

His sister placed her hand on his and nodded, smiling. She sure seemed different today.

"I like your friend Jarrod. He seems like a lovely guy," she said, tucking into her cake. "I know we've only met a couple of times, but I feel like I've known him all my life. He had me in stitches on the way over here. He sure is a lot of fun."

Cordell grinned. "He is that."

"And he's real fond of you," she went on, excitedly.

"Never stops going on about you — and Trinity. He certainly seems to be into her. What's she like?"

Cordell sniggered. *Where do I start?* "Well, she's real cute and tiny, like a little doll you wanna wrap up in cotton ball and keep safe. But she's as strong as an ox on the inside. You wouldn't believe what that girl's been through and yet she's as cheerful, friendly and lo—" He stopped himself short. *Loving? Was I actually going to say 'loving'?* When he'd held her in his arms, she'd seemed like she simply belonged there, somehow. And when he'd seen her with Jarrod, they could easily pass for a couple. She seemed to melt into them both, merging, becoming one. And the way she gazed at them just took his breath away. She was so accepting, so happy to be with them, so — yep, *loving*.

He was aware of his sister's gaze and quickly reached for his coffee to cover his embarrassment.

"It's obvious you both love her," Nancy-Ruth told him, matter-of-factly. She delved into her cake again.

This time it was Cordell's turn to gawk. He wanted to ask what made her think that. What on earth would give her that idea? But he knew her too well. She always had been good at reading people, and he and Jarrod were forever teasing each other about how they both wore their hearts on their sleeves. He sighed. There was no denying it.

"I can't wait for you to meet her," he said, shaking his head.

"Neither can I. I always knew it'd take a special woman to win your heart, but to get both of you in such a loved-up state, she must be really something."

"Oh, she is," Cordell assured her. "She sure is."

* * * *

Trinity felt hot tears burn the back of her eyes and she quickly ran down the stairs and out of the building. She took out her cell and called the cab company that had brought her here, asking for their first available ride.

147

"I'll be on the road leading away from the Fielding Ranch," she croaked, when she was told it would be at least ten minutes.

Instead of crossing the yard, she took the path that ran down the back of the stables and came out by a beautiful house that stood not far from the main gate. The drive narrowed as it got farther from the ranch, twisting a little, and pretty flowers and shrubs adorned each verge. Trinity didn't stop to admire the scenery, though. She merely kept running as fast as she could.

After a short while, she heard a car coming down the road behind her. Quickly, she jumped into the bushes to the side. It was the first time in her life that she wished she didn't have vibrant pink hair and such gaudy clothes. She hoped all her colors might merge like flowers among all the greenery — if any of it were visible — and she kept stock-still as she heard the car getting closer. As it passed her, she recognized it as Jarrod's SUV, and she held her breath as she saw his gorgeous face and his muscular, tanned elbow perched on the window ledge.

More tears flooded her face as the car sailed past her. He seemed to be in a hurry. She glanced at the time on her cell. It was a little after eleven. *So much for picking me up at eleven.* Their girlfriend had obviously distracted him and he'd forgotten all about her. If he *was* going to fetch her. It would be more than a little bizarre to expect her to join them and their girlfriend. And she had to be with both of them, as Trinity had seen them all hugging and holding her together. No, the old lady was right. They were into ménage and that girl was their third. It all made sense. What didn't make sense, however, was why they had told her that they were interested in a ménage relationship in the first place. *Surely they would know that I presumed they'd meant they wanted that relationship to be with me? Or am I even more boneheaded than I thought?*

She wiped her face with her fists as she ran down the road. A huge lump had formed in her stomach and she felt sick. She also felt stupid. *How did I not know?* She hadn't seen anything of the guys since they'd come back from Nebraska, which had been at least a couple of weeks. When they had all been out there, she'd gotten the impression that they liked her — more than liked. Waking up in their arms had been the best feeling in the world. And she'd thought them so chivalrous for lying on the top of the covers. Now she understood why. They wouldn't have wanted to be *that* close to her, given that they had left their girlfriend at home. When they had said they were interested in a ménage, they actually meant that that's what they were into, *not* that it was what they wanted with *her*. Why hadn't she even thought to ask the question? She sighed. Because she was too dumb.

She was relieved when she heard another car and saw a cab driving toward her. She signaled to the driver, who stopped, his engine purring.

"Where to, Miss?"

"Um." She stared at the back of his head. She had merely assumed she would go back to Aunt Sylvia and Uncle Frank's house, but what would they think? Especially given the state she was in. And she couldn't be sure that Jarrod hadn't gone there, anyway. *Where can I go?*

"Miss?" the guy turned his head to face her.

In that moment, she just wanted her momma. She had always made things right for her, somehow.

"Can you take me to St. Mary's Church, please?" she asked, her voice hoarse from crying.

"Over on Banham Moor?"

"Yes, that's it."

"Sure."

He turned the car around and she sat back in her seat, closing her eyes as she idly fiddled with her ring. It used to be her momma's ring and she wore it every day. Trinity was never told who gave it to her, but he must have meant a lot to her. She secretly hoped it had been her father.

Momma had been so kind and gentle, yet she had been

as strong as any man until the cancer had gotten her. She'd used to do everything for herself up until then, and she had virtually renovated the little cottage they'd lived in single-handedly. Trinity wondered what her home looked like now. She hadn't been back there since the funeral. Aunt Sylvia and Uncle Frank had been Mom's executors for the will and they had taken care of everything. At the time, Trinity had been happy to leave it all in their hands, clearing out the house and selling it. The money had gone into a savings account for her, and she had only used it for emergencies, hoping that it might accrue enough interest to afford her the deposit on her own house one day. Unfortunately, with everything that had happened lately, she'd had had to dip into the account a little more than she had hoped. But there was no denying that losing her home was a dire situation. Now she wished she'd had more of a hand in sorting out her momma's possessions, but at the time, it had been all too painful. There were so many little things, knickknacks, that she wished she'd kept. Now she had no idea where they had ended up.

"Here you go." The cab driver seemed a little apprehensive about leaving her at the church alone. It was tucked away on a lonely moor, miles from civilization.

"I'll be fine. I've got my cell," she assured him, showing him the proof.

"All right, if you're sure," he mumbled as he took her money and set off back toward Cavern County.

Trinity took the little winding path that led through the graveyard. She shivered as the wind cut around the corner of the little stone building, and she was glad that she'd thought to bring a sweater, even though it was such a warm day. Having expected to be riding up in the mountains, she hadn't forgotten how cool it could get up there at times, despite Jarrod's concerns about them getting too hot in the midday sun.

It was then that she realized she hadn't even thought about the guys for the past hour while she had been traveling up here. Thoughts of her momma had flooded her mind, leaving no room for the handsome — if deceitful — cowboys.

She gazed out over the hills that stretched for miles in front of her. The nearest town was twenty miles away, and all the little houses that used to be dotted among the moorland had been deserted and demolished years ago.

She didn't know how long it had been since the church had actually held a service other than a funeral, and they were only for people like her mother who had already paid for their plot to be with family members. Momma had reserved her plot when her mother died. Grandma was placed in the shared plot with Grandpa, and Momma wanted to join them when her time came. She hadn't reserved one for Trinity, though, as she'd wanted her to be able to travel the world and maybe settle somewhere else. She'd wanted her to be free. That's why she had encouraged her to go to university down in Nebraska instead of staying local. Momma was a free spirit and she wanted the same for her daughter.

Trinity strolled through the graveyard, strewn with plots that had long since been neglected. Weeds grew high in the flower beds and moss covered most of the headstones. She sighed. Momma's grave would be like that, as it had been ages since she had been up here. Momma used to love this place though. *'A little piece of heaven on earth'*, she used to call it.

She came to her momma's grave and balked in surprise. It must have been the neatest plot in the cemetery, with fresh flowers in the vase by the headstone and the most beautiful blue and white flowers planted all over the grave. The colors reminded Trinity of a small vase that her mother used to keep on the windowsill of their cottage, and she used to keep fresh flowers in it constantly, even if she could only afford to pick wild ones from the garden.

Her grandma and grandpa's graves had neatly-trimmed lawns and they, too, had fresh flowers in the vases by their headstones. Someone had gone to a lot of trouble to keep her family graves looking beautiful, and it lifted her heart to see it. Uncle Frank and Aunt Sylvia must have been responsible for this, she surmised, as she didn't have anyone else. They were both far too frail to do all this work, though, and it would mean driving miles out of their way on a regular basis. They must have been paying someone local to do it. Probably the old caretaker, she guessed.

She felt much better out here in the open air, and knowing that the graves were being tended to relieved her more than she'd expected. She did feel guilty for not being able to visit the graves very often, but, in her mind, her family wasn't there, anyhow. She toyed with her ring again. Her momma was always in her heart, not in a cold, dark hole in the ground. And she didn't remember her grandparents, as they had died when she had been very young, but she somehow knew they would be up in heaven, not down there.

Sitting on the side of her momma's grave, she pulled her knees up to her chest and wrapped her arms around them. The breeze wasn't as sharp down here as it had been up by the church, and it was actually quite refreshing on her face. She closed her eyes, letting the fresh air waft over her, clearing the confusion in her head and soothing the ache in her heart.

She wasn't sure how long she'd sat there for, but an idea slowly emerged in her mind. When she had come back to Cavern County, she'd thought she might want to settle here with Aunt Sylvia and Uncle Frank. They were the only family she had and she thought she would like to look after them. But they didn't need her. Jarrod and Cordell were obviously calling around on a daily basis before she'd come back, and they were doing all sorts of jobs to help out the elderly couple, jobs that even *she* couldn't manage. Just because she had gotten the wrong impression of the guys with regard to their feelings toward her, it didn't mean they weren't good friends to her aunt and uncle.

She wasn't needed here. They had all managed quite well without her up until now, so why would she think they would want her here, all of a sudden? Perhaps it was time to travel, like her mother had always suggested? It seemed that Cavern County wasn't the place for her, after all…

Chapter Eighteen

Jarrod was disappointed to arrive at the Crowthornes' house to find that Trinity wasn't there – disappointed and anxious.

"I'm surprised you didn't see her at the ranch," Sylvia frowned. "She left here over an hour ago. She took a cab to save you the journey, as well as some time. I got the impression she wanted to have as much time with you as she possibly could."

"She wasn't annoyed that I'd had to postpone an hour, then?" Jarrod was worried on all kinds of levels.

"No, of course not. She understands that you have work to do, the same as she does," Frank assured him with a chuckle. "Why would she be upset? You hadn't even canceled on her, simply put it back a while. She's quite easy-going, you know." He shrugged.

"She called the ranch to explain what she was doing. Didn't you get her message?" Sylvia piped up.

Jarrod shook his head, whipping out his cell. "Cordell, is Trinity with you?"

His heart sank as his buddy replied, sounding as concerned as he felt, "No, I thought you were fetching her?"

"She left here around ten. She was going over by cab to save time. We should have gotten a message. Can you ask around and get back to me? I'll stay here until I hear from you, in case something's happened and she's on her way back."

"Sure thing, bro."

"Have some coffee while you're waiting," Sylvia insisted. "I've made a lemon sponge cake."

"How can I say no to that?" Jarrod didn't feel much like eating. He actually was sick, but he didn't want to disappoint her — and Sylvia made a mean lemon sponge cake.

"I've had a quote for the new fencing for the east side of the garden," Frank announced. "Come on through. I've put it in here somewhere."

Jarrod followed him into his study, glad for the distraction. They were determined to get all the outside work completed before the fall and were well on their way to finishing it.

Frank sifted through some papers on his desk, muttering to himself, while Jarrod's eye was caught by the other desk, which was much tidier, where a small pile of sketchbooks and notebooks sat neatly by a brand-new laptop. The trashcan was half-full of screwed-up pieces of paper, and he stooped to pick up one that hadn't quite made it into the bin. It had been squeezed into a ball but had started to unwrap itself, which was possibly why it hadn't landed in the trashcan like the rest. As he held it, he became more and more intrigued by the scribbles and lines, and he opened it up fully to take a closer peek. It was a pen-drawing of a typical child's impression of a perfect little cottage with a picket fence around the garden, and honeysuckle growing up the walls either side of the door. In the corner of the page was a simple Venn diagram with the letter 'C' in one circle, 'J' in the other and 'T' in the overlapping portion. He grinned. *She does like us.*

"Here it is," Frank announced, then frowned over to him. "Whatcha got there, son?"

"This." Jarrod offered it to him. "I take it she's doing another children's book?"

"Yeah." Frank nodded then took the page from him. "Well, dang it!"

Jarrod frowned. "What's wrong?"

"This is the house Trinity always wanted. All the time she was growing up, she wanted a place just like this. She was determined that one day she would get it, too. It's her dream house, 'Honeysuckle Cottage'. He pouted. "I don't know what all these scribbles are about, though. Looks like she was doodling, unless she's planning to put that house in a book."

Frank shook his head and went to screw the paper up again.

"Mind if I keep that?" Jarrod asked, reaching for it.

Frank seemed surprised, but handed it back to him. "Sure."

"Coffee's ready," Sylvia shouted through.

"Come on," Frank said, eagerly, ushering Jarrod out of the room.

They sat on the terrace on the wrought-iron chairs.

"This cake's lovely," Jarrod remarked. His stomach still churned with worry.

Sylvia blushed. She always did that when either of the guys complimented her — which was quite often — and they found it quite endearing.

"Thank you. You're doing a lovely job with the garden," she replied.

"D'you think Trinity's forgiven us yet for pruning that lilac tree?" Jarrod grimaced.

"She's just a little possessive when it comes to her momma," Frank told him with a chuckle. "That tree was a big part of her childhood. She and her momma used to sit under it for hours making daisy chains. They were real close."

"I can see that." Jarrod nodded. His cell rang and he quickly reached for it. "It's Cordell."

"Hey, bro. It seems she *had* called here, but the message hadn't been passed on as neither of us was available."

"Dang!" Jarrod quickly recalled that he had been off-site and Cordell had been in a meeting. There hadn't been time for anyone to tell them.

"There's something else." Cordell didn't sound happy.

"Go on."

"Ashley said she came to see you and he had her wait in

the viewing area at the riding school. She was supposed to watch for you coming back."

Jarrod frowned. "Then why didn't she notice me? You can see the whole of the yard from there." As soon as the words left his mouth, a huge lump hit his stomach. "Oh, no."

"Yup. I checked the CCTV. She left not long after you got here. I couldn't see much as she took the back path, but she was wiping her face, so she was obviously upset." Cordell sighed. "Nancy-Ruth's real sorry. Thinks she may have given the wrong impression without knowing it."

Jarrod frowned. "You think our little pink-haired girl has got a green streak?"

"She'd have to care about us for that, bro."

"Exactly what I was thinking, buddy." He snickered. It was a nice thought, although it didn't help them right now. "I'll have a chat with Frank and Sylvia to see if they've any idea where she might have gone. She sure didn't come back here."

"Okay. Let me know."

"Will do." Jarrod slipped the cell back into his pocket, aware of the questioning expressions on Frank and Sylvia's faces. He quickly put them out of their misery by filling them in.

Sylvia put her hand to her mouth, turning pale. "I can tell she thinks a lot of you boys. She'd be so hurt to think you don't feel the same way."

"Don't worry about that, Sylvia. We love that girl." The words just fell out of Jarrod's mouth like marbles from a jar. They all stared at one another in silence for a moment.

"Good to know," Frank said with a nod.

"But where could she have gone? She doesn't know anyone, and she wouldn't know her way around. It's been ages since she was last here." Sylvia was close to tears.

"Don't worry, honey." Frank put his hand over hers. "She's an adult. She knows how to stay safe. She'll have probably gone off somewhere to be alone while she licks her wounds."

Sylvia's eyes were wide. "But that's just it, Frank. She's upset and in a strange place. Where could she go?"

Jarrod frowned, feeling a little guilty for the anxiety his news had caused. "Do you have a cell number for her? I take it she carries a phone?"

"Of course," Frank said, looking instantly relieved. "Why didn't I think of that? She always has her cell on her."

Jarrod was secretly pleased to have a legitimate reason for obtaining her number, and he quickly added it to his contacts before ringing her. His heart was beating heavily as he waited for the call to connect. It didn't. "She must be out of signal," he told them, despondently.

"Dang!" Frank scowled.

Jarrod's cell rang again. "Cordell, what's up, bro?"

"We're going mad here, twiddling our thumbs. Have they got any clues where she'd go?"

"No, sorry. I've tried her cell, but it won't connect. She must not have a signal, wherever she is."

"Dang!"

"Yup." Jarrod sighed. "We're still racking our brains here."

"Nancy-Ruth and I are gonna hit the road to see if we can find her. She was walking, so she may not have gone far. Let us know if you think of anything."

"Of course. And tell your sister not to worry. It's broad daylight and we've got good weather. That's something to be thankful for."

"I will," Cordell assured him.

"Is everything all right?" Frank asked with a frown, as Jarrod pocketed his cell again.

"Yeah. They're going to drive around to see if there's any sign. Someone must have noticed her." Jarrod did his best to sound positive, despite the ache in his heart. Last time she had been upset she'd taken a trip to Nebraska. She could be anywhere now.

* * * *

Trinity shivered as the evening brought a chill to the air and a foreboding dimness that shrouded the open landscape in a cloak of inky blue. Tears dripped from her face and a pain stabbed her heart. She didn't know how long she had sat on that hard ground, saying goodbye to her momma, and she didn't even care.

When she had lived in Nebraska, she hadn't worried too much about coming back to tend to this piece of land, as she didn't feel her mother's presence was here, but now she did. Now she didn't want to let go. She loved the bones of her momma, and those bones were lying beneath her right now. Leaving Cavern County for good would mean leaving this reminder of her momma behind, and she didn't know how she was ever going to do that.

When Momma had passed away, Trinity had cried here for hours, saying goodbye. Now she was going through it all again — saying goodbye. And it hurt. Bad.

Aunt Sylvia and Uncle Frank had been so good to her, and she worried that she hadn't shown them enough appreciation. She had gone back to Nebraska and not visited them often enough. A thought dawned on her and she reached for her cell. It was getting late and they would be worried about her. She needed to let them know that she was safe. *But am I?*

The rolling hills and lush meadows that had stretched out before her in the bright sunlight earlier now gaped like vast holes of nothingness. The mountains in the distance had turned to great black ogres and appeared to be getting nearer to her with each thump of her pounding heart.

"No." She shrieked into the fading twilight as she realized that she had no signal on her cell. There was no way of letting her kin know where she was, no way of calling that cab company to send someone out here to take her home. *Home. Where is that?*

Fresh tears poured down her cheeks and she hugged the hard, cold headstone in front of her. Her stomach gurgled and she realized that she hadn't eaten since breakfast. The lump in her stomach reminded her that she wouldn't be able to eat right now, even if she had food. The wind whipped around her, adding to her misery, and the stab in her heart reminded her exactly how lonely she was. So very lonely.

* * * *

Cordell had driven around the county for hours, stopping at each village to ask if anyone had seen a girl with bright pink hair passing through. The answer was the same everywhere he went. No, and they would have noticed. Trinity wasn't the type of girl they would easily forget.

"There's got to be somewhere we haven't tried yet," Nancy-Ruth mused, biting her knuckle. "It's getting cold and dark out here. Maybe she's found a motel or something for the night?"

"Why would she? I mean, she's staying at Frank and Sylvia's. Surely, she'd easily get a cab back there—unless something's happened to her." As soon as Cordell said the words he bit his tongue. Nancy-Ruth had turned white.

"I'm sorry, sweetheart. I didn't mean to worry you." He put an arm around his sister and led her back to the pickup. He knew he was only voicing what everyone had been thinking, but it didn't help the situation.

"It's okay. I have to admit it's crossed my mind a time or two," she told him. "I'll see if Jarrod's got any news."

Cordell nodded, knowing full well that if he had heard anything at all he would have been straight on the phone, but it gave Nancy-Ruth something to do, and she needed that right now.

Jarrod had also been driving aimlessly around Cavern County, while Frank and Sylvia waited anxiously at home for any news.

"Nothing," Nancy-Ruth reported back to Cordell with a frown. "He's scared she'll have gotten lost. Frank and Sylvia reckon she won't remember her way around, and what with the dark…"

"This is stupid." Cordell felt his anger rising with his anxiety, and hit his hand hard on the steering wheel. "We can't just drive around in circles hoping for a sign. We need to regroup and sort out some kind of strategy. Tell Jarrod to meet us back at the Crowthornes'."

Frank and Sylvia seemed pleased to see them all, although they obviously would have preferred it if they had brought news with them. Sylvia insisted they all have coffee and cake while they sat around the kitchen table, racking their brains.

Cordell sighed. He was the ranch foreman, for heaven's sake. He had to tackle this methodically like any other problem that might crop up at work.

"Okay, so we know why she's disappeared. We simply need to figure out where she might have gone," he said. "And we need to think fast. It's getting late.

"I thought she might have found a hotel or something," Nancy-Ruth offered. "She sounds like a real smart girl. Surely, she'd think of something like that?"

"Why, though, when she's got a perfectly good home here?" Sylvia clearly felt hurt. "I hope she didn't feel that she couldn't talk to us about it. We're her only kin."

Cordell shrugged. "Maybe she didn't want to see anyone for a while. You know, get her head straight before she came back here."

"But you said you'd checked at all the places in Pelican's Heath," Frank pointed out, indicating to Jarrod.

"Yes, sir, I did."

Aunt Sylvia shivered. "It's cold tonight, and even the moon has clouded over. If she's out in this, she'll freeze to death. She didn't even take a jacket or anything." Tears flooded her eyes again and she wiped them away with a cotton handkerchief.

"Don't worry, honey. We'll find her," Frank assured her, putting his arm around her and kissing her gray hair.

"We have to, Frank. She's all we've got." Sylvia sobbed

into his arms.

Cordell's heart went out to her and he caught Frank throwing him an anxious look. They were all thinking the same thing. There *had* to be something they could do. Frank and Sylvia were like family to him and Jarrod, and there was nothing they wouldn't do to help them. And Trinity was the girl they loved, they couldn't let her down.

"Hang on." Cordell finished eating his cake as he perused a thought. "Sylvia, you said she called a cab, right?"

"Yes." The old lady nodded wiping her eyes.

"And if she was going anywhere outside of town, she might well have called a cab to take her there. After all, she doesn't know her way around that much, does she? Anywhere even as far as Almondine would be strange to her." Cordell felt a grain of hope begin to grow inside him as he spoke.

"Yeah, of course. What cab company did she use, Sylvia? Chances are she'd have used the same one." Jarrod pounced on the idea, his eyes shining with optimism.

"It was Pete's firm. She put the number in her cell, too, so she's bound to have used the same one," Sylvia replied.

Cordell's cell was already in his hand. He quickly called the firm, asking if any of their drivers recalled picking up a girl with bright pink hair today. He gave the woman Trinity's name and explained the situation.

"According to the list here, Raymond picked her up from the Crowthornes' place shortly after ten and dropped her at the Fielding Ranch," the woman told him.

"Yes, ma'am, but what about after that? Did anyone get a call from her later in the day?" Cordell held his breath for the answer.

"Hmm, not according to this, but I'll check with the drivers. Someone might remember a girl with bright pink hair," she offered.

"She's checking now," Cordell told the others as he heard the woman ask the question over the radio.

After a lot of white noise and muffled voices he heard the

woman again. "Yes, sir. It seems one of our cabs picked up a girl with pink hair not far from the Fielding Ranch about quarter past eleven. He was worried about her because she was real upset."

"That's her. Where did he take her?" Cordell asked, his heart pumping like a steam engine.

He heard her talking over the radio again before she got back to him. "She went up to St. Mary's Church—the one on the hill outside town. He actually didn't want to leave her there, but she assured him she had her cell and would call someone to take her home afterward."

"St. Mary's? Thank you, ma'am. I'm much obliged to you." Cordell was on his feet before he even put his cell back in his pocket.

"Her momma's grave!" Sylvia was clearly shocked, while more tears streamed down her cheeks Nancy-Ruth put an arm around her.

"Now, why didn't we think of that?" Frank frowned as everyone stood up.

"You stay here," Cordell told his sister. "Me and Jarrod'll go."

"I'll see them to the door. You stay in the warm," Frank told the ladies.

Cordell could see that the old man was holding back tears as they left the room.

"Boys, I know you'll do your best," he whispered as they stood at the front door. "But she's all we've got. We just can't lose our little girl."

Cordell nodded. "Don't worry, Frank. Neither can we."

Chapter Nineteen

It was black up on the moors and the guys strained their eyes, searching for any sign of their girl.

"If she was at the church around lunchtime, she would surely be on this road somewhere," Jarrod said.

"Unless she's still up there." Cordell's stomach burned with a mixture of dread and hope as he drove carefully up the hill.

Their headlamps were on full beam, the only lights in the wilderness, and their only hope of finding Trinity. Wildlife darted in and out of the road before them, and the wind whistled around the sides of the SUV.

"She's gonna be freezing out here," Jarrod remarked, his teeth clenched with worry.

"We've got blankets in the back, bro," Cordell reminded him, trying to stop himself from panicking as much as his buddy. They were always covered for emergencies.

It seemed to take an age to finally reach the top of the hill, and they could just make out the light gray stone of the church. Cordell pulled up and left the headlights on to show their way, while they pulled on their jackets and fetched the flashlights and blankets from the trunk.

They ran down the winding path, heading directly for the graves that they had regularly tended every week since Sylvia had become too frail to keep bending down. Although they hadn't met Trinity's momma, Sylvia had told them so much about her sister that it seemed as though they knew her and they always spoke to her while tending the flowers they had planted at Sylvia's request.

"There she is." Cordell shouted as his flashlight found the

headstone, and as he got nearer he could see Trinity's vivid pink hair as she lay slumped over it.

She stirred as they peeled her away from the cold stone, her body barely shivering and her skin like ice.

"It's all right, sweetheart," Cordell assured her as he pulled her into his arms while Jarrod wrapped a blanket around her. "You're safe now."

He held her through the soft wool while Jarrod spread out the other blanket that they quickly draped over her. She moaned but didn't make any coherent sound as Cordell hoisted her into his arms and carried her, bundled up like a little pink baby, back to the SUV.

"I'll drive," Jarrod offered as he helped Cordell into the passenger seat.

"That's good, bro. 'Cause I'm never letting this girl go." Cordell was surprised to feel tears sting his eyes as he gazed down at the beautiful face that was half-covered by the blanket.

"Well, now, that makes two of us," Jarrod told him with a grin, kissing Trinity lightly on the forehead.

"She's hardly breathing, bud. You'd better step on it." Cordell couldn't keep the tremble from his voice as he searched fervently for her pulse. It was barely there. He held her close, fearful that they were already too late.

The heat of the car soothed them as they sped back down the hill, and Cordell couldn't take his eyes off the girl in his arms. He sniffed. "She must be badly missing her momma," he said, softly.

He caught a knowing stare from Jarrod. "You can't replace a momma's love, buddy."

Cordell sighed, getting the message loud and clear. He held Trinity a little tighter and felt her stir. "I know."

His heart went out to Trinity. As if reading his mind, she slowly opened her eyes. They were weak-looking and watery, and he guessed she had broken her heart out there tonight. He bent forward and gave her a gentle kiss on her cold lips.

"It's all right," he told her. "We've got you."

She was clearly powerless to respond. Cordell pulled the blanket even more securely around her and he held her close to his warm body. Her rigid frame relaxed a little and he knew she was aware of his presence.

"I think she's gonna be okay," he told Jarrod, who peered over with tearful eyes

The journey back to the Crowthornes' was spent mostly in anxious silence as they both reflected on the trauma of the day. They hadn't realized quite how late it was, and Jarrod yawned as they pulled up in the drive alongside a car he hadn't noticed there earlier.

"Hand her over," he told his buddy, as soon as he'd got out from behind the wheel and ran around to the passenger door.

Cordell gave Trinity one last kiss on the forehead before gently passing her into Jarrod's capable arms. He climbed down and followed them into the house, where Frank and Sylvia were waiting in the doorway.

"She was perishing cold," Cordell announced as they all crowded inside.

"Take her to her room, will you? The doc's here to check her over," Frank told Jarrod, hurriedly.

Nancy-Ruth rushed into Cordell's arms as soon as she saw him. "I was so worried," she told him.

He forced a smile. "Well, you shouldn't be," he told her, "especially not in your condition. You need to stay calm and take it easy, ya hear?" He loosened his grip on her, standing back to study her face. She looked tired, overwrought.

"Fat chance of that in this bunch," she scoffed.

He frowned. She had a valid point there. There was far too much drama going on for a pregnant lady to cope with, and it wasn't good.

"Not for long," he promised her, thoughtfully. "It's about time this group learned the true meaning of 'family'."

She narrowed her eyes at him.

Frank handed them each a cup of coffee. "You can't beat

it," he told them with a nod.

"You can if no one's watching," Cordell muttered.

Nancy-Ruth burst out laughing. Cordell grinned. It had been years since he'd heard her laugh like that. It wasn't a polite titter or a giggle. This was a real belly-laugh. It was so lovely to hear. He hadn't realized how much he'd missed that sound. It made him think. They all used to laugh like that at one time. They'd had so much fun when they were growing up, and even as adults, sitting around the kitchen table with Mom and Dad after a big Sunday lunch. They all used to get on so well. Dad would have been horrified at how the family had fallen apart without him.

"She's awake." Sylvia came into the living room a short while later, smiling.

Cordell felt his stomach churn. "How is she?"

The doctor was right behind Sylvia. "She'll be okay," he assured him. Jarrod had been helping Frank in the kitchen, and he now stood in the doorway, his arms resting on the frame above his head. Cordell noticed the way his face relaxed and Jarrod closed his eyes momentarily. Probably offering up a prayer of thanks, he surmised, doing the same.

"You can go see her for a minute if you want to," Sylvia told them.

Cordell watched Jarrod's eyes spring open, sparkling and lit up like a Christmas tree.

"You guys go in. I'll see her tomorrow," Nancy-Ruth whispered.

"You sure, sis?"

"Yeah. I'm gonna sit down with my coffee." She smiled, gesturing toward a large sofa, and Cordell nodded.

He and Jarrod went into the pretty guest room. The light was dim, with only one of the lamps from the nightstand giving a warm glow. The room smelled sweet, and Cordell recognized Trinity's perfume.

The bed was in the middle of the room and the men stood either side, smiling a little coyly at Trinity, who gazed up at them, warily. Her bed covers reached her face, trapping her arms inside. The heating must have been turned up as it was almost too warm for comfort. She still had a pinched expression and Cordell guessed it would be a while before she felt warm again.

"Darlin' I am so sorry," Jarrod whispered softly, crouching at the side of the bed. "I should've explained properly. I was only fetching Cordell's sister, Nancy-Ruth, from the station. That's the girl you saw us with."

"Aunt Sylvia told me." She whispered, nodding slowly. "I'm sorry. I was just…"

She gulped. Her eyes were still weak and watery, while almost too big for her face. Cordell's heart ached at how vulnerable and fragile she appeared. It was sad to see such a strong, feisty woman reduced to this, and mortifying to know that it was because of them. He gently sat on the edge of the bed, facing her.

"It doesn't matter now," he told her. "All that matters is that you're home safe and with the people who love you." He winked, wondering if she would understand what he was saying. *We love you.*

She frowned a little, thoughtfully, and he knew she was pondering his statement.

"Time to go, boys. She needs to get some rest now." Aunt Sylvia came in, clearly more relaxed than she had been all day.

"Yes, ma'am." Jarrod leaned over and gave Trinity a soft kiss on her cheek. Then Cordell reached over. Feeling a little bolder, he kissed her gently on the lips.

"Remember what I said, sweetheart," he whispered.

* * * *

Trinity slept until late the next morning. When she finally opened her eyes, her mind whirled, and she couldn't quite comprehend where she was for a few seconds. Warmth surrounded her and she sighed as the familiar scent of her bedroom permeated her befuddled brain. Her head ached and she was grateful that the drapes had been left drawn, as daylight peeped through the cracks where they met.

"Hey, honey, how're you feeling?" Aunt Sylvia came in, carrying a small tray that she set on the nightstand before sitting on the bed, facing her.

"I'm all right," Trinity whispered, her throat sore and dry.

"That's good. You gave us all quite a fright," Aunt Sylvia told her. "I've brought you some sweet tea. Doc said it would do you good. It's not too hot. Let me help you sit up a little."

Trinity nodded. She hadn't drunk tea for ages, although she quite enjoyed it. She put out her arms and held onto her aunt as the older lady helped her haul her weary body into a sitting position, fluffing the pillows behind her.

The tea was sweet and warm, just as promised, and Trinity was glad of it streaming down her raw throat. Memories of yesterday ran through her mind, though not all of it made sense, and she noticed the anxious frown on Aunt Sylvia's face.

"I'm sorry. I didn't mean to worry anyone," she whispered.

"That's all right." The old lady shook her head, her gray curls dancing around her ears. "We didn't know where you were."

Trinity racked her brain to figure how she could have gone off like that without saying where she would be, then the pieces of yesterday began to fall into place.

"I went to the ranch," she whispered. "Jarrod and Cordell were there, kissing a woman."

Aunt Sylvia nodded. "That's was Nancy-Ruth, Cordell's sister."

Trinity frowned as she recalled her aunt telling her that before.

"I thought..." Trinity shivered and took another sip of her tea. "Aunt Sylvia, I like them, you know?" Her voice was little louder, though hoarse and raw.

Her aunt smiled with a nod. "I know. They very much like you, too."

Warmth flooded Trinity's insides as she took in what her aunt was saying. She remembered seeing the guys last night. They had been here. She had gazed up into their gorgeous faces. She couldn't remember what they had said exactly, but she recalled feeling good about it. It was probably the only good part there had been of yesterday.

"They'd never do anything to hurt you, honey. You should know that," Aunt Sylvia went on. "They spent all day and half the night searching for you."

Trinity gawked at her. "They did?"

The old lady smiled. "That's how much they care about you. They must have covered the whole of Cavern County and goodness knows how many doors they must've knocked on, trying to track you down."

Trinity blushed. She hadn't expected to hear that. "I'm sorry. I took a cab to St. Mary's," she said, remembering the way she had felt as she'd made that journey. Desperate. Hopeless. Hurt. "I just wanted to talk to Momma."

"I know."

As tears flooded Trinity's face, she saw her aunt wipe her own eyes before leaning forward to hug her.

"I miss her so much, Aunt Sylvia," Trinity wailed, holding the warm, soft lady in front of her. She loved everything about her aunt. Even the sensible, steady beat of her heart was a comfort.

"I do, too," Aunt Sylvia admitted. "I guess we'll simply have to miss her together."

Trinity held her a little tighter, sobbing. It occurred to her then that she wasn't alone in her pain over her momma. She had been Aunt Sylvia's only sister and the poor old lady must feel the same way as she did. Until now, she had always thought she was alone in her grief. How selfish had she been not to realize that Aunt Sylvia and Uncle Frank were suffering too?

"Did it help talking to your momma?" her aunt asked when they finally recovered themselves.

Trinity nodded. "Yeah."

A vision of the graveyard flashed before her eyes. "Momma's flowers are beautiful, too. They reminded me of a small china vase that we used to have on the window sill in our living room. It was painted in tiny blue and white flowers, exactly like that. I wish I'd kept it now, but it was too painful at the time. Mind you, it would only have been ruined like everything else by now if I'd had it." She shrugged, recalling the pile of rubble which she used to call home.

"Or maybe not," Aunt Sylvia said, thoughtfully. "Drink up your tea, honey. I've brought you some soft croissants if you're up to a bit of food. The doctor said you had to eat and drink as much as you can manage. I'll be right back."

Trinity took one of the warm, flaky pastries from her aunt and set the plate on her knee. Croissants were one of her favorite things, and she devoured it eagerly. She couldn't remember when she'd last eaten, but she sure was hungry.

"Cordell and Jarrod have been taking care of the graves up there lately." Her aunt looked a little wary as she returned carrying a small box.

Trinity felt a pang inside her.

"I can't bend down as easily as I used to because of my arthritis," Aunt Sylvia went on, "so Frank and me took the fresh flowers up and the boys came with us and did the weeding and trimming the grass on your grandma and grandpa's plots."

"That's real kind of them," Trinity replied.

"Yes, it is." Aunt Sylvia seemed a little relieved as she took the dishes and put them back on the tray. Trinity noticed how frail her aunt was and cursed herself for not noticing it sooner.

"I've got some things you might like," Aunt Sylvia said, passing her the box.

Trinity opened it slowly and her heart almost pumped out of her chest.

"The vase!" She gaped at her aunt.

"I knew it was all too much for you at the time, hon,"

Aunt Sylvia told her, "but I wondered if one day you might regret not taking more of your momma's things. There's a few trinkets I thought you might want. I've been keeping them safe for you."

Trinity's fingers clutched the little blue and white vase while her eyes filled with tears.

"This was all I had left of her," she told her aunt, holding up her other hand to show her Momma's ring. "I hardly took any of her things and everything I did have was destroyed in the fire. Luckily, I never take this off or I would have lost this, too."

"Well, there's not much in there, but it's all for you." Aunt Sylvia sniffed.

Along with the vase, there was a silver-framed photo of Trinity as a baby, lying in her momma's arms, a pretty compact mirror, a small dish that Trinity had made her out of clay with the word 'Mom' etched into it and a tiny trinket box that held a few items of jewelry. Trinity gasped as memories of happier times whizzed through her mind, and the smell of her mom wafted over her.

"I worried about you not grieving properly for your momma at the time," Aunt Sylvia told her in a soft voice, as she choked back her own tears. "I could see you were putting on a brave face for the rest of us, but I knew it would hit you sometime. It looks to me like losing everything else in your life has churned up those feelings again, which is a good thing. You needed time to properly say goodbye to your momma, and now you've done it."

Trinity nodded as tears streamed down her cheeks. "I feel more like I can accept it now, Aunt Sylvia. I know she's not here, but I still have my memories. And these." She held up the trinkets. "Thank you."

She flung her arms around her aunt, and for a brief second, it was as though she were hugging her momma. Aunt Sylvia held her tightly and kissed the top of her head, the way her momma used to. Trinity was so grateful that she still had her aunt to share her grief and her memories with.

Her aunt sobbed with her, as they comforted each other. It was so liberating not having to hide her feelings anymore. Eventually, she loosened her grip and used the tissues from the nightstand to compose herself.

"Well, I'd best let you get some rest," Aunt Sylvia said, at last.

"Leave the tray. I'll bring it back," Trinity offered.

"No, you need to stay in bed. Keep warm," her aunt told her. "Doctor's orders."

She smiled and took the dishes.

Trinity snuggled back down into the bed. She was tired but strangely peaceful. Aunt Sylvia was an old lady and needed help around the home, as well as someone to share her memories with. And she was just the person to provide it.

Chapter Twenty

It was a few days before Trinity was allowed to get showered and dressed and actually venture outside for a while. Up until then, she had been kept warm indoors, with her only concession being the odd occasion when she was able to take a warm drink on the terrace, but that was only for a short while.

Summer had quickly turned to fall and the air was a little chillier, so she now had to dress in sweaters, thicker jeans and boots. At first, she had been horrified at how mollycoddled she was by her aunt and uncle, but she soon realized how much they worried about her, so she was glad to do as she was told. She was guilty for causing them so much concern and vowed to make amends.

"How's the invalid today?" Jarrod teased, strolling into the kitchen.

"Don't you start," Trinity moaned jokingly. "I'm absolutely fine, thank you. How are you?"

Jarrod grinned. "All the better for seeing you, darlin'."

She beamed. The guys had been around every day and she never tired of their jokes and flirting. She had met Nancy-Ruth, Cordell's sister, and they had gotten along really well. Trinity felt so close to all of them. They had even agreed to all go out together the next time a band came to play locally.

"Trinity's been working all morning," Aunt Sylvia said, placing a fresh chocolate cake on the kitchen table. "I'll pour us some coffee and we can sit down for a minute."

Trinity jumped to her feet. "Let me pour the drinks, Aunt Sylvia. You sit down. You've been working hard today, too."

Aunt Sylvia chuckled but did as she was told. Trinity smiled as she poured out the coffees. It seemed her aunt was slowly getting used to having her help. She had been afraid the older lady might resent her muscling in on her territory, but Aunt Sylvia seemed only too pleased to have an extra pair of hands around the place.

Uncle Frank joined them. "Ah, Jarrod. Good of you to stop by. That new fencing seems to be holding up well. With all that wind last night, I was worried we might not have set it deep enough, but it was absolutely fine.

"Great. I'll take a look after this." Jarrod smiled.

Trinity loved that smile. In fact, she loved everything about him and Cordell.

"Cordell's just getting some work done, then he and Nancy-Ruth will be dropping by later," he said, answering her unasked question. "William, Nancy-Ruth's husband will be here this afternoon, too. She wants him to meet you all."

Aunt Sylvia smiled. "Tell them to come for supper. I'll cook a couple of chickens."

Jarrod frowned. "Are you sure, Sylvia? There'll be quite a lot of us."

"Yes. I want to meet this guy," Aunt Sylvia replied with a smile. "If he's going to be part of the family, then it's only right."

Jarrod laughed. "All right, *Mom*," he said, cheekily. "I'll tell 'em."

Trinity smiled. It was lovely to think of them all as one big family. She had already noticed that Jarrod regarded her aunt and uncle as his parents, having lost his own. Cordell treated them the same, even though he had a momma who lived a couple of hours away. "I'll help with the supper," she promised.

"Don't you overdo it," Uncle Frank warned her.

"Uncle Frank, I've hardly done anything for days. I'd like to help out around the place. I need to earn my keep somehow." She beamed as she saw him smiling over at her.

"Looks like you're feeling a little better," Uncle Frank remarked.

"I keep telling you, I'm fine." She giggled, shaking her head. She could tell it would be a while before they stopped worrying about her.

They chatted for a while before Uncle Frank took Jarrod to examine the fence.

"I think that's the last of the work done out there now," Aunt Sylvia remarked as the men went out the back door.

Trinity felt a thud in her stomach. She had enjoyed seeing so much of the guys as they'd come over to help Uncle Frank. She helped carry the dishes through to the kitchen, and insisted on washing them while Aunt Sylvia went and put her feet up for a while. Her aunt must have been tired, and she knew that cooking supper for everyone would have been too much for the old lady to cope with on her own. She wiped down the counters and put everything away before she heard voices at the back door again, as the men returned.

"Thanks so much, son. I truly appreciate it," Uncle Frank said, shaking Jarrod's hand.

"Anytime, sir. You just holler."

Uncle Frank smiled.

"Well, I'd best get back to work. Ben's got another thoroughbred coming in today. I'll need to assess him before the light goes."

"I'll see you out," Trinity offered, wiping her hands in a soft towel.

Jarrod nodded and said goodbye to Frank.

"Aunt Sylvia's resting in the living room," Trinity told them. "In fact, I think she may be asleep by now. She seemed awful tired."

"Well, I won't disturb her in that case," Jarrod said with a smile. "You can tell her I said goodbye."

"Don't worry, son." Uncle Frank nodded.

"I hear you've finished all the work in the yard," Trinity

said, as cheerfully as she could manage, as they walked down the hall.

"Yep. It's all safe and sound." Jarrod smiled.

Trinity nodded. "So, does that mean we won't be seeing so much of you now?" She got a lump in her throat as she asked then held her breath for the reply.

She was surprised when he leaned in close to her and muttered in her ear, "You can see just as much of me as you want to, darlin'."

His voice was deep and rasping and did unholy things to Trinity's body. She stared up at him, the twinkle in his deep, brown eyes telling her that he had fully intended the innuendo.

"Oh," was all she could manage as her face flushed when he brushed his soft lips on her cheek as he held her in his strong arms.

Then he brought his lips crashing down on hers and his power ran through her whole body, igniting all her impulses on its way down.

"You still owe me a date," he murmured when he finally freed her mouth.

Heat raced right through her body and her pussy ached. "W-what?" Her brain had turned to mush.

He giggled, deep in his throat. "I seem to recall you and I were supposed to go trekking up the mountain not so long ago," he reminded her.

She gasped as embarrassment and regret smothered her. "I'm sorry. I didn't mean to spoil it all. I thought..."

"That me and Cordell were with another woman," he finished for her, with an incredulous smile. "As if we'd ever do a thing like that. You must know how we feel about you, darlin'? We'd never do anything to hurt you. You mean too much to us both."

Trinity gulped, her heart pounding. She had hoped that she had read the guys right but didn't dare ask the question. "You mean the world to me, too," she whispered before he took her lips in another searing kiss. She instinctively wrapped her arms around his neck and she ran her trembling fingers through his silky, dark hair.

She knew all about Cavern County. Ménage was practically the normal way of life out here, though she'd never considered it for herself before. She did now, though. In fact, she relished the idea. She wouldn't have been able to choose between the two hunks, so it was a relief not to have to. *And even more of a relief that I didn't misunderstand them, after all.*

"You get some rest and we'll see you tonight." His eyes were flashing with excitement as he said goodbye and Trinity watched him go, taking deep breaths to try to steady herself.

She shut the door, then leaned against it with a huge sigh, her eyes closed and arms folded around herself as she slowly drifted back to earth. When she opened her eyes, she was shocked to see Uncle Frank watching her from the kitchen doorway. He gave a massive grin but said nothing.

Trinity went straight to the study and tried to bury herself in some work to take her mind off the gorgeous hunk — and stop herself watching the clock until supper time.

* * * *

Cordell smiled as he drove up the Crowthornes' drive and they all piled out of the SUV. He felt a little nervous, somehow, although he didn't know why. He had been here for supper hundreds of times and was only introducing his brother-in-law to his best friends.

"Come on in." Frank was at the doorway, ushering them out of the cold. "The women are just finishing up in the kitchen."

The smell of roast chicken filled the warm air as they all went through into the living room. This house was always welcoming and Cordell loved coming here — especially now that a certain young lady was staying.

"Frank, this is Nancy-Ruth's husband, William Furrows,"

Cordell announced once they were all comfortably inside.

The men shook hands. Cordell watched Frank curiously, wondering what he would make of the quiet young man.

Frank smiled politely and offered them all a drink before Sylvia and Trinity came in. They both looked lovely in thick, warm dresses, and Trinity wore knee-length boots. He threw her a smile and watched her blush.

"Hey, sweetheart, how are you?" He couldn't resist going over and giving her a hug, and he relished the feel of her melting into his arms.

"I'm good, thanks," she told him, nodding, when he finally let her go.

"Great." He'd been to see her every day and was relieved to see her improving each time. "Come and meet William," he offered, steering her toward the others.

Trinity was beautiful and he honestly didn't want to take his hands off her. When they sat down to supper, he made sure he sat next to her, with Jarrod at her other side. William sat opposite him, with Nancy-Ruth next to Jarrod and Sylvia next to her, preferring to sit near Frank, who was, of course, at the head of the table.

"This is lovely," he remarked with a groan as they began to eat. The air was then filled with a chorus of agreement and gratitude for the meal, while Trinity and Sylvia flushed at the compliments.

Frank raised a toast to William, welcoming him to the family, and the guy looked like he was about to pee his pants. He nodded graciously, thanking everyone beneath his breath.

"So, what do you do, William?" Frank continued as they all resumed their meal.

"I work on a farm, sir. It's near where we live, a couple of hours from here."

Frank nodded his approval. "What do you do?"

William seemed shocked that he had been asked another question and stammered a little. "I-I work the land. It's fertile."

"What do you grow?" Frank was clearly finding it as hard as Cordell to make conversation with the guy. Cordell had been so relieved to hear they were coming here for supper tonight, as he had just had a couple of hours of the guy's company and was almost tearing his hair out. William sure was shy.

Trinity must have noticed the tension, too, as she suddenly stared up at Cordell. He caught her eye and grinned, knowing that she was alluding to the difficulty between the two guys. Suddenly she went cross-eyed and Cordell burst out laughing in surprise.

Trinity turned back to her meal as though nothing had happened, while Cordell tried to pretend he was having a coughing fit. Jarrod give a snort, clearly trying not to laugh.

Frank and William continued to have a stilted conversation across the table, with Nancy-Ruth chipping in occasionally, obviously trying to help her husband out.

The whole scenario made Cordell's eyes water and he could hardly eat for trying not to laugh. That girl sure was a lot of fun.

Sylvia peered over at him, curiously. *Dang.* He was hoping she wouldn't notice his outburst. He took a sip of his wine, trying to appear nonchalant.

"I think Uncle Frank's practicing to become a dentist," he heard Trinity mutter to Jarrod. "He sure is trying to pull some teeth out over there."

That was it. Cordell quickly stood, clenched his mouth shut and headed toward the bathroom where he burst into hysterics.

When he returned to the table, the conversation had moved on, and Trinity was asking Nancy-Ruth about how she and William had met. Cordell secretly wondered if Trinity wasn't actually wondering *why* they'd gotten together, not how, but he took his seat graciously and listened.

"I'll bet your wedding was lovely," Trinity went on. "What was it like?"

"Oh, you know, small and quiet. Just a few people there.

We had a meal at a local hotel. It was nice." Nancy-Ruth seemed a little uncomfortable.

"I'll bet it was a lot of fun, though," Trinity went on.

Nancy-Ruth nodded, staring over at Cordell for support.

"Aren't weddings always fun?" he chipped in, noncommittally.

"I'm sure they are if you're there," Trinity replied, smiling up at him. "I'd love to see a picture of you two all dressed up."

Someone could have cut the silence with a knife.

"They didn't come," William interjected unexpectedly.

Trinity's face fell and she stared at them, stunned.

"How could you not go to your own sister's wedding?" She frowned at Cordell accusingly.

"It's a long story. I'll explain later," he said, trying to pacify her. He was horrified by the expression on her face. She looked devastated.

"Trinity, give me a hand with the dishes, would you?" Sylvia stood and began gathering the plates.

He watched Trinity swallow hard before she busied herself with the crockery.

"We'll use the dishwasher for these. Would you load it up for me, hon?" Sylvia was saying as they left the room.

There seemed to be a collective sigh of relief as soon as the women left. Cordell didn't like it one bit. Trinity had been right to be so shocked. He was shocked at himself. *How in hell did I allow it to happen?*

"You haven't told her, then?" His sister scowled at him as disapprovingly as Trinity had just done.

"No, sis. It didn't seem the right time with everything that had been going on." He knew it sounded feeble but it was the truth.

William snorted derisively. "Why would you? It's not like she's related or anything. I don't think outsiders need to know family business, do you?"

Cordell stared at him in amazement. It seemed he was only the quiet type when he had to talk about himself.

When it came to defending his wife, he sure had some strong opinions.

"Trinity *is* family," Jarrod stated coolly.

"Not ours, she isn't," William replied, shaking his head. "I get that she's Frank's niece, but then they're no relation to us, are they?"

Cordell saw Frank's back straighten and his jaw tightened.

"Just 'cause someone isn't blood-related doesn't mean they're not family," Jarrod said. "And it's a darn good thing Trinity isn't our blood or we wouldn't be able to have a relationship with her, now, would we?"

William shook his head. "But having a relationship with someone doesn't make them family, either. I'm not being funny or anything, but that girl's no more a part of our family than you are."

Cordell had heard enough. He stood as hot-red anger boiled through his veins. His breathing was strong and his heart pumped almost out of his chest. No-one got to speak about his family like that—even if they *were* family.

Chapter Twenty-One

"You be careful what you say in there," Aunt Sylvia warned Trinity as they filled the tray with apple pie and cream. "There's been a problem in that family that's got nothing to do with the rest of us, so best just keep out of it, ya hear?"

Trinity nodded. She recalled that the guys had mentioned some sort of rift, but she didn't know what it was about. It must have been bad, though, if it had resulted in Cordell not attending his own sister's wedding.

"Hope you all like apple pie," she announced cheerfully, as she took the tray into the dining room.

She was surprised to see Cordell on his feet with a face like thunder — gorgeous thunder, but thunder all the same — and William cowering in his seat. The atmosphere was as thick as pea soup and she knew they had interrupted something.

Aunt Sylvia totally ignored the whole situation and carried on serving out dessert and passing the dishes down the table. "Help yourselves to cream," she told them cheerfully.

"Smells delicious, ladies," Uncle Frank told them with a smile. "What do you think, Cordell?"

Cordell stared over at Uncle Frank incredulously. "What do I think?" His voice was curt, his face tight as a drum.

"About the food. It's time for dessert." Frank held Cordell's stare, as though telepathically having a stern conversation with him.

After a few seconds, which felt like minutes, Cordell nodded and took his seat. "Looks lovely," he replied.

Trinity was amazed how calm he suddenly seemed, and

she quickly put the pie dish on the tray that they had placed on the sideboard, before resuming her own seat.

"Did you have a hand in this?" Uncle Frank asked her.

"I sure did, Uncle Frank. So, if you find any fingers in there, remember they're mine." She smiled and was relieved when her uncle burst out laughing and Jarrod joined in. The women giggled and Cordell smiled at her.

Only William had an expression that could turn milk sour, and Trinity longed to know what had been said while she had been out of the room. She was conscious that an awkward quietness was settling around the table again, so she searched her brain for something to talk about.

"You must be thrilled about the baby," she said, smiling at Nancy-Ruth and William. "Have you thought about names yet or is it too early?"

"We shouldn't have, but we have started discussing it," Nancy-Ruth admitted with a smile. "We've got so many to choose from. It's going to take forever to decide."

"You've only got a few months," Jarrod reminded her with a smile.

"Yeah, we'll probably be choosing a *family* name," William interjected.

Trinity didn't much like the way he sneered at Jarrod, and she guessed it was some kind of jibe.

"Do you have a big family, William?" she asked.

He seemed surprised at her question and balked a little. "Yeah. Four brothers, three sisters and a whole heap of cousins. Momma and Dad are both from big families."

"You've still got both your parents?" she asked.

He seemed incredulous. "Yeah."

She was desperate to know whether this massive family of his all got along but daren't ask. "Did many of them get to your wedding?" She hoped that wasn't too invasive.

He gulped. "Some. At least my momma and dad came." He stared pointedly at Nancy-Ruth.

"That must have been wonderful. I'll bet both your mommas cried. I know mine would if she could go to my wedding." Trinity was trying to keep the conversation light but could see by the expression on Nancy-Ruth's face that she had hit a nerve. She looked questioningly at Cordell.

"Our momma wasn't at their wedding," he told her softly.

A thud hit her stomach. "Oh. I'm so sorry."

Nancy-Ruth stood, and after excusing herself, headed out of the door. Trinity felt awful.

"Shall I go after her? I didn't mean to upset her." She glanced over at Aunt Sylvia.

"No, hon. You just eat your apple pie. Nancy-Ruth's not stupid. She'll realize you simply didn't know. It's a safe assumption that someone's momma would be at their wedding. You didn't say anything wrong."

Trinity swallowed hard and took another sip of her drink before finishing up the dessert. It truly was delicious.

"It sounds like you'll have plenty of help with the baby," Aunt Sylvia said calmly to William. "Are all your family local?"

"Fairly."

"That's good. It's a shame when families aren't able to see each other too often," she went on, seemingly oblivious to his sulky attitude.

"Yeah, I'd want my family around when I have a baby," Trinity added, as a sudden warm feeling flooded her body. She was surprised and delighted to feel Jarrod's hand cover hers, while Cordell's hand went on her knee. A thrill of excitement ran though her, and she immediately knew that this was what she craved. A baby with these guys would be the ultimate.

"You got a big family?" William asked her.

"Just who's sitting around this table," she replied with a smile.

William's face dropped. "You're not related to all of us," he pointed out as Nancy-Ruth returned to her seat.

"That doesn't mean I can't relate to all of you," Trinity replied coolly.

William frowned. "But you're not actually family then,

are you?"

"William, leave it, will you?" Nancy-Ruth urged him irritably.

"It's okay, Nancy-Ruth. I'm not offended. I hope I didn't upset you, by the way. I simply didn't realize about your mother." Trinity told her.

Nancy-Ruth managed a weak smile. "No, it's okay. We had a falling out and she didn't come. We've made it all up now and she's real happy about the baby, so at least she'll be around for that."

Cordell's hand tightened on her knee and Trinity realized that that was another thing she would miss sharing with her mother.

"That's great," Trinity told her with a smile.

Nancy-Ruth's face suddenly dropped and she shot to her feet, her hand covering her mouth. "Oh my God, I'm so sorry." She quickly came around the table and held her arms out to her. "I didn't mean to..." Her voice was muffled as Trinity stood to give her a big hug.

"It's okay," Trinity assured her.

"Please don't think I'd say anything to hurt you, Trinity. I honestly didn't mean it like that." Nancy-Ruth was clearly mortified.

"It truly is okay. I didn't mean to upset you earlier," Trinity told her. "We're just finding out about each other. We're bound to hit the odd raw nerve. It can't be helped."

Nancy-Ruth held her tightly again, and Trinity was pleased to feel genuine warmth from her.

"How about some coffee?" Aunt Sylvia asked, easing the atmosphere again.

"Good idea. I'll help," Trinity offered, as Nancy-Ruth went back to her seat.

"Phew!" Aunt Sylvia exclaimed once they were safely in the kitchen. "That boy's sure got a chip on his shoulder about something."

She made the coffee while Trinity got the cups together.

"A chip? I'd say he's got the whole tree on that shoulder

of his," she said, making them both giggle.

They served coffee, trying to keep the conversation light.

"The garden looks lovely at night," Aunt Sylvia remarked. "Cordell and Jarrod have installed lights all around it. We could put them on tonight as it's getting much darker these days. Perhaps you'd all like a little stroll after supper?"

"Good idea," Frank replied with a knowing smile. "I think a little fresh air would do everyone some good, especially after such a big meal."

"Big and *delicious* meal," Jarrod added.

Aunt Sylvia blushed and Trinity giggled.

"We managed to get it all done right on time," Frank said with a smile, "but only thanks to these guys." He nodded toward the window.

"I knew someone, someday would find a use for my brother," Nancy-Ruth said with a chuckle.

Cordell feigned indignity. "I don't know what you mean."

Trinity smiled at their banter. "This is family," she told William.

He snorted.

* * * *

Cordell awoke the next morning feeling irritable. William had thoroughly annoyed him last night and he was determined to have it out with his brother-in-law. Frank had been right to talk him down at the dinner table — that wasn't the place for an argument — but here, in his own home on a Saturday morning was perfect.

"What're you doing, bro? It's the weekend. You don't need to get up yet." Jarrod frowned, passing him in the corridor on his way to the bathroom.

Cordell rolled his eyes. It would be lovely to stay in bed for a while longer, but he knew he had to get this crap off his chest first before it ate away at him. Besides, there was no way he'd get back to sleep. He'd had enough of a job last night, which was why he'd got showered and dressed as soon as he'd woken up.

"I'm just going to take a walk, clear my head a little," Cordell told him with a smile. "You go back to bed."

"Want me to come with you?"

"Nah. You stay here. I need some time to think."

"Think? About what?"

Cordell sighed. "Family," he told him.

He was glad no one else was up when he went through to the kitchen and grabbed a glass of cold milk.

The air was still and mild when he walked down the driveway that led to their house. He had been looking forward to bringing Trinity here one day, but now he wasn't so sure. The house was big. There was no denying it. He had hoped it might be a family home, with loads of kids and maybe a dog or two. There was certainly enough room for them all. But would Trinity like it? Probably not. He'd seen the picture she'd drawn of her ideal home, which was the total opposite to what they had to offer. He sighed. It sure seemed like he'd be packing his cases soon. He hoped, anyhow.

As he walked down the country lanes, his mind ran over the conversation at the dinner table. William sure had a bee in his bonnet when it came to families. He must have felt that he had a raw deal coming from a huge family and marrying into such a small one — not that it should matter.

He took a break, sitting on a low fence. Nancy-Ruth had been real unhappy getting married without her momma — and rightly so. He was glad they had made up, but he desperately needed to work things out with his brothers. It had been such a relief when he contacted Nancy-Ruth to find her so responsive and eager to meet up and resolve their differences. He just wished the guys had been.

He turned to go back and was surprised to see William walking toward him. The sun was still splashing pink and orange streaks across the sky, and he was surprised that his brother-in-law was up so early.

"Hey, bro, you wet the bed, too?" Cordell joked as he got

nearer.

"Something like that," William grimaced. "Actually, it's Nancy-Ruth's pillow that's wet. She's been crying half the night."

"Is everything okay with the baby?" Cordell frowned, his stomach churning.

"Yeah, yeah, the baby's fine," William assured him. "It's me. Well, me being an asshole. I'm sorry if I embarrassed you in front of your friends last night. I didn't mean to. I guess I was quite tired and a bit on edge."

Cordell stopped walking and turned to face him. William looked worried and sure didn't seem as opinionated as he did last night. "You wanna tell me about it?"

They walked on slowly.

"I know you've got this problem in your family, but it's seriously hurting Nancy-Ruth, you know?" William said. "It was horrid not having her mother at the wedding — or you, of course. She cried her eyes out about it on the day. That's why I didn't invite all my folks. I didn't want to rub it in that I'd got all this family and half of hers hadn't even been invited."

"It can't have been the day either of you wanted," Cordell said with a scowl.

William shrugged. "We loved each other and we thought that was all that mattered. And, in a way, it is. But when you get married, you have certain ideas of how it should be, don'tcha? That day was nothing like either of us imagined." He shook his head sadly. "I don't want the same scenario for the christening."

"You won't, bro," Cordell assured him. "I'm gonna talk to Jacob and Martin. Do they know about the baby?"

"Not yet. Nancy-Ruth wanted you and your momma to be the first to know. We haven't got out to see the guys yet." He shrugged again.

Cordell narrowed his eyes in thought. It was obvious William was completely bewildered by the whole thing and didn't know what to do to rectify it. He was relieved to see how much he cared for Nancy-Ruth, though. And he'd done the right thing coming to his big brother-in-law for help. Maybe he was the family guy he claimed to be, after all.

By the time they returned to the house, the others were already up and having breakfast.

"Your wife sure cooks a mean pancake," Jarrod announced as they entered the large kitchen.

"And your buddy must have a hollow leg to put away so many," Nancy-Ruth giggled.

"Tell me about it," Cordell replied, rolling his eyes.

They sat around the breakfast table and Cordell was aware that everyone was staring at him.

"So, bro, what're we doing today?" Jarrod was tucking into yet another pancake.

"We're going over to Huron," Cordell announced.

Nancy-Ruth stared at him. "All of us?"

"Yeah, why not? We're all family." Cordell mentally dared William to dispute the fact, but he didn't say a word.

"I don't think Jacob'll be all that happy," Nancy-Ruth warned him.

"I don't care how happy he is. It's time he grew up," Cordell replied calmly.

He grabbed his cell and rang their eldest brother. He didn't answer. Martin, his other brother, didn't live far from Jacob and the men often worked together. Cordell rang him.

"Hey, Martin, it's Cordell."

There was silence.

"I'm calling to let you know that we're coming over to see you and Jacob. We need a family meeting. Nancy-Ruth and William are coming, too. Where's the best place to meet you two?"

Martin was quiet for a minute. "Er… we're kinda busy right now. We're both working."

"I appreciate that, brother. That's why I'm ringing. It'll take more than a couple of hours to get over there, so you'll have time to do whatever it is you're busy with. This is important. We've got some news for you." Cordell wasn't taking no for an answer, and he winked at his sister.

He could hear the worry in his brother's voice. "I-is everything okay?"

Cordell guessed Martin would be worried about their mom. "We'll tell you both when we get over there. Shall we come to your place or Jacob's?"

"Um, Jacob's."

"All right. You'd better let him know we're on our way. We'll give you a ring when we're nearer to give you an idea when to expect us." Cordell was firm but calm.

"Er…okay. We'll see you later."

Cordell smiled as he tucked his cell back into his pocket. This was going to be interesting.

Chapter Twenty-Two

Trinity hummed to herself as she designed the cover of a new children's book. She smiled at the little characters she had created and thought how much a young child would love them. Nancy-Ruth's child — or maybe…

The phone rang in the hallway, pulling her from her reverie. She had been in a kind of daydream ever since last night. She had relived every squeeze of her hand and knee, every smile and laugh of those gorgeous guys, and every hug and kiss they had given her.

She heard Uncle Frank answer the call and was surprised to hear her name mentioned. Jarrod had already texted her to explain that they were going to visit some of Cordell's family and would be out most of the day, so she wasn't expecting to hear from anyone. It was nice to hear from them more often now that they'd finally exchanged cell phone numbers. She went into the hallway where Uncle Frank was frowning as he hung up the receiver.

"The police in Nebraska have been searching for you," he said. "They wanted to make sure you were okay after the explosion."

She felt a lump in her stomach. She had just about put all of that behind her now. The insurance still had to pay out, but that was the only connection she had left to it all.

"Why did they want to know about me?" Her voice was croaky as her mouth had suddenly dried.

"It's nothing to worry about," Uncle Frank said, although he didn't actually look convinced.

"Come and sit down," Aunt Sylvia urged from the kitchen doorway.

"You're not in any trouble or anything," Uncle Frank assured her as they sat at the kitchen table. "Your driver's license was found in a car parked in the street. They wanted to return it to you, but when they saw the address, they were concerned that you were caught up in the explosion. Someone's going to send it over now that they know you're here."

"Well, that's good of them," Aunt Sylvia said, handing around cups of coffee.

Trinity frowned. "I lost my license ages ago," she said. "I meant to renew it, but I haven't needed it, so I didn't rush, in case it turned up. Did you say it was found in a car?"

Uncle Frank took a swig of his coffee before replying calmly, "A car registered to Kevin Pulver."

Trinity felt a jolt inside her. Kevin loved his car and she hardly ever got to drive it, though it didn't matter. She was able to walk to the shops, and when she was on her own, she never needed to buy much, anyhow. Of course, she was working from home, so that wasn't an issue. He, on the other hand, was a salesman. She had often commented that his company should provide him with a vehicle, but he said he preferred to drive his own. Now, of course, she wondered whether he really was a salesman. He certainly didn't make much money out of it.

"How did they find me?" she wondered.

"I've no idea. Someone will be over with it in a day or two, he said. They'll just need to verify it's yours, I guess." Uncle Frank shrugged.

Trinity couldn't help feeling a little unnerved by the call, and her mind whirled.

"Did they say who found it?" she asked.

"Nope. I presumed the cops," Uncle Frank told her.

Something didn't sit right with Trinity and she was agitated all afternoon. Trust this to happen on the one day the guys were out of town. They always had a way of making her feel better about things.

She tried to settle back down to her work, but nothing

seemed to go right. There was another project she was working on, so she tried that. Her head wasn't in the right zone at all and she found it hard to concentrate on that, too.

After a couple of unsuccessful hours, she went to help Aunt Sylvia. She was able to hang out all the laundry and enjoyed feeling the cool air on her face.

"I think I'll take a walk," she said, once they had finished. "I could do with some fresh air and the exercise will do me good."

"Wrap up warm and take your cell," Aunt Sylvia told her, looking a little concerned at the idea.

"I will," she promised before going to her room to fetch a sweater.

She picked out a warm, wooly one and hugged it to herself as she made her way back down the staircase. Checking her back pocket for her cell, she smiled at Aunt Sylvia, who was waiting in the hall.

"I've got everything," she assured the older lady.

"Good. Just be careful." She kissed Trinity on the cheek as soon as they reached the door.

"Of course. I won't be long," she promised her aunt before heading down the drive.

The cool air was bracing and she was glad of its bite as she breathed it in. Her head cleared and she inwardly laughed at herself for getting so worried about the situation. She supposed it was just the reminder of the whole trauma that had upset her, and she cursed this for happening right when she had put it all behind her and moved on.

She smiled as she thought of the two men who had come into her life since then. It had been a great consolation to her to remember that if the dreadful incident hadn't happened, she might not have met the gorgeous pair. By the time she next visited her aunt and uncle, they would probably have found someone else. It was comforting to find something good among the bad. And those two sure were good.

She wandered through the meadows and down the country lanes for a good few hours, and only checked the time when she realized that it was starting to become dark. She quickly called Aunt Sylvia to assure her that she was okay and was on her way home. Her aunt sounded concerned, but pleased that she'd rung.

When she got back to the house, she was exhausted but much happier than when she'd left. Her head was much clearer and she was refreshed and ready to tackle her work again. She was planning to work into the night if the muse hit her, as she had wasted so much of today.

A large black SUV was parked in the driveway next to Uncle Frank's truck and Trinity frowned. She didn't recognize it at all.

"There you are," Uncle Frank said as she went in. Aunt Sylvia came out of the living room. "You've got a couple of visitors." She seemed a little concerned and Trinity's stomach lurched.

She went into the room and immediately recognized Poppy and a man whom she assumed to be her dad.

"It *is* you!" Poppy stood up as soon as she saw her and pointed at her accusingly.

Trinity frowned as a mixture of anger and anxiety roiled inside her. She wanted to cry, but instead did what she always did. She took a deep breath and forced a smile. She held out her hand to her. "I don't believe we've met properly," she said. "I'm Trinity Ellis."

Poppy looked as though the wind had been sucked from her sails and she balked. "We have met, actually. At my fiancé's internment."

"We spoke in the ladies' restroom, I believe," Trinity corrected her. "I didn't get your name."

Poppy was clearly stunned, then she became angry. "Poppy Witherington," she said pointedly. I happen to have been Kevin's fiancée, in case you didn't know."

"Why don't we all sit down and have some cake," Aunt Sylvia suggested, bringing in a fresh chocolate cake while Uncle Frank followed with a tray of coffee. This seemed to be Aunt Sylvia's fallback method for keeping the peace, cheering people up, forcing everyone to take a break—any excuse, really. Trinity could see she was going to start piling on the pounds if she stayed here much longer, not that it was a bad thing.

"I don't know if you've met my aunt and uncle?" Trinity asked politely as she sat down.

Poppy huffed and sat back down on the sofa next to the man. "Yes, when we arrived," she said sulkily.

"And this is Poppy's dad, Eric," Uncle Frank interjected.

Trinity held out her hand and the man shook it, hesitantly. "Now, we don't want any trouble," he said firmly.

"I should hope not," Uncle Frank said incredulously. "We invited you into our home as you said you were friends of Trinity's. Why would there be any trouble?"

"Because her driver's license was found in my fiancé's car. That's why." Poppy gave them a supercilious smirk, which they all chose to ignore.

"Oh, great, you've found it. Thanks so much. I've been searching everywhere for it." Trinity held out her hand as if expecting to be given the card.

"The cops've got it now," Poppy told her piously.

"Oh? Have I committed a crime?" Trinity feigned confusion, making her point as subtly as she could.

"Well…no," Poppy relented.

"Thank goodness for that," Trinity tittered.

"Why was his address on it?" Poppy demanded.

"I think you'll find *my* address was on my driver's license," Trinity told her. "That's the law."

"Quite right," Uncle Frank said, nodding.

"Okay, let me spell it out," Poppy said, sarcastically. "I want to know why your driver's license was in my fiancé's car, why it had his address on it and why you were at his internment." She glared at Trinity, who flushed—more with anger than embarrassment.

"And I want you to remember your manners while you're in my home and speak with a little respect, please." Aunt Sylvia's voice was quiet but firm, and Poppy was evidently taken aback by it.

"She's right, sweetie pie," her dad told her, appearing a little embarrassed. Poppy looked livid.

"My fiancé died recently," she said, in a whiny voice.

"I know, dear, and I'm very sorry for your loss," Aunt Sylvia said. "But you need to remember that you're not the only one grieving for him and everyone deserves a little respect and kindness, especially at a time like this."

That clearly wasn't the response Poppy had hoped for and her whole face tensed as she seethed.

"Who found my license?" Trinity asked calmly. Aunt Sylvia certainly set a good example and she was glad she was here.

"Poppy's boyf...er...friend," Eric replied. "We had retrieved the car from where Kevin had parked it. Had to get someone to come and open it for us, as we didn't have the spare key."

"No, I had it," Trinity interjected, matter-of-factly. She knew exactly what he had started to say and it rankled that Poppy's father was aware of her boyfriend and still allowed her to come here playing the victim. She had intended to be kind to the girl — after all, she had lost her fiancé — but now she was just annoyed that she'd had the audacity to turn up. If she had been here when they'd arrived, she probably wouldn't have let them over the threshold.

"Why?" Eric asked indignantly.

"Because I used to drive it."

"What? He never let anyone drive that car!" Poppy's face turned red and her jaw tightened. Her whole body seemed to stiffen as she visibly fumed.

Trinity shrugged. "He let me." She had a great sense of one-upmanship and had to stop herself from smirking at the idea.

"Oliver and Patricia agreed to let Poppy have Kevin's car, so we wanted to empty it before having it valeted," Eric went on. "We moved the seats and found the license wedged between the driver's seat and the edge of the car.

We didn't understand why it would be there and went to the police. We thought they'd come find you."

"It was good of you to be so concerned about returning it," Aunt Sylvia said soothingly.

Eric and Poppy stared at her as though she was mad.

"We weren't planning on *returning* it," Poppy sneered. "We wanted to know why it was there and why it had Kev's address on it. It was the cops who started asking questions about who Trinity was and whether or not she had been in the apartment when it exploded."

"It was good of you to allay their fears," Trinity said calmly. "I guess you recognized me from the bar that night when you were with your boyf...er...friend," she said pointedly.

The expression on Poppy's face told her she had got the message, loud and clear.

"I didn't know for sure it was you. You looked different." Poppy pouted and Trinity guessed she had denied all knowledge of her.

"So, who gave you this address? The cops?" Uncle Frank asked with a frown.

Poppy rolled her eyes. "As if. They wouldn't tell us anything."

"I happen to be friends with the manager at The Winchester Hotel," Eric admitted. "Poppy saw the resemblance with the photograph on the license and the girl who had been in the bar that night and I...er...persuaded him to give us the details from the register."

Uncle Frank frowned. "I believe that's illegal, isn't it?"

Eric gulped.

"Uncle Frank's a lawyer," Trinity piped up.

"Well, it was only because we were worried," Eric added quickly.

"Worried?" Uncle Frank was still frowning.

"Well, isn't it illegal to have a false address on your driver's license?" Poppy gloated.

"Yes, it is. That's why I had my own address on my

license," Trinity said slowly, as though spelling it out for her. "Excuse me a minute."

She heaved a sigh of relief once she had left the room and headed for the study. Her insurance documents were on the desk, and she picked them up with a grin. Poppy wasn't going to like this any more than she liked Poppy's attitude.

She presented the documents to her as soon as she went back into the living room. "Here," she said. "This is my insurance document stating that I am the sole tenant of that address." She pointed to the line that she was referring to.

Poppy shook her head. "But Kevin lived at that address. He told me. It's where he stayed whenever he had to go over that way. He only rented it because it was cheaper than paying for a hotel."

"What did Kevin do for a living again?" Uncle Frank asked, innocently.

"He was a salesman. A real good one, too," Poppy gloated.

"Then why didn't his company pay for his hotel bills? That's the usual practice, isn't it? They give you a company car and pay all travel and accommodation expenses." Uncle Frank looked surprised.

"Well, he wanted to save the firm some money, I think he said." Poppy frowned thoughtfully for a moment.

"Why would he do that? They clearly weren't paying him much. And he was already using his own car," Uncle Frank asked.

"He's got a point there, sweetie pie," Eric told his daughter, frowning. "Are you sure he was a salesman?"

"What else could he have been?" Poppy sounded incredulous.

"A cheater," Trinity said quietly.

"How dare you speak about my fiancé like that!" Poppy shouted. "You didn't know him."

"I think you'll find I did," Trinity told her softly. "I lived with him for the better part of a year. I believed he was a salesman, too, although we had loads of arguments about why he never had any money and why he insisted on using his own car. We hadn't got on very well for the past six months or so before he died. We'd talked about splitting up and he was already searching for somewhere to live as the apartment was mine before he moved in with me. I'm sorry, but it seems like we were both duped by him."

"You're lying!" Poppy shot up and shouted fiercely at her.

"I wish I was," Trinity told her, shaking her head. "If you were actually engaged to him, it looks like you had a lucky escape."

"So, he was leaving me and going to stay with you every weekend?" Poppy frowned but it was clear from her face that she knew Trinity was telling the truth.

"Not every weekend," Trinity told her. "Every couple, usually. It all depended on 'where his work took him'." She used air quotes to explain those were Kevin's words.

"But he told me he never worked during the week, apart from some computer stuff he did from home. Sometimes he had to put in an extra Friday or Monday or something, but usually he was only away at weekends." Poppy had lowered her voice and sat down.

"Well, maybe he was seeing someone else besides us," Trinity said with a sigh. "I feel sorry for her, if he was." Her mind immediately drifted back to the conversation she'd overheard in the bathroom of the hotel. Hadn't there been another of Kevin's exes on the scene? Lydia? Perhaps she wasn't so 'ex' after all.

"So, where does that leave us with his life insurance?" Eric frowned.

Trinity balked. "What?"

"His life insurance. It should go to Poppy, as they were going to be married if this hadn't happened. Don't tell me you thought you were going to claim it?" He sneered at her, which made her angry again.

"His parents are his next of kin. That's who it's going to, surely?" Trinity was shocked they'd even mention such a thing.

"But I was engaged to him." Poppy pointed to a ring on

her finger.

"Yes, but you weren't married. That means that legally, you weren't related," Trinity explained. Echoes of last night's conversation with William sprang to her mind.

"This is ridiculous!" Eric shouted. "She was going to marry him. That makes her closer to him than anyone else."

"Good luck contesting that one," Uncle Frank told them. "I'm afraid in the eyes of the law, his next of kin are still his parents, and if he named them on his insurance documents, I think you'll find the court will uphold it. My advice to you is to forget it and move on."

"Yeah, at least you've got another guy now, haven't you? You don't need to live in the past," Trinity told her, kindly.

"What? My private life is no business of yours!" Poppy suddenly exploded, standing up again. "And besides that, what about you? I heard all about those two guys coming out of your bedroom that morning. Judging by the look of them, you must have had a great time!"

"And my private life is no business of yours," Trinity told her calmly. "And, for the record, yes, we had a very nice time, thank you."

Poppy was clearly flabbergasted.

"Trinity has moved on with her life. What happened to Kevin is a tragedy and something she won't forget, but she still has to live for the future," Uncle Frank said firmly. "And she has no interest in Kevin's life insurance, so she's no threat to you."

Trinity was amazed at how well her uncle had taken the news that both of the men had been in her room—not that she had anything to be ashamed of.

"But it doesn't alter the fact that she's a whore!" Poppy shouted. "She had them both in her bedroom. She was seen."

"Yes, I did," Trinity admitted. "I had two guys in my room who were the kindest, sweetest people I've ever met. And they think more of me than Kevin ever did. I know that. They would never cheat on me or lie to me like he did. And I've learned from them that I never actually loved him. Now I know how it feels to be in love. I know that what Kevin and I had didn't even come close—not really. So, yes, I have moved on with my life, and, as my uncle said, it might be a good idea if you did, too."

Aunt Sylvia and Uncle Frank beamed in Trinity's direction, while Eric and Poppy simply stared. At first, she was surprised, as she didn't think that what she'd said had been profound enough to provoke such a reaction, but then she turned around and saw Jarrod and Cordell leaning against the doorjamb, grinning.

Trinity's whole body flushed and she closed her eyes momentarily while she realized what they'd heard. When she opened them again, they were still smiling at her, and she noticed that Nancy-Ruth and William were right behind them. *Damn.*

"Well, I think we'd better go now." Eric got up, appearing a little nervous, and urged his daughter to do the same.

"I hope it helped," Trinity said to Poppy as she walked past her. Poppy sneered at her and eyed the two men in the doorway.

"I'll see you out," Uncle Frank offered as the guys moved back to allow them through.

"I'll go make some fresh coffee," Aunt Sylvia said with a smile, as she gathered up the dishes.

"Can I do anything?" Trinity started collecting the cups, grateful of something to do to save her blushing at the handsome hunks.

She heard a deep chuckle and knew they were onto her.

"I think I can manage, hon," her aunt told her with a wink.

As soon as she turned around, Trinity found herself being whisked into the air by Cordell. His smile was glowing as he gazed at her and when his lips touched hers, she never wanted to move, especially when Jarrod put his arms around her shoulders. Jarrod nibbled at her neck before Cordell freed her lips to allow him to kiss her, too.

Chapter Twenty-Three

"How could you come sneaking up on me like that?" Trinity demanded playfully when they finally let her go.

Cordell shook his head as they all took their seats. He and Jarrod sat on the sofa with Trinity between them, each with an arm around her shoulder. She sure was cute when she was embarrassed.

"Well, we tried knocking, but there was so much hollering going on in here that no one could hear us," Jarrod told her. "We thought something might be wrong, so we came in anyhow, just in case we were needed."

"Trinity had it all under control," Frank said with a proud smile.

"So we saw." Cordell grinned at her and relished her blush.

"I see she's still wearing poppies to remind her of her name," Jarrod added, referring to the flower in Poppy's hair.

"I feel sorry for her," Trinity admitted.

"I got the impression they only came around here to lay into you," Frank said, ruefully. "They were determined to accuse you of all sorts of things. You sure shot them down with that insurance form."

"They thought I was going to contest Kev's life insurance," Trinity explained to the guys. "It's going to his parents as next of kin, but Poppy wants it for herself, them having been engaged and all."

"As soon as they found out Trinity was sharing a place with him, they assumed she'd be after his insurance, too." Frank sounded incredulous.

"Fancy tarring our Trinity with the same brush as that girl." Sylvia was handing around coffee and sandwiches and seemed totally shocked at the idea.

Trinity wouldn't be interested in anything like that, Cordell could tell.

"Well, you sure put her in her place," Jarrod said, clearly impressed.

"Good for you," Nancy-Ruth piped up. She and William had sat on the other sofa and looked far more relaxed than they had been the previous night.

"What about you guys? How did you get along at your brothers'?" Trinity peered up at Cordell.

He grinned. "It was…enlightening."

"Now what in the world's that supposed to mean?" Sylvia was obviously keen to hear their news. "Come on. We wanna know, word for word."

Cordell chuckled. It had been a long day but a fruitful one.

"Well now, I rang this morning and told Martin that we were coming over and had something to tell him," he began. "They hadn't yet been told that Nancy-Ruth was pregnant, see? Anyhow, they seemed to think we were coming to say that our momma had passed on."

"Oh, no." Trinity's face fell, and he couldn't resist squeezing her a little tighter.

"Actually, it didn't do them any harm," Cordell continued. "We got over there to find them both upset and feeling sorry for the way they'd treated her."

"He didn't put them straight at first," Nancy-Ruth said, shaking her head at him.

Cordell chuckled. "How was I to know that's what they'd think?" He tried to appear innocent and everyone laughed.

"To be fair, as soon as we arrived, they said they knew what we were there for then started on about how much they blamed themselves for not making up with her. Jacob admitted it was a stupid fight that should never have happened." Nancy-Ruth took a sip of her drink.

"Yeah, it was good to hear," Cordell said.

Jarrod sniggered. "So, then he asked them if they had their time over again, would they do things differently, and of course, they said 'yeah'."

"That's when I told them they needed to go take their chance while they still had it. Momma would be only too pleased to forgive them," Cordell added.

"They weren't happy at first, accused you of all sorts of things, didn't they?" William piped up.

Cordell said, "Like I told 'em, I never said anything about Momma. That was all on them."

"Guilty consciences," Sylvia stated.

"That's what I thought," Nancy-Ruth told her.

"They were so relieved when they heard what we'd actually come for, and they were thrilled about the baby," William said, with a smile.

Cordell grinned. It had been wonderful to see their faces when they'd heard that Momma was okay, then to hear that they were about to become uncles was just the icing on top. Neither of them had married, so this was going to be the first baby in the family.

"Looks like your little one's brought the whole family back together again," Trinity said with a dazzling smile.

Cordell and Jarrod both tightened their grip on her shoulders as they exchanged a grin. They had spoken last night about how fantastic it would be if they could have a baby with Trinity. She would make a perfect momma.

Nancy-Ruth stroked her stomach and William placed his hand over hers. Cordell knew that the stress of the family feud hadn't been good for his sister, and he was glad that it was finally over. She already seemed far more relaxed and hadn't stopped thanking him for arranging it all. Not that he'd done much. Most of it had been due to Martin and Jacob's imaginations—and, as Sylvia had said, their guilty consciences.

"The guys rang Momma while we were there and you could hear her crying on the phone," Cordell told them.

"She was so happy to hear from them." He grinned.

"Yeah, they're going up to visit her tomorrow," Nancy-Ruth added with a smile. "She's so excited to see them after all this time."

Cordell clicked his fingers. "Dang. I guess that means I won't be the favorite son anymore."

Everyone laughed. The atmosphere was so much easier than last night, with everyone so relaxed and happy. He smiled over at William. Joining the family in the middle of a feud must have been hard for him. Now, it looked like he had joined the kind of family he wanted to be in, one more like his own. A perfect family to bring a baby into.

* * * *

The next morning, Cordell and Jarrod were up early to say goodbye to their house guests. Jarrod cooked breakfast for everyone before it was time for them to leave, and Nancy-Ruth said a tearful farewell to her brother. He was surprised when William took him to one side.

"Jarrod, I want to apologize for the dumb things I said the other night," he said, shaking his head. "I had some really crazy ideas back there that I'm totally ashamed of. I've seen you in action and I know that you're just as much a part of this family as anyone. You're obviously a good friend to Cordell — more like another brother — and I wish you nothing but the best." He held out his hand and Jarrod didn't hesitate in shaking it.

"Hey, no worries, man." Jarrod was surprised but grateful for the acknowledgement.

William narrowed his eyes thoughtfully. "And you wanna hang on to that little girl of yours, too," he went on. "She talks a lot of sense. I'll never forget what she said about family and relations that night."

Jarrod grinned proudly. "Don't you worry. We intend to hold onto her," he assured him.

"Nice one, bro." William winked knowingly as he turned

to go.

Jarrod was glad to have the guy's approval—not that he needed it, but it was good, all the same. He watched Nancy-Ruth tear herself off Cordell and she turned to smile at Jarrod before flinging her arms around him.

"I'm sorry. I must be real hormonal this morning," she told him, sniffling. "I'm so glad Cordell's got you for a friend, Jarrod. You're a lovely guy."

"So, they tell me," he said, modestly, merely to make her laugh. It worked.

"You two are obviously real close. I'm so sorry we didn't invite you to our wedding. I know how left out of the family William feels sometimes, and I really didn't want to do that to you." She looked sad and like she was about to cry again.

"Hey, don't sweat it," he told her, cheerfully. "You'll just have to do it again. That's all."

She laughed then stared at him, computing his words. "Of course. There's nothing stopping us from renewing our vows, is there? We can get everyone there this time and have the day we should have had." She jumped back into his arms and clung to him like a leech.

"What a great idea," William said, excitedly.

"I do have them occasionally," Jarrod said, raising his eyebrows.

"You do that, bro," Cordell nodded.

Jarrod chuckled.

"We'll get it all planned out and send you three the first invitation," Nancy-Ruth promised, her eyes shining with glee.

"And don't forget the christening," Cordell told them as they made their way toward William's car. "We wanna come to that, too."

"Of course," Nancy-Ruth shouted through the window as William started the car.

Jarrod grinned as they watched them disappear from view. He knew it would be hard on him for a while. It always felt a little flat after guests left, but when they're family, it must be even harder. "You okay?"

Cordell seemed thoughtful as they slowly went back into the house to tidy the kitchen.

"Yeah." He nodded. "It was just all that talk about marriage and babies. It got me thinking."

Jarrod grinned. He had been thinking the same. He was sure of that. "Wanna finish up here and go see if a certain little girl wants to come out to play?"

Cordell burst out laughing. "Hell, yeah!"

They quickly loaded all the plates into the dishwasher and got ready.

"D'you think we should call her first?" Jarrod checked as they flew out the door.

"Nope." Cordell seemed quite sure about that.

"You don't think she might be working or something?"

"It's Sunday. It's a day of rest."

"So?"

"So, I wanna spend the *rest* of the day with her—and you, of course."

Jarrod nodded. "That goes without saying."

"You're very sure of yourself today," Cordell remarked with a chuckle.

Jarrod sighed. "I'm very sure of a lot of things." He glanced over at his buddy and smiled.

Cordell raised his eyebrows in question. "Such as?"

"Such as the way a certain young lady feels about us."

Cordell beamed. "Yeah, we heard it straight from the horse's mouth now, haven't we?"

"In front of Frank Crowthorne, too. Best lawyer in Cavern County. She can't go denying it."

"Hmm, legally binding and all that," Cordell said with a nod.

"Absolutely."

They both laughed as they made their way toward the Crowthornes' house and were still chuckling when they got to the door.

"You're happy this morning," Sylvia said with a smile as

she let them in.

"We are, ma'am," Jarrod told her as they followed her into the kitchen. Fresh bread sat on the counter, obviously not long out of the oven, its smell drawing them in. "Is Trinity about?" They removed their hats, looking around for her.

"Somewhere," Sylvia said casually. "Cordell, would you mind bending down there and fetching that cake out of the oven for me, hon?"

Cordell took the oven gloves, crouched down and removed the tantalizing fruit cake from the bottom shelf. He placed it onto a cooling rack just as Trinity appeared in the doorway.

"Aunt Sylvia, I was about to do that for you," she said, shaking her head.

"That's all right. I merely didn't want it to burn," her aunt told her, smiling. "Besides, I thought I'd make the most of them while they were here. Something tells me they're not planning on hanging about today."

Jarrod grinned at Trinity's bemused expression. She was real pretty in her tight jeans and a close-fitting pink and yellow striped top. He loved how she had taken to wearing her thick, vibrant makeup again and she looked stunning, her hair all spiked and her lips glistening.

She folded her arms and jutted out her chin as she peered up at him. "Is that right? You got plans today?"

"Yup," Jarrod told her.

"You going somewhere nice?"

"Yup."

She stared at him questioningly. He loved her defiant attitude.

"Got any boots, sweetheart? You can't ride in sneakers," Cordell piped up.

"Ride? Who said anything about riding? I'm helping Aunt Sylvia today." She raised her eyebrows mischievously.

"Oh, no. I'm all finished here," Sylvia said, putting a hand up to her. "I'm spending the rest of the day with your Uncle Frank. We thought we'd have some special time together."

She smiled.

"Sounds like the grown-ups want you out of the way for a while, darlin'," Jarrod told Trinity with a grin. "You may as well come out with us instead of spending the day on your own."

Trinity narrowed her eyes at Sylvia, as though she had just betrayed her. Sylvia raised her eyebrows innocently.

"Besides," Jarrod went on, "I did remind you about it the other day. You seem to think it's okay to go around reneging on your arrangements, don't you?"

Trinity whipped her head around and stared up at him. "Now how in the world are you figuring that?" She seemed incredulous and he found it hard to keep a straight face.

"You promised those few hours of trekking up the mountains, if you remember? I'm simply cashing it in." He tried to appear officious but wasn't sure how well he was carrying it off.

Trinity gaped at him, her eyes wide.

"Sounds fair to me. A deal's a deal, ain't that right, Frank?" Cordell spoke up, as Frank entered the room, smiling.

Trinity turned toward her uncle as if hoping for some support. She was clearly disappointed.

"You can't argue with that, sugar," Frank told her, shaking his head. "If you said you'd go with him, then you're honor-bound to stick to your word."

Trinity rolled her eyes. "I might have known," she said, feigning resignation. "I'll go get my boots."

Everyone burst out laughing as she left the room.

"You can take that cake with you," Sylvia offered. "I made it for you young 'uns, anyhow. And I'll make you up some sandwiches."

"That's real good of you, Sylvia," Jarrod told her. "But we don't expect you to do all that."

"Nonsense. You're making my niece happy, and that's good enough for me."

"Then, at least let us help," Cordell offered, and both guys started buttering bread and slicing some ham.

"She's afraid Trinity might leave again or something," Frank confided in a low voice as they worked.

Jarrod felt a thump in his stomach. "Why would she do that? Has she said something?" It suddenly occurred to him that she might not take kindly to all his clowning around. What if she took him seriously and thought he really was an arrogant bully?

"Nope. She hasn't said anything. That's just it," Sylvia told them quietly. She cut the pile of sandwiches. "I don't know what she's planning and I dare not ask in case she thinks I'm asking her to leave, which is the last thing I want. I've become used to having her around again and I'm loving it. She's such a help to me and I don't know what I'd do without her." Tears filled the old lady's eyes as she packed up the food for them, and Frank went over and put an arm around her.

"Leave it to us," Cordell said softly, putting a hand over Sylvia's.

Jarrod nodded. Cordell sure was on a roll. "Come on, Mr. Fix-it. We need to get going," he said, as he heard Trinity coming down the hallway.

Cordell took the food, thanking her again, and they followed Trinity out the door, as she called back her goodbyes. They knew Sylvia wouldn't want Trinity to see her upset.

"Nice boots," Cordell said, nodding approvingly as they climbed into the truck.

"Sorry we haven't got the SUV today, darlin'," Jarrod told her, "but we kinda prefer this one." He climbed into the driver's seat as Cordell sat the other side of Trinity.

She beamed. "Me, too. I get a crick in my neck in the SUV," she told them. They laughed and Trinity was glad they were all on the same wavelength. Being able to all sit together in a less-comfy vehicle sure beat sitting separately in the comfy one.

Chapter Twenty-Four

Despite being early fall, the sun was quite warm up in the foothills. Trinity was relieved that she slipped quite easily back into riding, not having had the opportunity for quite some time. Cordell and Jarrod were great fun, and she hadn't stopped giggling. Even back at the house she had had trouble not to laugh at their subtle way of asking her out.

"D'you think Aunt Sylvia was serious about them wanting some of that 'special time' she was talking about earlier?" she asked, thinking aloud.

"Well, I know they're getting on a bit, but I'd say they still have needs, you know?" Jarrod winked at her.

She giggled. "No, I mean…you don't think I'm in the way, do you? After all, they lived there quite happily without me before. I just wondered if maybe they'd rather I gave them back their space."

She noticed a nervous exchange of glances between the two and it occurred to her that she had said something wrong.

"You have got to be kidding," Cordell told her, "They love you to bits and would hate it if you left."

"Besides," Jarrod added, "where would you want to go?"

She shrugged. The thought had crossed her mind. She didn't have anywhere else *to* go. "I don't know. I can do my work from anywhere," she said, "so, from that point of view, it doesn't really matter where I am."

"Where would you *want* to be?" Cordell asked

She frowned thoughtfully. "I'd want to stay here, in Cavern County," she told them. "Even if I didn't live with

Aunt Sylvia and Uncle Frank, I'd need to be near to them. They're the only family I've got and I think they need me, even perhaps a little bit. Momma's buried here, too, so I'd like to stay near her. And I feel like I fit in here—even with bright pink, spiky hair."

They all chuckled and she was aware of Jarrod's horse getting closer to her. "Is that the only reason?" He lifted one eyebrow salaciously and she felt her insides instantly melt. Of course, she had thought about mentioning them, but he seemed so sure of himself today she wouldn't want to do anything to stroke that ego of his anymore than he'd done himself. It was fun to see him on the back foot, if only for just a minute.

"Hmm, I'm not sure," she said, as though thinking hard about it.

"Why don't we stop here for a bite to eat?" Cordell suggested, as Jarrod huffed. "It might give you a little brain power."

They dismounted next to a little stream and led the horses over to drink.

Cordell took out the food and Jarrod spread out a blanket for them all to sit on while they ate. The bread was delicious and they hummed and groaned their appreciation. The fruit cake was still warm and very tasty.

"Did you help make all this?" Cordell asked Trinity.

She nodded, her mouth full.

"I was kinda hoping you'd say that," he admitted with a grin.

Her insides turned to mush and her face got hot.

"You're even more beautiful when you blush," Jarrod murmured into her ear.

She rolled her eyes, aware that he was only making her blush even more.

Her whole body had gone hot and she had to remove her jacket.

"It sure is getting warm up here," Cordell remarked as the guys both removed their jackets, too.

Trinity shook her head. Subtlety really wasn't their strong point, but she had to admire their efforts.

She wiped her hands to get rid of the crumbs when Jarrod suddenly bent forward and took her fingers in his mouth. Her pussy clenched as he licked his way up each finger, sucking and lapping at them slowly.

Her whole body lit up and she gasped at the sensations. Then Cordell leaned over and took her lips in a sensual, loving kiss. They gently laid her backward on the blanket, the soft grass underneath providing a comfortable bed, while Jarrod let go of her hands to allow her to grasp Cordell's shoulders to steady herself.

Cordell's spicy cologne mixed with the fresh smell of the mountain, swathing her in an intoxicating cloud. He moaned softly into her mouth as he continued to kiss her, a little more intensely now but no less gentle, and she realized Jarrod was pulling the boots from her feet.

She was surprised to feel her socks being taken off, too, then Jarrod licked at her toes. It was quite weird at first and she giggled and kicked her legs, but he held her feet firmly in his hands and soon her pussy grew wet as the sensations ran through her whole body.

Trinity held onto Cordell even tighter as her emotions ran rampant. She had never felt anything like this before. The peacefulness of the rippling stream and the birds chirping were completely at odds with the tumultuous pleasure that ripped through her body, and she gasped as every nerve within her seemed to ignite. She closed her eyes as electric pulses seemed to bombard her and she was getting hotter by the second.

When Cordell swept kisses down her neck, she moaned, willing him to go a little farther south. He chuckled and she knew he had read her thoughts. He lifted his head, kicked off his boots and moved slowly down her body, kissing her breasts as far as her top would allow then soaking the material by sucking at them through her clothes.

"Take it off," she pleaded in a hoarse whisper.

"You sure, sweetheart?" His voice was low and soft.

"Yeah."

He pulled it over her head and when she opened her eyes, she saw that both guys had also divested themselves of their shirts. She gasped at the sight of their ripped muscles. Cordell had tiny, fair hairs on his chest, while Jarrod's were much darker, though just as sparse.

Jarrod moved up her body and smiled at her before planting tiny kisses all around her mouth. He then plunged his tongue into it and she sensed his desperation as he invaded her space, owning it like no one else had ever done.

"You better know how much we love you, darlin'," he murmured when he finally came up for air.

Before she had chance to reply, he covered her mouth again and she moaned with pleasure as his long tongue danced with hers. His fresh scent surrounded her and her whole body relaxed into their ministrations.

She yelped as a sharp pain shot through her right nipple. In the next second, Cordell was soothing the hurt with his mouth then the pain morphed into the most exquisite pleasure. She moaned at the sensation and pushed her breast toward him, encouraging him to continue.

He did it again and this time the pain was even sharper. Her pussy convulsed and she tried to clasp her muscles tightly as his warm breath eased the pain once again.

They continued their loving assault until it became unbearable. Trinity found herself getting more and more agitated, willing them to do a little more, go a little further.

"Please," she whispered as soon as her mouth became free again.

"Please what, darlin'?" Jarrod's teasing eyes danced with mirth as he grinned down at her. He really was gorgeous. The soft scruff around his face gave him a roguish appearance that perfectly matched his expression. He knew darn well what she wanted.

Cordell trailed his slightly rough hands over her stomach and her entire body clenched as he found the waistband of her jeans.

"Yes." She nodded frantically, gazing down at him.

He was watching her carefully and she knew they wanted to be sure their advances were welcomed.

"I want you to," she assured him. "Please."

Cordell slowly undid her button then her zipper, clearly giving her plenty of time to change her mind. *As if!*

She reached up and ran her hands through Jarrod's slightly longer hair, toying with his waves, fisting them in her hands with anticipation as Cordell pulled the jeans from her legs. The cool air was welcome as it wafted gently over her.

"What about this?" Jarrod ran a long finger over the silky edge of her bra.

"Yes." She didn't need asking twice. It was soggy and uncomfortable now that Cordell had sucked the life out of it, anyhow, and she was relieved when Jarrod lifted it from her flesh.

As Cordell had moved a little farther down her body, Jarrod took the space on the other side of her. He took her left breast into his mouth and sucked hard, while he massaged her right.

Trinity gasped at the heady sensation. His slightly whiskered face was deliciously rough against her smooth flesh and she welcomed its bite. Arching her back, she tried to push her breast farther into his mouth. His chuckle reverberated through her skin, adding a tingling current to the cocktail of sensations already running through her.

Cordell trailed his finger gently over her silk panties, which she knew must be soaked by now, as they lay plastered to her aching pussy.

"Take them off," she pleaded, desperate for the relief.

"Sure?" Cordell asked.

She immediately felt the zing of delicious pain rip through her breast as Jarrod nipped her once again and she screamed into the stillness of the air.

"Just do it," she pleaded, gasping for breath. Another

trickle had escaped her pussy and rendered her underwear a source of discomfort.

Cordell pulled the sodden silk from her and she heaved a huge sigh as the cool air invaded all the heated, wet cracks and crannies of her throbbing pussy.

Cordell's mouth covered her mound and he sucked at her, licking his way around her most sensitive area while she moaned and thrashed her head from side to side. She knew she was so close to her release that there would be no time for theirs, but they didn't seem to mind.

Both guys stepped up their game, rampantly licking and sucking at her body, driving her wild. The heat rose inside her and she clung onto Jarrod's hair for dear life as he sucked and pummeled at her soft breasts.

She'd parted her legs as far as she could for Cordell and pulled her knees out to her sides to allow him all the access he could need, as he continued to suck at her, using his tongue to torment her. Suddenly, he swiped the tip of his tongue over her little hard nub and she screamed as the pleasure tore through her whole being.

Before she came down to earth, they whipped off their shorts and Cordell tore open what she assumed to be the packet of a condom.

"I want you," she assured him, her body still racking with aftershocks.

"I love you, sweetheart," he told her directly before aligning his thick cock to her soaking pussy.

"Ever had it round the back?" Jarrod asked, as lust painted an exquisite film across his gorgeous face.

She shook her head and thought she might be about to cry.

"No matter," he told her. "How about here?" He poked a finger into her mouth and she instinctively sucked it hard. "Good enough," he said quickly.

She saw his long, meaty cock as he swung his leg over her and knelt astride her shoulders, keeping his weight off.

Trinity breathed in his raw scent and eagerly opened her

mouth wide to take him in. "Slowly, darlin'. There's a lot of it," he warned her.

"Bragging again," Cordell said with a sigh.

"What can I say?" Jarrod replied.

"You can say you're ready. I'm dying here," Cordell told him.

Trinity loved their banter and found it eased the tension somewhat. She toyed with the tip of Jarrod's huge cock as it twitched on her tongue.

"Ready, sweetheart?" Cordell was clearly restraining himself, and she hummed her assent as she took more of Jarrod's delicious member into her mouth.

Jarrod moaned loudly and she guessed he had experienced the reverberation of her hum through his skin. Cordell let out a growl as he pressed his humongous cock into her, and she forced herself to take deep breaths to try to relax her muscles enough to accommodate him as she gasped around Jarrod's dick.

Cordell held her hand with one of his, his palm enveloping her fingers.

Jarrod's groans became even louder, and Cordell's thrusts became harder as his grunts became deeper. The sounds of her men becoming more and more aroused spurred Trinity on and she had never heard anything so erotic.

The fire in her pussy suddenly erupted like a volcano and she moaned uncontrollably, while Cordell's cock became even more engorged—who knew that was possible?—and he roared his release as his hot seed filled the rubber sack. Jarrod quickly pulled back and jumped off her, groaning uncontrollably, but not before a little of his salty nectar had trickled down her waiting throat.

She lay on the blanket, naked, panting at the fresh mountain air, while the guys disappeared for a moment. She closed her eyes as the euphoria gradually dissipated and she felt as though she was sinking into the ground.

"D'you think she's asleep?" Jarrod's jovial voice cut into her thoughts and she quickly opened her eyes.

"Make that a no," Cordell replied.

She sat up, surprised at how fresh they both appeared, then recalled they had stopped near some water.

"It gets a little deeper downstream," Cordell informed her, clearly reading her thoughts.

She smiled, gazing approvingly at their ripped bodies. Every inch of them was delicious and she looked forward to tasting them sometime very soon.

"I love you both," she told them and it seemed as though her smile was wide enough to tear her face in two.

"Funny you should say that," Cordell told her with a grin, "as we were just saying something very similar about you."

She jumped up and hugged them both, putting an arm around each broad back. They smothered her in their warmth, enveloping her with love. Skin against skin, they stood on the fresh mountain, wrapping each other in their adulation. Then she quickly pulled away. "I'm all sticky," she explained.

"So are we, now," Jarrod said, in mock horror.

"Only one thing to do then, bro." Cordell chuckled as they all headed for the cool water of the mountain stream.

They had been right about it being much deeper farther on, and Trinity relished the coldness as she submerged herself in the clear water. Although she was shivering when she came out, she was much cleaner and fresher.

"Let's get you dressed," Jarrod urged her as they went back to where they had left their picnic.

"Now that's something you don't usually hear him say," Cordell muttered.

"I heard that," Jarrod said, as he took something from his saddle bag. "I just don't want her getting hypothermia all over again. Frank'd never forgive us." He threw them each a towel.

"Nah, I reckon it's Sylvia you'd need to worry about," Cordell told him, winking at Trinity, who giggled.

Jarrod threw Trinity a pair of rolled-up jeans from one of the saddlebags. "Here. They'll be a bit big on you but it's better than nothing."

Trinity gawked at him.

"Oh, I don't know…" Cordell winked at her again.

"But mine are—" she began.

"Wet," Cordell finished for her.

Dang. He'd noticed. She had to admit she hadn't exactly relished the idea of putting them back on.

"Same as your underwear. You'll need to go commando like us," Cordell added matter-of-factly.

She narrowed her eyes at them as she pulled on the jeans, which almost fell right back off again.

Jarrod frowned. "Here, try this." He handed her his belt as he continued to get himself dressed.

There weren't enough holes on the belt to make it fit so she tied it in a knot around her waist instead, making her jeans look like a large sugar bag.

She pulled on her top and was glad she had her sweater as she was still shivering. Cordell put his arms around her and hugged her tightly. "Did you dry your feet properly?" he checked as he rubbed her wet hair with the towel.

"Yes, of course."

"Well, that's good."

She smiled. Cowboys always had a thing about their feet, she recalled. She caught Jarrod's eye and noticed his grin. She flushed as she suddenly remembered that *he* seemed to have a thing about her feet, too.

Chapter Twenty-Five

They climbed back onto their horses and headed back down the mountain track.

"It's so beautiful out here," she said, wistfully.

"It sure is," Jarrod agreed. "Makes you wonder why folks'd want to live anywhere else."

"They can't all live here," Cordell remarked.

"Why not? Look at all this room." Jarrod waved his arm out to emphasize his point. "You'd fit a fair few people down there."

"It wouldn't be the same." Trinity giggled. She enjoyed their simple way of seeing things.

"Things don't always have to stay the same, do they?" Jarrod asked, peering back at her.

"Some things do." She got his message loud and clear.

"Such as?" Jarrod grinned at her.

"You two, for a start," she told them with a giggle. "Don't you ever change. I love you just the way you are."

"Right answer." Jarrod chuckled. "We love you, too, darlin'." He blew her a kiss, which she caught in one hand.

She heard Cordell sniggering behind her, too, and turned back to throw him a smile. Both of them were gorgeous, their faces radiant and sated, and their manner so content and happy.

They reached the ranch and returned the horses, which Cordell instructed one of the hands to take care of for them, before clambering back into the truck.

"We'll get changed over at our place, if that's okay?" Jarrod asked her, a little warily.

"Great." She certainly didn't relish her aunt and uncle

seeing her until she was able to wear her own jeans again, although she had to admit that these were quite comfy.

She hadn't seen their place before and expected it to be smaller than the Crowthornes' and much more masculine. She stared when they pulled up in the drive of large, luxurious home with several garages and set in its own vast grounds.

"You live here?" She felt slightly giddy. This was so far removed from what she'd envisioned that it was almost laughable.

"Yup." Cordell appeared uneasy as he scooted out of the car and held a hand up to help her down.

Her heart pounded. She frowned as Jarrod came around from the other side of the car, having taken their things out of the back of the truck on his way past.

"So, how many people live here?" She suddenly had visions of it being some kind of commune or a house divided into several apartments, although she knew in her heart it was highly unlikely.

"Just us." Cordell shrugged, but she could sense the uneasiness in the air.

"You rent it, right?"

"Nope. We own it." Cordell told her. "Come and take a look."

She almost didn't want to see any more of the house and was tempted to ask them to take her home, regardless of her attire. Maybe they weren't who she'd thought they were at all—not if they lived in a place like this.

"When my parents died, they left me everything," Jarrod explained. "It wasn't until Cordell lost his dad, too, that we decided to invest it all in property while having a go at a little building and restoration work ourselves. Hence…"

He opened the door and she was met by a huge reception area with wooden paneling and a staircase that swirled up to the next story. The floor was wooden and a large, circular rug sat in the center, with an ornately-carved circular table that held a beautiful arrangement of fresh flowers.

Trinity gasped. She tentatively followed Jarrod as he showed her a huge, well-equipped kitchen, a dining room that could easily accommodate twenty people or more and a massive, plush living room with chandeliers and claw-footed furniture.

It was all far too ostentatious for her taste, especially when she was shown the study, the den and the family room.

Cordell had disappeared part way through her tour and he showed up again just as they were about to go upstairs.

"Your clothes are in the dryer," he announced. "I gave them a quick wash. They should be ready by the time you've taken a shower."

"I was about to show her the bedrooms," Jarrod told him.

"It's fine. I'd rather just take a shower for now, if that's okay? I'm really uncomfortable in these." She gestured to the baggy jeans she was wearing, which were actually not causing her any bother—it was the house that was doing that. It was all too much.

"Of course. Jarrod'll show you to one of the bathrooms, and when you're done, there's something else we want you to see."

Trinity forced a smile and followed Jarrod up the massive staircase. It opened out onto a spacious galleried landing with several doors leading off it. She didn't want to know how many bedrooms there were. She already knew that—too many.

"My room's in here." He steered her toward one of the doors at the far end of the hall. As she predicted, the room was like something from a high-end hotel. Cream walls and dark-wooden furniture graced the scene, with a hugely over-sized bed and drapes that must have cost a year's wages.

She gaped. It was truly gorgeous, though not to her taste—and certainly not what she had expected. She inwardly chastised herself for misjudging them. When she had first seen them with her aunt and uncle, she had thought they were trying to wheedle themselves into their affections to get their hands on the elderly couple's money. Now, she realized they didn't need to do that. And they were so close to her family because her aunt and uncle almost replaced the parents they had lost.

She felt as though she were in a daze as he showed her through to the en suite bathroom with its gold taps and luxurious tiles.

"Use anything you need," Jarrod told her with a smile. "I'll get Cordell to put your clothes in the bedroom. Don't forget to come down as soon as you're ready, though. We want to show you something."

Trinity managed another smile as he left, but as soon as he closed the door, she burst into tears. She had fallen in love with these guys, but she should have known it was too good to be true. They weren't who she thought they were at all. They might live out here in Cavern County, but they were more like Lords of the Manor in their gorgeous mansion.

She was pleased for the warm water that gushed over her as she took her shower, and she actually began to feel a little better once she was able to get washed up. She closed her eyes and relaxed as she took a few minutes for herself and realized how silly she was being. They were still the same people, even if they were a lot richer than she had assumed. And they'd never lied to her. She had made presumptions about them that had been wrong. It was her own fault. And they loved her. That was really all that mattered. Would she have worried if she'd found they had no money at all? No, of course not. So, it didn't matter how affluent they were. Cordell and Jarrod loved her. She smiled. They had *made* love to her and it had been wonderful. Nothing could ever change that. And she was glad.

Putting on her laundered underwear was a joy, and she smiled at how thoughtful Cordell had been to do her clothes for her. Once she was back in her own jeans, she felt much more like herself and she sighed at her reflection as she spiked up her hair with her fingers. Her makeup had washed off in the shower and she thought how different she appeared. The guys had accepted her, no matter what image she had portrayed, and she would pay them the same courtesy. It's what was on the inside that counted. Her momma had drummed that into her from a very early age.

She took a deep breath, preparing herself for whatever delight they had to show her downstairs. It was bound to be either another grand room or piece of priceless furniture. Whatever it was, it had excited them and anything that made them happy would be fine by her.

As she went down the stairs, she tried to imagine herself living here. It wasn't what she had envisioned for herself, but she had to admit it was beautiful. Jarrod had even mentioned a gym in the basement with its own pool.

"Wow, you look gorgeous." Cordell met her at the bottom of the stairs, his face shining. Judging by his change of clothes and damp hair, she guessed they'd also managed to get cleaned up. His spicy cologne hung in the air and she breathed it in with a smile.

"Thank you."

He put his arms around her and gave her a lingering kiss that burned her insides deliciously. He was so tender, so loving.

"What do you think of the house?" He gestured to their surroundings as he led her toward the dining room.

"It's very…grand," she replied, thoughtfully. "I mean, it's beautiful," she added hurriedly. "It's just not what I expected." She wondered if the guys had noticed how quiet she had been when they had shown her around and hoped they didn't think her rude.

She was relieved when Cordell chuckled. "Come and see this," he said, opening the door.

Jarrod stood by the huge table with lots of large sheets of paper spread out in front of him. He glanced up and gave her a dazzling smile when he saw her.

"Hey, gorgeous."

Her cheeks warmed and she went over to where he held out his arms and gave him a hug. He smelled fresh and seemed more relaxed than earlier.

"You have a wonderful home," she assured him.

Jarrod chuckled. "Nah, it'll do for now," he said with a shrug.

She frowned.

"What do you make of this one?" Cordell showed her the large plans that were laid before them.

"What is it?" She picked up a photograph from the few which were scattered about on top of the blueprints.

"It's a house," Jarrod explained. "We're building it down near the river and plan to give it its own garden."

Trinity peered at the plans and saw that it was a small, country-style cottage with a large breakfast kitchen and a chimney for a real fire. There was a thud in her stomach.

"This is the sort of house I used to dream about living in," she admitted quietly.

"It's going to have a small garden at the front with lots of flowers. We thought maybe honeysuckle growing around the door," Jarrod said with a grin.

She stared at him.

"Something like this." He pulled a screwed-up sheet of paper from his pocket and showed it to her.

"Honeysuckle Cottage." She gaped at it as she recalled doodling it recently while she was supposed to be working.

Cordell put his arms around her and tears pricked her eyes.

"Like we said, we're investing in property," he told her softly. "This house is going to be sold and we're using some of the land we got with it to build our own home. We wanted it to be a little closer to Frank and Sylvia so we could keep a better eye on them, and far enough from this place to feel secluded." He kissed the top of her head gently.

Her heart leaped and she turned around and flung herself into his embrace.

"I think that means she likes it," Cordell said, over her head.

Jarrod whooped. "Does that mean you'd like to live in it? With us?"

Trinity gaped up at him as Cordell put an arm out to include him in their embrace.

"We love you, sweetheart. How would you feel about moving into our home with us?" Cordell asked, his eyes twinkling.

Tears of joy streamed down her cheeks. "I'd love to," she whispered. "I love you."

Maggie's Man

Excerpt

Chapter One

Maggie smiled at the good-looking cowboy who had planted himself opposite her at the counter. He had come in here every day for the past few weeks and wasn't showing any signs of getting tired of her cooking — or her company — yet.

"Morning, Maggie. I'll take a coffee and one of those cinnamon buns, please." His baby-blue eyes twinkled as he removed his hat and placed it on the stool beside him.

"Coming right up. This is getting to be a regular habit, isn't it?" She grinned at him. "Not that I'm complaining, of course."

"Yeah. No one cooks like you do. It's well worth the trip." He took the plate from her, sniffing the fresh cinnamon.

"Oh, right." She felt a little disappointed.

He must have noticed her expression. "You sure know

the way to a man's heart," he added quickly.

Good save. She snickered. "Well, I wish that was all it took," she joked.

He raised his eyebrows, taking a swig of his coffee. "You're not gonna tell me you're single?"

She giggled. "I sure am," she told him, admiring his subtle way of asking. "I know it's hard to believe, isn't it?" She put a hand to the back of her head, posing like a model. Sticking her nose in the air, she gave him a blasé look before bursting into laughter. She knew she was a little too old and a lot too fat to pull off a super-model appearance, but she was having fun pretending. In truth, she was still in her twenties, but she felt more like a hundred and twenty.

"I can't for the life of me imagine why you're not wed." He sounded serious, much to her amazement.

She sighed, quickly turning away from his handsome face while wiping her hands on her apron.

"Can we get some coffees over here, miss?" An older gentleman had just sat at a window seat with a lady, whom Maggie guessed would be his wife.

"Of course." Maggie suddenly felt flustered. She hadn't taken any notice of them coming in, as she'd been too busy laughing with Aiden Fielding, the gorgeous cowboy.

Her hand shook as she poured the coffee, and she tipped one of the cups over with the edge of the coffee pot, sending the hot, black liquid running all over the counter.

"Damn!" She felt herself go hot and knew she was blushing. Panic overtook her as she quickly tried to rectify the mess.

"Hey, hey. Are you okay?" Aiden was on his feet in a second, moving everything out of the way of the stream of coffee that was threatening to engulf everything in its wake. His voice was calm and gentle, and Maggie wished she could be as composed as he was.

"Yeah, I just..." She took a cloth and soaked up the spill, surprised to see Aiden dive behind the counter and grab a clean cup.

He quickly poured the drinks and placed them on a tray while she cleaned up the counter. "Did you scald yourself?"

He was right next to her, and she was surrounded by his fresh cologne. She had admired his scent from across the counter, but he was even closer to her now, and she was immersed in the heady aroma. He was a gorgeous-looking guy and seemed to really care about her. But she had to remember he was way out of her league – and age range. Although he must have been a year or two her senior, she usually went for much older men than him – not that she'd had that many.

"Er...no. No, I'm fine. Thank you," she stammered as he stared at her with his big, concerned eyes. "I'd best take these over." She took the tray, brushing past him as she squeezed from behind the counter to serve her customers.

"I can recommend the cinnamon buns," Aiden called over to the elderly couple as Maggie served their drinks.

"Now that sounds like a good idea," the man remarked, looking first to Aiden then to his companion. "What do you think, Sylvia? Cinnamon bun?"

Maggie noticed the lady's face light up, much the same as she was sure hers did when someone mentioned food.

"Ooh, yes please." The lady smiled excitedly.

"We'll take two, please." The man nodded at Maggie.

"No problem." She quickly returned to the counter and placed two of the warm buns onto a plate. She loaded up the tray with knives and side plates, as well as a couple of napkins then smiled at Aiden before taking them over to the couple.

"Thanks for that. You're good for business," she told the cowboy when she arrived back at the counter. He had already returned to his seat opposite her and was sipping his coffee.

"Gotta keep you employed," he said with a laugh.

"Ain't that the truth." She sighed, rolling her eyes.

He frowned. "Now that's the second time this morning I've said the wrong thing," he said, narrowing his eyes. "Is everything all right, Maggie?"

She balked, shocked that she had given away her feelings. "Oh, of course. No, you didn't say anything wrong." She tried to assure him but could see he wasn't convinced. "Everything's fine, really."

She busied herself tidying away some dishes so she didn't have to look at him, but she could feel his eyes boring into her.

"Do you like working here?" he asked after a few minutes.

She turned back to him, smiling. "Yes, of course."

She followed his gaze as he looked around the little café. It was a cozy place with red-checked tablecloths on wobbly-legged tables, surrounded by old, mismatched chairs. A couple of booths occupied one end while a row of tables stood in front of the large window. At the other end was the door to the small kitchen that backed from the counter where Maggie served coffee. Tall bar stools lined the counter from the patron's side so customers — like him — could easily perch up there and have a quick drink or chat to the waitress.

"Does it ever get busy in here?" he asked.

"Not really," she told him. "Which is just as well, being as the boss refuses to take on any more staff. He reckons I cost him enough, already. Ha!"

She thought back to the pittance she earned working here every day. Her only consolation was that it was easy work and she didn't have to travel far to get here. Trouble was, Bracken Ridge, where they were situated, was so far away from anything that they hardly had any customers. The Melrose Motel stood opposite them, but business wasn't exactly booming there either, so she didn't get many residents to cook for. Most people just drove right on through the tiny village to get to the more interesting towns of Almondine or Pelican's Heath, a short trip down the road.

"But surely if business picked up, he'd have to?" Aiden appeared thoughtful.

"Yeah right. Like that's gonna happen." She wiped her hands in her apron again. "Between you and me, it's more likely to close down altogether," she told him in a hushed tone.

Aiden looked surprised. "So where does that leave you?"

"Oh don't worry about me. I'm likely to be out of a home before I'm out of a job anyhow, so it won't make much difference either way."

His shocked face told her she had said too much, and she inwardly admonished herself for letting her tongue run away with her. There was just something about Aiden. He was so easy to talk to.

"Thank you very much, dear. That was lovely." The elderly couple left their table, calling over to her from the door.

"Glad you liked it. Come again." Maggie was grateful for the distraction and hurried on over to clear their table, noticing that they had left a large tip along with their payment.

When she returned to the counter, Aiden was taking a call on his cell. "Yeah, tell him we're interested," he said. "Definitely. We want that land at the best possible price, ya hear? Thanks for that."

"Everything all right?" she asked, sad to see him stand up.

"Just peachy. I'm hoping to accrue more land for the ranch, expand a little." Excitement shone from his eyes as he nodded, smiling. "Say... How about a drink tonight? What time do you finish?" He put his hat on.

She frowned in surprise. "Don't you think I'm a bit old?"

"Too old to go for a drink?"

She snickered, her heart racing. She really liked the guy, and she did enjoy his company. He had a point, though. They were only going for a drink. "Okay. I get off around seven." Something burned inside her, and she couldn't help smiling at the thought of spending more time with the hunky cowboy.

"I'll be here, then," he told her with a grin, throwing a handful of notes on the counter.

"I'll look forward to it." She was sad to see him go, but it was nice to think it was only for a few hours.

* * * *

Aiden climbed into his truck. He liked Maggie Welch a lot and was pleased that he'd finally plucked up the courage to ask her out. It had been several weeks since they'd met, and he'd liked her from the start. She always seemed quite happy and cheerful, so it was a shock to see her flummoxed and a little pensive today. Something must have happened.

He drove down the back road toward Pelican's Heath, looking forward to seeing her again tonight. It was obvious he'd said the wrong thing when he mentioned her being married. He'd meant it as a compliment but could see he'd hit a raw nerve. And what about losing her home and job? That poor girl always seemed to put on a brave face, but it seemed things weren't quite as they appeared with her.

Ben, his older brother was waiting for him when he pulled up at the ranch. "No prizes for guessing where you've been."

Aiden grinned. "I've got a date with her tonight."

Ben hooted with laughter. "Well now, you actually did it? What in hell kept ya, bro?"

"Very funny. I just wanted to wait for the right moment. That's all. I don't think she's as confident as she makes out, you know?"

He followed Ben over to one of the meadows that looked out to the south of the Fielding Ranch.

"I can't wait to meet this one," Ben murmured, shaking his head.

"Maybe in time, bro." Aiden wasn't so sure his family would approve of Maggie.

Ben chuckled, looking out over the land in front of them. "Well, you'll sure be able to impress the girl if we get all this," he remarked.

Aiden sighed. He knew money and land weren't going to impress a girl like Maggie, and he was glad of it. He couldn't explain that to Ben, though.

"Well, I've told Walker we're interested," he said, "but at a reasonable price. We can't let this guy know how much we want it."

Ben nodded. "Yup. I don't even know this guy, Rossington. Seems he just recently acquired the spread, and now he wants to sell it on. I knew old Jake Parry had passed away, but I thought his family was keeping the place on."

"Maybe they're finding it hard to cope," Aiden mused. "Perhaps we should've offered them more help?"

"If they were anything like the old man, they'd have had to beg for it." Ben snorted. "That old cuss wouldn't give you the time of day. He sure wouldn't thank you for offering any kind of help. Probably misinterpret it as an insult, if you ask me. No, I reckon we were right to leave well enough alone there, bro."

Aiden sighed. Ben was probably right. Jake Parry was known for not being the friendliest of men, and his family seemed to be behind him all the way. He'd been a wealthy guy, though, and owned a lot of land hereabouts. If they could just get their hands on the few acres that bordered their land, it sure would provide a much-needed boost to the Fielding Ranch.

"I'd love to see a few thoroughbreds over there," Ben remarked wistfully, pointing to one of the fields.

Aiden shook his head. "Nah, I reckon we should get more quarter horses. They're good all-rounders. And if we're gonna start giving riding lessons, as Josie suggested, they'd be perfect for the job."

Ben frowned, looking back at him. "But think what it would mean to get some more real good thoroughbreds. It'd give a good impression to folks who came to take your lessons, too. Let them see how affluent we are. We've got to make it look good, and the few we've got don't exactly stand out."

Aiden sighed. This argument was getting old. Ben had always been more interested in how things looked to the outside world, instead of what was practical.

"But we won't be that affluent if we go throwing good money away on show horses," he objected. "We can get more quarters for the same money, and they'll be a lot more useful to the ranch as a whole."

"Nah, we've got enough. We don't need to bring in any more, at least not yet a while. I reckon we need to lift the prestige of the Fielding a little, and the best way to do that is to buy the best."

Aiden rolled his eyes. "Well, let's think about that once we've got the land, shall we? One step at a time."

Ben nodded and smirked, which let Aiden know that, as far as he was concerned, he'd won the argument. Damn!

More books from
Totally Bound Publishing

Book three in The Cowboys of Cavern County series

When he opened his mind, she opened his heart.

Book one in the Roughstock Sweethearts series

Traditional cowboy Cotton and tattooed Emmy couldn't be more different. That's part of their attraction, but different worlds can make for a lot of heartache.

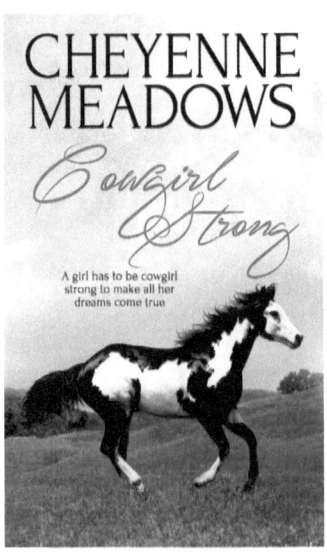

When life is full of lemons, a girl has to be cowgirl strong to make all her dreams come true.

*She never knew what heat was until she met her cowboy —
then fire consumed them.*

About the Author

Bella Settarra

Bella Settarra is a British Erotic Romance author and lives in the beautiful English countryside.

She has several published novels to date, with subject matter including cowboys, BDSM and Myth/Fantasy. She has also written short stories for anthologies and has even had some raunchy poems published.

She likes to keep busy, cramming as much into each day as she possibly can, while battling—and is determined to win—against breast cancer. She loves to hear from her readers, so please get in touch!

Bella Settarra loves to hear from readers. You can find contact information, website details and an author profile page at https://www.totallybound.com/